Xin Publishing

Going Forth

Clive K Semmens

Xin Publishing

Published by Xin Publishing
an imprint of Xin He Ltd.
Hill Quays
14 Commercial Street
Manchester M15 4PZ
United Kingdom

ISBN: 978-1-326-23956-5

Foreword

Going Forth is a sequel to *Pawns*. When I planned *Pawns* and started to write it in the late 1970s, it was, I thought, a complete story in itself. I still think it is. But while I was completing *Pawns*, *Going Forth* began to form in my mind.

You could read *Going Forth* as a story in itself, I suppose – but I think it would be much better to read *Pawns* first.

A different leg of the trousers of time?

After I planned *Pawns* and wrote half of it, it languished for over thirty years. At first I considered updating the first half to take account of changes in the world in the meantime, but quickly realized that it wouldn't work.

So *Pawns*'s leg of the trousers of time had diverged somewhat from ours.

Going Forth is much further still down that other leg of the trousers of time.

Spelling of place names

There are quite a lot of real place names in *Going Forth* that are not spelt the way they usually are nowadays. They're spelt the way they were spelt in the big 1983 Times Atlas that Pete, Persie and Merly found in *Pawns*.

Chapter 1

The first day I really remember was the day we raided the military vehicle depot, and saw the army trucks for the first time. I was pretty excited, but the thing that sticks in my mind most was how excited Granny Persie was. She was like a small child with a new toy.

I don't remember much else about that day, but I've heard all about it so many times that I know a lot about it.

Grandad – his name is Grandad Pete, but there's only ever been one Grandad, so we just call him Grandad – and Uncle Sid had spent two whole days watching the depot through the big binoculars, from some rocks near the top of a big hill overlooking it. It took them that long to be confident it really was completely abandoned, even though Grandad hadn't seen a living person apart from the family for thirty-three years, and Uncle Sid never had.

We were a long, long way from home, staying at a farm just a few kilometres from the depot. It was a place we'd stayed for the odd night a couple of times before, but we'd not found the depot on our previous visits.

We were 'just exploring,' as Granny Merly put it. We didn't need to go so far for raiding – there were plenty of places we'd not raided yet within half a day's drive of home, even with the roads beginning to get pretty bad in places. But we always did a bit of raiding while we were exploring. Grandad said we might as well take stuff from further afield while we were there, and save the places closer to home for later.

'We'd not really exhausted Østerby yet, never mind some of the other villages within easy reach. By then, less of the stuff in each house was any use than when we first started raiding, but tinned and pickled stuff was still mostly okay. But we didn't need as much of that kind of thing anyway since we'd got better at farming.'

Then Granny Merly got to talking about the old days, before they'd learned to catch fish, before the shellfish had recovered, and when there were so many rabbits that if you missed one you'd hit a different one. It was before the foxes and wolves and skuas arrived, but even so I think she was exaggerating.

There were still plenty of rabbits really anyway, and fox and wolf meat isn't bad. 'As long as you cook it thoroughly,' Grandad always says, but Granny Persie always points out that you've got to cook any kind of meat thoroughly anyway, if you want to avoid a bad tummy – or worse.

Then Grandad gets to grumbling about the stink when he's gutting a fox or a wolf or a badger, but we all know he's just teasing Granny Persie really. Rabbit guts smell pretty foul too.

'Skua meat would be okay too, wouldn't it, Grandad?'

'Probably, if you cooked it well. But they'd be hard to hit with a rifle, and we don't have an inexhaustible supply of ammunition. Plenty, but not inexhaustible. If we used a shotgun we'd end up biting on lead pellets, however carefully I picked them out. Lead's not good stuff to bite on.'

I think I remember that it took a long time to get the trucks started, with lots of faffing about doing this and that before they could even try, but I might really have muddled up the actual memories of the day with the memories of what I've been told later.

One of the best things from Granny Persie's point of view was the batteries, but I certainly didn't understand that until years later. Most of the trucks didn't have batteries in them, and in those that did, the batteries were quite, quite dead. What pleased Granny Persie was that there was a battery store, and the batteries in it were dry. The acid was separate, which meant that the batteries would last much, much longer. Effectively they were brand new. They'd only start to deteriorate after the acid was put in. There were loads of them in the store, waiting to have their acid put in. We could have brand new batteries again whenever we needed them.

'We've been having to start all our vehicles with the little generator, for years and years. Once these batteries are charged, we'll be able to start these trucks from their own batteries!' Granny Persie had said, and she was right.

There weren't any batteries in the store that would fit any of our old vehicles, apart from the Jeeps. Granny Persie didn't care. 'All our old vehicles are pretty old and knackered now anyway. We're much better off with these trucks. They're just as old as the others, but they're designed to be more robust, and they've been under cover and unused for the last thirty-four years. And with their big wheels and four wheel drive, we can get through in places our old vehicles would get stuck. Even in the area we've explored, the roads are getting pretty bad in places. What they're like further afield, I dread to think.'

I vaguely remember the old vehicles, but I don't remember much about them. But I remember some of the stories.

One time when Mum and Dad and Uncle Sid were little and the rest of the aunts and uncles weren't even born – so it must have been 1995 or 1996 – the whole family had been quite a way away from home in one of the Jeeps. They'd left the engine running while they raided some houses, but when they came back the engine had stopped. They'd left the Jeep on a slope in case that happened, as they always did, but it wouldn't restart. They had to walk back to the farm – many kilometres with three small children. They had to spend the night in a farm they didn't know on the way. 'There were corpses. Well, just skeletons really, by that time. And there were rats.'

There was a pick-up like ours in the yard, but after so many years they knew there wouldn't even be enough juice in the battery to run the heater plugs, so they'd no chance of bump starting it and they didn't even bother to look for the keys.

Back home, the generator had stopped, too. Fortunately the weather was cold, so the contents of the freezer were still okay. I've seen freezers, and I've been told what they were for and even how they worked, but I've never seen a working one.

'For years after our freezer packed up, we would try other freezers whenever we found them. But we never found another working one. I could kick myself for not collecting a few and keeping them running. We'd probably have had a few more years use out of one of them.'

With no batteries, the only way they could restart the big diesel generator was using the little petrol generator.

'After that, we kept our eyes open for another little petrol generator – or two – and always carried one with us whenever we went out raiding. We preferred to use the pick-up after that, because we didn't like the smell when we carried a petrol generator inside the Jeeps. But the pick-up only lasted a few years, and we never found another one that would start at all.'

After we found the military trucks, there was a big family discussion. The decision was finally made to move out of the farm, and head south. 'South of France, or Italy, or Spain.'

I'd no idea where those places were. Grandad showed me on the map, but it didn't really mean anything to me at the time.

'We can always come back here if things aren't better there.'

Granny Merly wasn't so sure.

'Assuming we don't bump into real trouble somewhere.'

'Real trouble could find us here in the end. And if we take a convoy of ten big military trucks, we'll be a fairly intimidating force. We wouldn't be likely to run into human trouble at any rate.'

'I'd rather take just five. That way we've got two drivers for each vehicle, and can do about twice the distance each day. It also means we've got twice the range with the same amount of fuel.'

'If we take a tanker, we've got range of several thousand kilometres anyway.'

'Refilling that tanker at a filling station will take forever! Best if we could do it overnight.'

'It might be worse than you think. The pumps are designed to fill fuel tanks on ordinary vehicles. They might not have the pressure to get the diesel all the way up to the top of the tanker. We might have to lift it up a jerry can at a time.'

Granny Persie thought the pressure would be plenty, 'but you're right, it would take forever. I wonder if we can find a more powerful pump somewhere? It would be easier anyway. We wouldn't have to rewire the station's pumps up to our generator. I wouldn't be surprised if there's a suitable pump at the depot. We'll have a good look when we go back.'

Aunty Anna suggested that we could split up, half of us staying at the farm with Granny Merly, and half of us heading south with Grandad and Granny Persie. Granny Merly wasn't having that. 'Either we all stay, or we all go. There's not enough of us to want to separate.'

I think Granny Merly couldn't stand the idea of being separated from Grandad and Granny Persie anyway. None of us really wanted to say goodbye to anyone. We knew it would almost certainly be goodbye forever. Well, the grown-ups did, and maybe I did. The three little ones couldn't possibly have understood at all.

There were fourteen of us then. Granny Merly and Mum were still alive, and there were only four of us children. I was the eldest. I was five.

Granny Merly used to laugh about there being ten grown-ups. 'There were only supposed to be six children' – she meant Mum and Dad and all the aunts and uncles – 'and we had the first five on schedule, no problem. But we waited and waited and waited for the last one, and then Aunty Belle and Aunty Dot came along two at once.'

Then Grandad would laugh, 'Like buses!'

It was years before I understood what he meant. I've seen some buses now – loads and loads of them – but it's still hard to get my head around the idea that there were ever enough people to need more than one or two of them. As for trains!

And aeroplanes. The Grannies had both flown in aeroplanes several times. Grandad sometimes tells the story of the one time he flew in an aeroplane, but then he gets all nostalgic and sad[*], and Granny Persie has to cheer him up.

We ended up taking three trucks with big trailers, one of the two tankers, and a Unimog. The tanker had a big, powerful pump built in.

'We were worrying about nothing!'

'We'll still have to rewire a pump when we want petrol for the little generator.'

'We won't need to do that very often! We'll run both the generators every now and then just to keep them in running condition, but I can't see us actually needing them much on the journey, as long as we don't need power tools for repairs or anything. We can keep petrol in most of the jerry cans, anyway. We'll keep a couple for diesel, but we probably won't need more than that.'

We filled both tankers with diesel from the huge underground tank at the depot, and twenty-three jerry cans with petrol from our local petrol station.

---

[*] And if you don't understand why, you'll have to read *Pawns*.

'One thing that worries me is whether we'll be able to get the pumps working at another petrol station, when we eventually need to do that. We've managed to keep this one running all these years, but we've run it every now and then to keep it going. The next one we want to use will very likely have seized up.'

'God, I hope not. We can't dig the guts out of this one to take with us – and it probably wouldn't fit another station unless we were lucky enough to find one of the same type.'

'Well, we could, I suppose. You can see the pump type straight away. We could just drive past petrol stations until we saw the right sort. It's probably better to do that anyway, because I already know how to wire up the generator to this sort. I hope we never need to use it, but it's probably worth taking the guts of this pump.'

And that's what we did. Well, what *they* did, really. I was still only just six.

Granny Persie was chuffed to bits when she realized that the trailers had driven axles, with a shaft drive from the truck. 'With wheels this size, and every wheel driven, we can get through pretty much however bad the roads are.'

Uncle Jake was a bit worried about the tanker. 'It's only got its own four wheels – no trailer to help push.'

Granny Persie laughed, 'No, as long as all the wheels are driven, it's as good as it gets. What I was worried about was trucks pulling trailers that were just dead weight. No problem in most places, but climbing out of muddy holes, or on hills or rough places in snow and ice things could get very difficult.'

She was pleased that the vehicles all had winches on the front, too.

'What we can't do is get these big trucks across from Sweden to Denmark. We might manage to find small boats to get ourselves across, and probably even a good stock of most things, but I can't see us managing to get these across. Even if we could somehow manage to get a big ferry's engines started, we wouldn't know how to operate it.'

The only option was to go all round the Baltic. Some of the grown-ups seemed quite excited at the idea of such a huge expedition, but Granny Merly and some of the others were a bit worried about it.

'We've no idea what conditions are like in Russia or Poland.'

'We've no idea what conditions are like anywhere except around here. But we've no idea what conditions will be like here by the time the little ones grow up. Another couple of bad winters like the last two and things could be getting really difficult around here, whether or not we've still got the place to ourselves.'

'We've all said it before, but I'll say it again. If there's anyone left in the world apart from us and the old camp, we really ought to try to meet up with some of them.'

'Who knows how they'll react to us? Or how they'll be organized? Would you really want to meet up with another camp like the one we left?'

'Not really, no. But at least other camps aren't likely to try to force us to join them if we don't want to, or to shoot first and ask questions later.'

'A convoy of five military trucks, even if more than half of them are driven by small women most of the time, isn't a force anyone is going to take lightly, not even a camp like our old one. As long as we don't act aggressively, no-one's likely to bother us much. A camp like our old one would just let us drive past, I'm pretty sure, if that's what they could see we wanted to do and they'd no idea who we were. And we'd want to get out of their area as quick as we could, too. It's small independent groups like our own that I'd actually like to meet. Or a large, organized group who don't think they need a secure perimeter fence to keep everyone in.'

'We don't actually know whether our old camp has a secure perimeter fence any more. Maybe that was just a temporary arrangement.'

'I expect they've extended the fence by now. But I bet they've still got one. And armed guards. I can't see the soldiers giving up their privileged position that easily.'

'I wonder if anyone else has escaped?'

'We don't even know if they survived the first winter. I guess most of them probably did, even if they didn't all. But if they'd opened the fence, I'd have thought we'd have bumped into some of them by now. Some of them would surely have come in this direction. Even if we'd not actually met any of them, you'd think we'd have seen evidence of their raids.'

'I'm not sure. We're a long way away.'

'It's only a couple of days' drive.'

'It was then. With the state the roads are in now, it'd be three or four at least, and you'd need a four wheel drive vehicle.'

'If they're still using those coaches, they won't be going far.'

'I'd be amazed if those coaches are still running. Actually, I wonder whether they've got motor vehicles at all any more. If they'd got a military vehicle depot in their raiding area, I'd have thought they'd have replaced the coaches straight away. And I can't think of anywhere but a military vehicle depot where they'd be likely to find any batteries without their acid in them already.'

'They might have kept the coaches for a while because they were easier to decontaminate than a military truck.'

'They were using that tractor with a trailer. A military truck would have been no worse than that.'

'The farm would be damned hard work without any motor vehicles. They don't even have horses or bullocks to pull ploughs.'

'Nor do we.'

'That's a chilling thought. How long could we keep the tractor going if we stay here? Will we manage to get a tractor going wherever we actually end up?'

'Quite likely not. The Unimog makes a pretty good tractor, though, and it'll probably outlast most things. But the day is coming when we, or our descendants anyway, won't have motor vehicles – and probably no draught animals either. Unless there are still factories working somewhere, and I rather doubt that. Or someone somewhere kept some draught animals in a shelter, and they're successfully breeding them somewhere. I'm not confident of that, either.'

Before we went, Granny Persie insisted that we pretty well cleared out the depot. We left a tanker, full of diesel, a truck, a Unimog, several batteries and some acid for them in the big barn at the farm, and a truck or two in barns at several other farms we knew we could find again – places where we'd spent the odd night at one time or another.

'If we ever come back to this area, we want to be able to find at least some of these vehicles. The most likely place for anyone else to raid would be the depot, if they were looking for this kind of stuff..'

Grandad was sceptical. 'If no-one's raided it in thirty-four years, I don't think anyone's going to.'

Grandma Persie wasn't convinced. 'We didn't raid it for thirty-four years. Better safe than sorry.'

She made sure that only five batteries got filled with acid.

'If we're going to leave a vehicle behind, we only need a battery in it while we're actually moving it. We can put the same battery in one vehicle after another. Every battery with acid in can end up being the battery for one of the vehicles we actually take.'

We couldn't distribute the acid around the various farms: there were just two big carboys full. We left one in the barn at our own farm, and took the other one with us in one of the trailers.

'There's not much point distributing the unstarted batteries, since we can't distribute the acid. We'll take half of them with us, and leave the other half at our own farm.'

But we ended up taking more than half with us.

'We're not expecting to be back, and if we are, there's still plenty here, and anyway, any we've still got we'll bring back with us.'

I wasn't aware of much of that at the time, but I do remember noticing that one trailer was almost full of spare wheels – not just tyres, whole wheels. I think the trucks we'd left behind probably only had three wheels each. Granny Persie's cunning like that.

Granny Persie was very reluctant to unwire the big diesel generator from our own farm, but they wanted to take two with us, and they'd only kept two in running condition. She and Uncle Sid scoured the surrounding farms without success looking for another one they could start, but they didn't want to waste time working on any of them.

'We could spend a lot of time, and still have nothing to show for it. We'll just have to take these two. If we do come back, all being well we'll bring both of them back with us.'

All our big preparations were towards the end of autumn, and we actually set off at the beginning of spring the following year. We wanted to make sure we weren't stuck somewhere in the far north when winter came.

'We should have plenty of time, but better safe than sorry. The roads will be pretty bad in places.'

Chapter 2

I remember the day we moved out very well, too. Grandad, the Grannies, Mum and Uncle Sid had been at the farm for twenty-nine years – almost the whole of Mum's and Uncle Sid's lives – and all the rest of us had been born there. I remember the tears in nearly everyone's eyes. But there was a lot of excitement, too. We were going on an expotition.

Okay, I know it's an expedition really. That's one of Grandad's little jokes. It's from one of his stories. He's got lots of little stories, and I remember how much I loved them when I was little. Tell the truth, I still do love them – but I love the way the littler ones enjoy them even more. I know Grandad enjoys telling them, too, especially because of the effect they have on us kids.

He draws hilarious pictures to go with the stories. He says they're not very good, and that he wishes he had the original books, especially for the pictures.

'Maybe one day we'll raid a bookshop that has them. Maybe they'll be Finnish or Russian or Polish or German translations, but the pictures'll be the same, and I can remember the words. I can remember the pictures too, but I can't draw them properly.'

But he never has found those books.

At first, the going was very good. There were potholes in the roads, of course, but there was a recognizable road almost all the way. Here and there it had been washed away completely, but with big wheels, all driven, we just drove through the mess – slowly and carefully, but pretty much straight through. We did nearly two hundred kilometres the first day.

Grandad says he still translates distances into miles every time, but Granny Persie laughs at him.

'The trucks think in kilometres, all the road signs are in kilometres, all the youngsters think in kilometres. You don't know how long a mile is any more than you know how long a kilometre is, anyway!'

'Yes I do. A mile is one point six kilometres.'

'Of course, but how far is that? How far away are those rocks on that hilltop?'

Then Grandad laughs. 'Okay, you win. I've no idea.'

I'm not sure Granny Persie knows, either, but I don't say anything.

Most of the road signs were illegible, the writing either peeled off or covered with lichen. Or a bit of both.

Granny Persie had an ancient opisometer, and had shown me how to measure distances on the map with it, but nobody used to bother. They estimated distances just by looking at the maps and knowing the scales.

'Even the opisometer doesn't really give you an accurate distance. The map doesn't show you the smallest wiggles, and they can make a huge difference, especially in the mountains. The distance doesn't tell you much anyway, because both time and fuel consumption depend so much on the condition of the road.'

We crossed over into Sweden somewhere on the third day. Grandad talks about the border crossing, but I don't remember it, and borders don't mean anything any more anyway. I didn't understand about borders at all at that time, and they don't really make much sense to me even now.

The further north we went, the worse the roads got. The washouts got bigger and more difficult to cross. Eventually we came to one where the second truck got stuck. I was in the first truck, with Granny Persie and Aunty Dot. Aunty Dot had been driving, but Granny Persie took over for the difficult bit through the washout. Whether it was that Granny Persie was a more expert driver than Grandad, who was driving the second truck, or whether it was because our truck had made some deep ruts that Grandad got stuck in, we'll never know.

Uncle Sid was driving the tanker. He'd been waiting at the edge of the washout for Grandad to get through before he drove into the mud himself. He got down out of the tanker, put on some huge boots that came halfway up his thighs, and waded into the mud. They'd worked out the procedure beforehand, and he knew exactly what to do. He grabbed the big hook on the end of the winch wire on Grandad's truck, and signalled to Grandad to release the winch.

It was quite a struggle for Uncle Sid, getting through the mud pulling the winch cable to hook it up to the back of Granny Persie's truck, but he managed. He signalled to Grandad when it was hooked on safely. With six big wheels driving and the winch pulling, Grandad drove through the mud, up the bank, and onto the road behind Granny Persie's truck.

'I'm not sure about getting the tanker and the other truck through there, though. I don't think the Unimog will have much trouble, but what are we going to do about the other two?'

There was no question of leaving them behind! Not that we'd have had to leave any of the people behind, of course, or even all of the stuff. But the truck was worth a lot to us, and the tanker full of diesel was vital.

Granny Persie and Uncle Sid walked up and down the banks of the river that had washed the road away, looking for a place they could cross more easily on foot. They found a place they could wade across in their long boots. Then Granny Persie took over driving the Unimog from Granny Merly, and they drove up and down that side of the river looking for a better place to take the trucks across the river.

I waited anxiously with Grandad and Aunty Dot, and Aunty Belle, who'd been in the second truck with Grandad. At first we were standing on the last bit of road, right at the edge of the washout, waving at the rest of the family standing on the last bit of road on their side; but then it started to rain, and we all got into the cab of Truck Two, and the others all got into the cab of the tanker. They could see our trucks, but we could only see theirs in one of the mirrors.

I felt as though they might as well be a thousand kilometres away. At least we had the intercom, so we could talk to them. At first, we could talk to Granny Persie in the Unimog as well, but then the link became intermittent, and finally broke completely.

'They're either too far away, or hidden behind a hill. Don't worry, Mikey.'

But the time stretched out, and there was still no sign from Granny Persie. I began to worry. I think it took longer before Grandad and the twins started to worry, but after a while I could tell they were worried, too.

Eventually Grandad spotted the Unimog in the distance. He wasn't sure which side of the river it was on.

'Persie! Can you hear me? I can see you now!'

'Really? I've not spotted you yet! Oh, I see you. We're on your side of the river now, with a drivable route to a place I'm pretty sure we can get the trucks across. But I've not found a drivable route back to the road on this side yet. It doesn't look good, in fact. I think we might have to go back and try to find a different place to ford the river – either further upstream still, or maybe downstream.'

Granny Persie and Uncle Sid spent all that afternoon searching up and down the river for a route, without success.

'We'll spend the night here now, obviously. If we can't find a route tomorrow morning, I've got an idea how we can get through here.'

There really wasn't an alternative crossing with a drivable route back to the road, and Granny Persie's method had to be used.

'I just hope the spare wheels survive, that's all. I'm pretty sure we'll get the trucks through all right.'

They unloaded six of the spare wheels from the trailer, and with much grunting and puffing and swearing and getting very muddy, the four men managed to manhandle them into position across the deepest ruts in the mud. They hooked up the winch before the third truck even entered the washout.

'If we can possibly keep the truck moving, hopefully we'll avoid making any more big holes for the next one.'

Granny Persie's trick worked perfectly. The tanker and the last truck, with its trailer, came across steadily with no problems at all, and the Unimog came across easily without even a winch cable.

Getting the spare wheels out afterwards was harder. Grandad took one look and knew they couldn't possibly manhandle them out. The only way was with the Unimog's winch. Granny Persie insisted that Grandad and Uncle Sid should put another two spare wheels on top of the winch cable, near each buried wheel, before she pulled.

'I don't fancy having a flying wheel coming crashing into the front of the Unimog when it comes free!'

They certainly came out with a big plop and knocked the piled wheels about, but I'm not sure they'd really have catapulted all that far. Better safe than sorry, though.

'I'm glad the Unimog was able to pull them out. Turning a truck round to use one of the bigger winches would have been a real pain.'

Then they had to fetch bucket after bucket of water up from the river to wash down the wheels before they loaded them back onto the trailer. One of them had lost all its air – the valve had got wrenched out – but the rest were okay.

'We'll keep that one anyway, even though we don't have a spare inner tube for it. It's still a good wheel and a good tyre.'

'We don't have any way to get a tyre on and off a wheel.'

'No, but we'll find a place that has the equipment. It'll be more of a problem to find a tube for it, for a tyre this size. If there's rubber solution that's still any good, we'll cut a valve and a few centimetres of rubber out of a different size tube, and patch it into this tube.'

'It would've been better if we'd had some big baulks of timber – railway sleepers or the like – rather than risking spoiling our spare wheels like that. But even if we find some, we've no room for them in the trucks or on the trailers.'

'But there'll be more washouts like that, beyond a doubt. Probably worse than that. We'll have to decide what to leave behind if we're lucky enough to find some timbers.'

'Or find a farm trailer, and pull it with the Unimog. We could regard a farm trailer as disposable, and just leave it behind if it gets stuck. There's hundreds of them around.'

'We'll always be able to pull through with the winch, I'm sure. And we won't want to leave a trailer stuck, even if we do regard it as disposable, because we might want to go back and we won't want anything blocking the road. Even if we're not going all the way back home, we might want to backtrack a little way to find a different route somewhere. We've been assuming the 88 is likely to be less broken than the E4, but we don't know that for sure. Even some of the minor roads might be better in some places.'

We found a farm trailer easily enough.

The timbers to fill it took longer. By the time we found them – a pile of rough cut timbers Grandad and Uncle Sid could barely lift, and so long that they overhung the trailer quite a lot – we'd been through several bad washouts, but only once had we had to use the spare wheels again, because Granny Persie and Uncle Sid had worked out a new procedure.

Whenever we got to a washout that looked the least bit difficult, the Unimog went through first, without its trailer, with the tanker's winch cable, running free, already attached. Then the tanker went through, pulling the next truck's winch cable, and so on. But the Unimog went back before the last truck came through, so its winch cable could be attached. Finally, the Unimog came through pulling its own trailer.

That way, none of the vehicles dug themselves into big holes at all in most places.

Later, we found a bigger trailer and wondered if we should swap them.

'It's heavier, but it's got the same size wheels as the trucks, which is better than those little ones. And we won't have to rope the timbers on.'

'Yes, but it'll be a lot more awkward getting the timbers on and off.'

That was a telling point, and we kept the smaller one.

Several days later and still heading north, we reached a place where there was obviously no chance of getting the vehicles across, even though we had found the timbers by then. The road went along the crest of a dam that had failed. The river had cut a channel through the dam, right down to the natural floor of the valley. The road ended in an almost vertical drop of about fifteen metres, facing a similar cliff maybe twenty metres away.

Granny Merly wondered why we'd ever set off on this hopeless expedition. Grandad was a bit disappointed, and wondered whether we'd have to go back after all. Even Granny Persie was a bit worried.

'Even if we manage to find a ford somewhere upstream or downstream this time, with passable routes to it on both sides of the river, sooner or later we're going to get to a place we really can't get past, come what may.'

It was Uncle Sid and the twins who persuaded everyone not to give up hope.

'We'll find a way round, even if we have to make a bit of road to do it. We've come all this way without getting stuck, and we're doing fine for time. We could take a week moving rocks to make some spot passable, and it wouldn't matter as long as it didn't happen too often. Look how far we've come already, and this is the first place that's really been difficult.'

'I know we want to get well south again, the other side of the Baltic, before winter, but even if the worst comes to the worst, we can survive the winter stuck in the far north if we have to. We've plenty of food and fuel.'

'We've been passing farms often enough, too. We've not even been bothering to raid them to replace food we've eaten. I know we've only eaten two weeks' worth, and we've got enough for about a year, but even so.'

In the end, Granny Persie and Uncle Sid, in the Unimog, found a route around the big washout. It involved several places where we had to put timbers down and use the winches to get across boggy ground and we lost several of the timbers, but it was a detour of only a few kilometres. We were back on the road.

'We'll find some more timbers I expect.'

After that, we raided the next few farms. At one of them, Grandad had a brainwave.

'I hate being so destructive, but what the hell? There's more farms here than what's left of humanity will want in a hundred years, and they'll all have fallen down before then.'

He hooked the Unimog's winch to a big beam in the old farmhouse, and pulled the whole place down. Then one by one, they pulled out several hefty joists, and loaded them into the trailer. We'd got plenty of timbers again, and we knew how to get more if we needed them.

Then we gave up raiding farms.

'We'll wait for a village, where we can raid several houses relatively quickly.'

And that's what we did.

We had to make detours off the road in a few places, and in one place we had to fill in a ravine with rocks, which really did take about a week. The Unimog went back and forth, fetching trailer load after trailer load of rocks from a boulder-strewn hillside a couple of kilometres away. All four men were exhausted by the end of each day, manhandling the biggest rocks they could manage on and off the trailer. I helped too, but looking back on it, the little stones I loaded and unloaded can't have made much difference, and I was probably getting in the way really.

When it was done, the trucks rolled across with no problems at all.

Heading north up through Sweden, that was the worst place. We were beginning to feel confident we could cope with anything by one means or another. At one point, we stopped at a filling station, and topped up the tanker with diesel. 'We've only used a tiny fraction of a tankerful anyway, but it's no trouble stopping and I feel more comfortable with the tanker full.'

'It's reassuring to know it's so easy to get at the tank in a filling station, too.'

'It might not be as easy at some of them. That's part of why I'll feel more comfortable if we fill up long before we need to.'

'The pumps are the same sort there were back at Østerby.'

That was reassuring too, but we didn't actually need to run the station's pumps, because we'd not used any petrol at all.

We'd seen no signs of any human activity more recent than the war – or the cull, whichever it had been, if there's really any difference anyway – all the way.

Although our farm had been overrun with rabbits, and we'd seen quite a lot in the south, there didn't seem to be any further north. We'd seen hares, rats, a few birds of various species, a few foxes, and traces of wolves – but not the wolves themselves. Granny Persie and Uncle Sid had shot a few hares, which made a nice change from tins, pickles, dried stuff and root vegetables. Grandad and Mum and Dad had managed to catch a few fish, too.

I remember that I was missing Granny Persie's seaweed stews. By the time I was born, the freezer had been dead for years, so I'd only had seaweed when we'd been down to the coast – trips I don't remember at all. If I hadn't got to know seaweed again later, I expect I'd have forgotten what it was like by now – but I definitely remember missing it.

All the grown-ups say it's very sad that I don't remember the Norwegian south coast, that was so near our old farm. They say it was a wonderful place.

Late one morning, Granny Persie and Uncle Sid were investigating a possible ford just a few yards upstream of a place where a bridge had been washed away. They were on foot, poking about in some mud, seeing whether they thought the vehicles would be able to get through without having to put timbers down, when Uncle Sid shouted, and Granny Persie ran over to him. Watching from the road, we all heard him and saw her running. Then Uncle Sid came running back to the road, leaving Granny Persie crouching down looking at something in the mud.

'Come and look! Mum (that's what Uncle Sid calls Granny Persie) isn't sure what they are. She thinks you might know, Dad (that's Grandad) or Aunty Merly might.'

Granny Merly didn't know, and Grandad wasn't sure either.

'I'm no expert. It might be goats, but maybe a bit big for goats. I *think* it's some kind of deer. Up here, probably reindeer.'

'That was my guess, too. Looks like there's quite a few of them.'

'Those prints can't be thirty-four years old. In fact, I reckon they're pretty fresh. They'll be gone the next time this river rises – maybe even next time it rains. They'd surely at least have lost their crispness if it had rained since whatever made them was here.'

'So they're probably just a few hours old, unless the rain we had earlier on was just local.'

'I vote we make camp here tonight. We don't absolutely have to press on as hard as we can, all day every day. If we sit quietly, maybe they'll show their faces again.'

'I wouldn't want to shoot a reindeer, though. We get plenty of meat from the hares, and we couldn't finish a whole reindeer before it went off.'

'I'm not so sure about that, with ten adults. How big is a reindeer? I don't know. But I wasn't thinking of shooting one anyway. I'd just like to see them.'

'So would I. But is it worth hanging around half a day, just to see reindeer? As you say, we don't need one for food. If there's been a herd of them here, it's likely there'll be more.'

'I don't know how big reindeer are, either, but they're certainly a good deal bigger than hares or foxes or wolves. Biggest animal we know to have survived in the wild. Unless of course they were in a shelter somewhere.'

'Maybe the war didn't really reach here.'

'It must have done. There'd be lots of people up here if it hadn't, and they'd have spread south by now. Even if we hadn't actually met any, we'd surely have seen signs of their presence.'

'I don't know. With the roads this bad, and most vehicles surely knackered by now, even if there were still lots of people we'd be pretty unusual being on the move like this. People won't be migrating very fast. Migrating on foot, thirty-four years isn't long enough for people to be likely to have spread very far at all. I doubt you'd migrate more than a long day's march in a generation.'

'They could be migrating by boat. You could carry more, and move small children more easily, that way. You might go a lot further in a generation.'

'You might. The whole coast might be getting repopulated, and we wouldn't have known until they got right round to the southern tip of Norway.'

'This is all just speculation. Let's just keep on moving, and we'll see what we see.'

Granny Persie never lets Grandad get away with that.

'There's nothing wrong with speculation, Mr Collins. Without speculation, you don't know what you're looking for, and you'll miss important observations that might support or confirm your speculations, or make them seem less likely or impossible.'

She only ever calls him Mr Collins when she's making a point like that, and we all think it's hilarious. Even Grandad himself laughs. Every time.

'Okay. What I'm still wondering is whether it was just a few odd reindeer that survived, like the few odd rabbits down south, and they've gradually re-established themselves, or whether they survived in big numbers in the first place. They obviously don't breed as fast as rabbits, but I'm pretty sure they breed a lot faster than humans.'

'So if there's a lot of them – and this doesn't seem to have been a very small herd – you're thinking that a lot must have survived, and that maybe quite a few humans survived, too?'

'You seem to be thinking that as well.'

Granny Persie and Grandad often score points off each other like that. Granny Persie nearly always wins. It's all entirely good-natured though. They're still very much in love even after all these years.

'Sort of. But we've increased from three to fourteen in a generation and a half. If reindeer reach sexual maturity in say six years, and each female has one calf each year, they'll have increased an awful lot in thirty-four years. Rabbits absolutely exploded in just a few years.'

'Maybe we should look carefully to see if there are any human footprints here before we go, anyway. If I remember aright, the Sami people often travel with herds of reindeer.'

'There's lots of our own footprints around here by now anyway. We've no hope of telling which are which.'

'Except that ours are on top of the reindeer prints. Any that have reindeer prints on top of them can't be ours. And we could follow where the herd went for a little way. Then we'd have a better chance of seeing any prints that weren't ours.'

But away from the muddy area, we couldn't see where the herd had gone at all. 'An expert could probably tell. But until we meet the Sami and they teach us, we don't have any hope.'

Granny Merly laughed. 'IF there still are any Sami, and IF we find them, you're going to spend a few months with them learning to track reindeer? You'll have to learn their language first. Some of the old ones might know Swedish, so Persie and I might be able to talk with them, but I'd be very surprised if any of the young ones even know Swedish. Seriously, I'm pretty sure that the last Sami must have died thirty-four years ago.'

They drove the Unimog through the ford, and decided that it would be best to put timbers down in a couple of places before driving the trucks through. So it took a few hours to get past that point. They'd not used a lot of timbers, but getting them out after the trucks had driven over them was always a slow process. As usual, a few were impossible to dig out, and a few others were so badly damaged they weren't worth retrieving. Uncle Sid thought it was probably quicker to get fresh timbers out of an old farmhouse than to dig used ones out of a bog, but nobody really liked pulling farmhouses down. It just seemed so destructive.

'You never know who might want to use them one day, even if they're in very decrepit condition by that time. It could be the difference between life and death for someone.'

'If there's anyone left apart from us. But you're right, it's not a lot of extra trouble, if any, to rescue as many as we can. And we really don't know whether there might be other independent survivors around. There can't be all that many in this part of the world at the moment, or we'd have met them or seen evidence of them, but there could be some, or people from somewhere else might arrive here later.'

By the time we'd finished digging out the last of the reusable timbers, it was the middle of the afternoon. Then there were two more washouts. They weren't as bad, and we didn't need to put down any timbers, but we did use the winches just in case, and even that takes time. All in all, we didn't get much further that day.

We reached yet another washout late in the afternoon, and Granny Persie, driving the Unimog at the front of the convoy, decided to call a halt.

'We don't want to be halfway through crossing this place when it gets dark.'

There was still about an hour of daylight left, and Grandad and Uncle Sid decided to climb a steep little hill a kilometre or so from the road, to scan the surrounding countryside with the binoculars. They took the Unimog across the rough country to a point as close to the hill as they could, and scrambled up the hill from there. It was beginning to get dark by the time they got back to the Unimog, and they drove back with the headlights on. It was the first time the headlights had been used, apart from checking that they worked when we first got the trucks.

'Interesting. I wish I hadn't had to use the headlights though. It might have scared them away.'

'Scared what away? Did you see reindeer?'

'Better than that. There are people here, with the reindeer. Not very many, I don't think, but some, I'm pretty sure. From up there we could see what look like two herds of reindeer, and each one seems to have a tent nearby. They're a long way off, and I can't be absolutely sure they're tents from this distance, but they look like it. I'd guess they're made out of reindeer skins, by the colour. They could just be rocks, but the other rocks around don't look the same.'

'If they're so far away you can't really make them out very well through the binoculars, do you think they'd even have seen the Unimog's lights?'

'Unless they were all inside their tents, I'm sure they would have. They might not have known what they were, if none of them are much more than thirty-four years old, but no-one could miss beams of light dancing about like that, I'm sure. If you didn't know what they were, they could be pretty scary. And even if you did know what they were, if you'd not seen any for donkey's years you'd probably be pretty worried about whose they might be.'

'I suppose you're right. It would have fairly put the wind up us, back at the farm, if we'd seen headlights around.'

'And we can be pretty sure there's been no-one else around with motor vehicles for a good long time. There's no roads for anyone who's less well equipped than we are.'

'I'd love to be up that hill in the dark, actually. I bet they've got fires. We'd be able to see fires further away, or in more camouflaged locations. We might be able to see more than just two small encampments.'

'I'm not sure you'd see their fires anyway. I'm pretty sure the fires would be inside their tents, and whether much light would escape I'm not sure. You might see the smoke if you were up there at dusk.'

'We were up there at dusk! If there was smoke, it was too well camouflaged – harder to see than the tents.'

'Without a torch, we can't get up or down that hill in the dark anyway, and I certainly don't fancy spending a whole night up there.'

I'd never seen a torch, but I'd heard about them. For the first few years after the war, Grandad and the Grannies had had a big rechargeable torch. They'd been able to raid deep into shops where daylight didn't reach, without having to trail cables from a vehicle; but the torch's battery had eventually died like all the rest. They'd been disappointed, but not surprised, that there hadn't been any small batteries in the battery store at the depot.

I've seen torches now, but I've still never seen a working one. Museum pieces, like so many other things. Not that they're in a museum – except in the sense that most of the world is a museum now.

Grandad's told me lots about museums, but I've never seen one of them, either. I wonder if I ever will? Grandad says there must have been some in Oslo, but we never went looking for them.

Chapter 3

In the morning we tackled the washout that had stopped us the previous afternoon. It wasn't a bad one, and we got through it using just the winches, no timbers at all.

'We could probably have just driven the trucks straight through really. Just a waste of time using the winches.'

'Quite likely. But not worth risking it. I'm not looking forward to the day we lose a truck, and I hope to high heaven it's not the tanker if we do.'

'Before we go on too far, we ought to think about whether we want to try to meet the people around here, and if we do, how to go about it. Even in the Unimog, we can't just drive across country and go visiting. We'd probably scare the living daylights out of them anyway, if we could.'

'For the next few miles, we're getting closer to one set of tents, and not really any further away from the other. But after that, we'll be getting further away. So unless this is just the beginning of an area with more people, we've got to think what to do pretty soon.'

Granny Persie laughed. 'You and your miles!'

Grandad stuck his tongue out. 'I mean for the next slightly-more-than-a-few kilometres. I'm sorry.'

Granny Merly said it seemed she was probably wrong about the Sami.

'Anyone camping alongside reindeer herds is far more likely to be Sami than anyone else.'

'And whoever they are, they're independent survivors, not a fenced-in camp. We really ought to make an effort to meet them. We could learn a lot from people who know how to survive right up here, and maybe we've got something to offer them, too.'

'So how do we get to meet them? I suppose all we can do is get as close as we can in the trucks, and then walk. But it's not going to be an easy walk, there's an awful lot of very boggy areas, and they're a devil of a long way away from the road.'

'I doubt if they'll stay in the same place anyway, and they know the place and will move much faster than we can. Even if they're not deliberately trying to get away from us, we'll never be able to catch up with them. I think we should just set up camp somewhere visible from a long way off, light a fire in the evenings, and hope that they want to come and see who we are.'

'A pity we don't have any tents. A convoy of military trucks isn't the most inviting kind of camp.'

'The best we can do is make our fire a little way away from the road, and hope they're curious enough to come close enough to see that we're just a family with little children.'

Late that afternoon, they parked the vehicles in a place where the road went through a patch of trees, so they weren't visible from a distance.

'They've probably seen them already, or heard them, or they saw our headlight beams yesterday, but that can't be helped.'

Granny Merly and Mum and Aunty Anna got on with cooking the evening meal. Grandad and Uncle Sid chose a couple of the less substantial timbers, that hadn't been used at the previous days washouts and were still dry, and split them into firewood, with some slenderer bits for kindling. Granny Persie made a few torches – not electric torches, wooden rods with rags ready to be soaked in diesel tied round one end – for the grown-ups to carry when we wanted to walk back to the trucks in the dark later on. Then all of us carried everything up a little hill a couple of hundred metres away from the road, and Granny Merly lit the fire.

I remember that evening very clearly. The atmosphere was magic, with all of us sitting on rocks, facing the fire, with

sparks flying up into the night, and the shadows dancing
behind us. I went to sleep with my head on Granny Merly's
lap, hearing the grown-up's voices discussing the world, the
future, what they thought they might or might not be able to
do, and whether they'd move on the next day, or stay put for
a couple of days to see if anyone would come and investigate
us and our fire.

I remember vaguely waking up as I was being put to bed
in the truck, too.

What I absolutely do not remember is hearing all the
conversations in faltering Swedish that happened that night.
But I've heard all about it.

After I'd gone to sleep, Grandad was a little surprised to
see a face staring out of the darkness behind the twins. It
seemed unreal, too improbable that it would happen so
easily. At first he wasn't sure if he was imagining it, whether
he could really see a face at all, it was so dark so far away
from the fire. Then he wasn't sure whether he was just
getting used to staring into the night, or whether the face was
getting gradually closer, but after a little while he was certain
there really was a face there.

He says he hesitated for a moment about whether to say
anything to the rest of the family, and then realized that the
owner of the face almost certainly wouldn't understand
English, and that the whole family had been chattering away
without alarming them.

'Don't look round now, but just opposite me there's
someone back there behind the twins, watching us.'

'I was about to mention the same thing, Pete,' said Granny
Merly, 'except that the person I can see is behind you. I
thought at first that maybe I was imagining them, but I think
they've moved a bit closer.'

Then Granny Persie said, 'Welcome, come and join us by
the fire,' in Swedish, and two young women stepped out of

the darkness. They were very skinny, and dressed in rough clothing made of reindeer skins.

Their knowledge of Swedish was far from perfect, and the Grannies hadn't spoken it for thirty-four years. There was no other common language, so conversation was very difficult, but each side recognized the other's friendly intentions.

It transpired that there were three of them: two women, Lieđđi and Suonjar, and one man, Gealbu – three cousins. Gealbu had stayed with the reindeer while Lieđđi and Suonjar came to investigate us.

The three of them were the only survivors of their community, and apart from two other families of reindeer herders, we were the first people they'd seen in a very long time. They thought there were at least a few others though, because they'd occasionally seen traces of where people had been, in places they were pretty sure the other families they knew didn't go.

The last of their parents' generation had died when they were still children. There had originally been two older cousins as well, but they had both died not long after the older people.

Lieđđi and Suonjar didn't know what everyone had died of, and either they couldn't describe the symptoms very well, or the Grannies couldn't understand the descriptions. They didn't know how old they themselves were, either, but the Grannies guessed they were in their mid-twenties.

Late that evening, Lieđđi and Suonjar had slipped off into the night, after extracting promises that we wouldn't leave in the morning before they'd come back with Gealbu.

'I don't think they can possibly be thirty-four years old, and anyway, their parents obviously survived a good few years after the war. So either the lethal agents, whatever they were, didn't reach here and their parents' deaths are coincidental, or the agents were diluted or decayed by the time they reached here, and resulted in much reduced expectation of life rather than fairly rapid death.'

'Much reduced expectation of life, but no loss of fertility. These two were born long after the war, obviously.'

'Could be some reduction in fertility, who knows? And how much older were their older cousins? Were they perhaps small children at the time of the war, or even foetuses? Were small children or foetuses particularly vulnerable, perhaps?'

'If so few people survived around here, it's pretty certainly only quite isolated pockets where the agent, whatever it was, was so weak it didn't kill everyone.'

I do remember the following morning, when Lieđđi turned up with Gealbu. Suonjar had stayed with the reindeer.

I thought Gealbu was a very funny little man. He was all curled over, and leant heavily on a stick.

Lieđđi was carrying a large piece of meat. It was evidently a present. She looked up the hill at the remains of our fire, and seemed very puzzled that we'd let it go out. She had a conversation with the Grannies, which I remember being amazed at, because I couldn't understand a word of it. Gealbu said not a word, but nodded and gestured at intervals.

Granny Merly took Lieđđi into the back of the truck we slept in – and cooked and ate in – and lit the stove. Granny Merly told me later that Lieđđi was visibly astonished at the stove. She'd obviously only ever cooked over a fire.

The meat was reindeer, of course. What none of us knew at that stage was that it had been kept underground for more than a year! It was delicious, anyway. Grandad and the Grannies discussed what present we should give them.

'We could give them some clothes. We've got more than plenty, and can get more easily when we next reach a town, or even a farm or two. We've nothing that will fit them well, but some of Jake's and Dot's and Belle's clothes will be a lot better than what they've got.'

'Would they really, though? Their clothes look rough, but I don't suppose they care what they look like, and I bet they're warm and hard-wearing. And they obviously know how to repair them as necessary.'

'I'd happily take them with us, but I have the feeling they're better off here with their reindeer. They know what they're doing here.'

'If we'd really be happy to take them, we ought to ask them what they'd like to do. Maybe they'd really like to move on. At least we should give them the option. I don't know whether they've thought about their old age, but I can imagine them having a pretty bad time.'

'When I heard they'd got a male cousin their own age, I was a bit surprised they've not got any children. They'd have an even bigger problem with inbreeding than we do, all being cousins, but having lost their parents while they were still children I don't suppose they know about that. But I think I can see now why it's not an issue anyway. Is Gealbu even fertile? I guess that's a serious congenital defect he's got.'

Lieđđi and Gealbu were apparently quite at ease not understanding a word, while our grown-ups discussed all this. The decision to make the offer, not particularly expecting it to be taken up, was easily reached.

Then Granny Persie spoke to them in Swedish. They seemed quite surprised by the offer, but smiled broadly.

'We'll have to ask Suonjar, and we've got the reindeer to think of. They wouldn't want to ride in a truck, even if you could take them.'

'Wouldn't the reindeer be okay on their own?'

'I suppose so, although I think they'd miss us a lot. And if once we've left them on their own, we can't change our minds. We'd never find them again. We're not really expert like our parents were.'

While Granny Persie was talking to Lieđđi, Granny Merly was telling the rest of us what was going on.

Gealbu hadn't said a word, but it was obvious from his nods and gestures that he was following the Swedish perfectly well. We later found out that he *couldn't* talk, although he understood both Sami and Swedish, the latter better than his cousins did. Whatever else might have been wrong with him, there was nothing wrong with his brain.

After a little while, Lieđđi and Gealbu went off to talk with Suonjar. It was more than two hours before Lieđđi and Suonjar reappeared. They'd obviously been having a very serious discussion.

'We're not sure. It's a very difficult decision. We've got everything we need here. We know how to live here. We're not as expert as our parents were, but we're managing. Our biggest worry is how we'll manage when we get old.'

'Won't your children be grown up by the time you get old?'

'We don't have any children, and without husbands we won't have any.'

'Aren't there any men in the other families you know?'

'They've got their own wives, and anyway, they don't like us. We're Sami.'

'I thought they were Sami, too – they're herding reindeer just like you, aren't they?'

'Of course they're Sami, but they think they're better than us because we speak Sami, and they speak Swedish.'

'You can speak Swedish too.'

'Not very well. It's not our mother tongue, and we don't speak it amongst ourselves. Anyway, our parents were proud to be Sami and speak Sami.'

Mostly it was Lieđđi who was talking, but Suonjar joined in, 'To be honest, there's another thing. It's Gealbu. He's our cousin and we love him and we couldn't possibly leave him on his own, he'd die. But the other families don't want to be near him.'

'That's true. They're horrible to him. It's really unfair. I think they're jealous of him actually, he's so good with the reindeer. He's good with his hands, too – our clothes are much better than theirs, and he does them all.'

'There's another things that's worrying us, actually. You tell them, Lieđđi.'

'Oh, yes. You were living a long way away from here, is that right?'

'Yes. Why?'

'What's the weather been like where you were, these past few winters?'

'Bad. Much worse than it used to be when we first arrived there.'

'Hmm. So it's not just around here, then. As long as we can remember, each winter has been longer and colder than the last. We're worried that if it gets much worse, we'll be in trouble.'

'That's part of why we're going south. It's warmer down south.'

'But you can only go south so far. You get to the sea in the end.'

'We've come north so we can go further south, round the other side of the sea.'

'No, you get to the sea again that side.'

'Not if you go far enough east.'

But Lieđđi and Suonjar didn't know what east meant at all, and they'd been assuming that 'south' – well, söder, since they were talking Swedish – meant downhill. They thought we were planning to go over the tops of the mountains and down the other side. It took a while for the Grannies and Lieđđi and Suonjar to work out what each other were talking about. Lieđđi and Suonjar's knowledge of geography didn't extend as far as the south of Norway and Sweden, never mind the sea crossing to Denmark, and the idea that there

were places where the ground wasn't covered in deep snow
for months every winter was completely new to them.

Their wits were sharp, though. They'd never seen maps
before, but Granny Persie got out the maps to show them,
and in no time at all they were working out how all the
places they knew fitted onto the map. They could scarcely
read, but they kept asking Granny Persie what each bit of
writing said, and they excitedly recognized a lot of the place
names – more often the names of rivers and hills than the
villages. Suonjar thought some of them were wrong, but
Lieđđi suggested that it was simply that the Swedish name
wasn't the same as the Sami one. 'The map seems to use
Swedish or Sami names at random – or maybe some of the
names are the same in both languages, or nearly the same
anyway.'

Lieđđi had even noticed the contour lines on the larger
scale maps of the immediate vicinity, and that the smaller
scale maps covering larger areas didn't have them – and
worked out that they had something to do with hills and
valleys. Granny Persie was impressed, and explained all
about contours. Lieđđi seemed to have no problem grasping
the principle – and although she could read words only with
difficulty, she could read numbers perfectly well. Granny
Persie had to show her how big a metre was, though, and she
found it hard to relate one metre to the heights of hills in
metres, or distances in kilometres. But she caught on very
easily to the idea that a thumb joint length on the local map
was about a day's walk, or on the big map about four days'
walk.

'It's much quicker in winter, though. We can ski at nearly
twice the speed we can walk.'

'How does Gealbu get on with skis?'

'Oh, he's like a different man. On the flat and uphill, he's
almost as quick as us two, but downhill he's really good. You
should see him. He does things we wouldn't dare to try, and
he never makes a mistake. We don't worry about leaving him

behind a bit, because we know he'll catch up, and overtake, as soon as we get to a down slope.'

'You're exaggerating, Lieđđi. Some days at the end of winter we're going up nearly all day. We have to hang back for him a bit then. We used to have a big bull reindeer – Oaván, we called him – who was happy to have a harness on and pull him, but he died a couple of years ago. He was just servicing one of the cows and suddenly keeled over, with a sort of strangled bellow. He wasn't even very old.'

You could see in Lieđđi's face the pain that the memory brought back.

They'd travelled a good deal more widely than Granny Persie had imagined, but they were amazed at how far we'd come in just three weeks.

'You should be able to get a long way south on the other side of the sea long before the snow comes again!'

'I don't know. The roads might be much worse in Finland and Russia and Poland, and the weather is colder there in winter, too. We don't know how early the snow might come there.'

Granny Persie had to show them where Finland and Russia and Poland were on the maps, and then she had to explain that while in general it was warmer the further south you went, it was more complicated than that.

'We must go and talk with Gealbu again. How much longer can you stay here before you have to move on? We might take some time to make up our minds. We'll need to ask you more questions. And you ought to ask us more questions too, before you really agree that we can join you.'

'Stay to eat with us before going to talk with Gealbu.'

'No, we must get back to him. He'll be worrying.'

'Take some food with you, for him as well.'

'If you're sure...'

'I hope you like it! It's not what you're used to, of course. That's one thing you have to think about before you decide. We won't have reindeer meat when we go south.'

'No, we realized that. But you're fat, you must have plenty of food of some sort! You'll have to explain to us how, when you don't have any reindeer. But later – we must get back to Gealbu. But you haven't told us how long you can stay here.'

Granny Merly was still translating for the rest of us, of course. Granny Persie looked at Grandad, and said, in English, 'We could stay a few days, at least, couldn't we?'

'You're a better judge than I am, Persie, but surely we could. Seriously, we could surely stay a whole winter and set off south next Spring, if we wanted to. We'll talk about that when they've gone.'

Persie turned back to Lieđđi and Suonjar. 'A few days at least, maybe longer. We'll talk about it, and tell you more accurately when you come back.'

'The reindeer ought to be moving on, really. There's a road to the left a little way further along this road, that goes near where our next stop will be. Can you move your camp up there? It would be an awful long way for us to walk back to you otherwise.'

'It's not marked on our map. I hope it's in good enough condition to drive the trucks on. What's it like?'

'Oh. We don't know, we only cross it in one place normally.'

'We don't know how far we should go along it to meet you, either.'

'About a thumb joint on the map. We'll find you, no problem.'

'We're probably best to leave the trucks here. We'll take just the Unimog. We can all cram into that somehow. If the road's okay, we can come back here at night. A thumb joint isn't far for a vehicle!'

'But we won't get to you until evening.'

'That's okay. We can drive in the dark.'

'Oh, yes, we saw your lights the other evening. They're amazing. See you tomorrow evening then.'

'What will you do if we can't get there?'

'We'll come back here – maybe just one of us. It'll be a couple of days, though, and it'll be hard going for me to catch up with the reindeer again. But what can't be helped, can't be helped.'

Lieđđi and Suonjar disappeared. They moved remarkably fast.

'Hard going for me to catch up with the reindeer again. No kidding. Her thumb joint is about thirty kilometres, no joke on foot on this terrain. But she knows what she's committing herself to, she's no fool. A real toughie.'

'They were giving us the chance to back out of the offer. No risk of that! If they want to come with us, we'd be honoured to have them.'

'That's for sure.'

'Gealbu could be a bit of a liability.'

'I don't think so. If he's been coping with their way of life, he's a lot tougher than he looks. Nothing wrong with his brain, and they say he's good with his hands. He manages to communicate with his cousins somehow, and he'll learn to communicate with us, too – or we'll learn to communicate with him. What more do you want?'

'I got the feeling Lieđđi was positively trying to sell him to us, that's all.'

'Oh, I think she was, but only because she was afraid we'd think he'd be a liability, not because she thinks he really would be. I'm sure of that.'

Granny Persie could see the doubt still in Grandad's eyes.

'Take my word for it, Pete. He'll be an asset, just as much as those two girls, you'll see – if they decide to come with us. I don't think they will, though, in the end. It'd be a hell of a wrench to leave the reindeer, and a whole way of life.

Remember what it felt like for us, to leave the farm? And we had plenty of time to think about it.'

Uncle Jake hadn't said a word up to this point.

'Dad said something a little while back, that made me think. We really could stay here over a winter. We'd learn a bit about living off reindeer, we'd get to know these three, and they'd get to know us. Our own future is pretty uncertain. It might be better if we joined them here, rather than them coming south with us. We'd all be in a better position to make up our minds by next spring. I'm not saying we should necessarily do that, but we should think about the possibility.'

Grandad smiled. 'Yes, that was what was running through my mind. But I know what you're thinking. Two more women, about your age.'

Granny Persie laughed out loud. 'Don't be rotten to him, Pete. You're a fine one to make a comment like that, anyway. It's a good thing if he finds someone who's not his half-sister. Or two someones, like you did. Who knows? We might yet find someone for Belle and Dot who's not their half-brother, too.'

Dot looked thoughtful. 'We might have already. Just because Gealbu can't talk and has something wrong with his back doesn't necessarily mean there's anything genetically wrong with him. Even if there is, it's probably recessive.'

'But do you fancy him?'

'I don't know. Maybe more than I fancy Jake. Much as I love Jake, he's still my half-brother. I'm not saying anything against Greg and Fi or Sid and Anna, of course! But I'm sure I could get used to Gealbu. What do you think, Belle?'

'He's sort of cute. He's got a very expressive face, and a lovely smile, even if it is a bit crooked. You can just see he means it, and you can see that he's taking everything in. I'd want to learn to understand his gestures, though, like Lieđđi and Suonjar do.'

Uncle Jake picked up on that point. 'I'd have to learn Swedish, too, before I'd want to commit myself to Lieđđi and Suonjar. Or they'd have to learn English.'

'We'd all have to learn Swedish, or they'd have to learn English, or a bit of both. But I think we'll have to make the commitment first anyway. If we stay the whole winter with them, we surely won't want to split up again next Spring. Either we'll all stay, or we'll all go. And if they come with us straight away, that's an even firmer commitment.'

'Here we are, talking like arranging marriages. We don't know what they're thinking.'

'You don't? Didn't you see Suonjar eyeing up Jake? And the way they were talking about not having children unless they had husbands?'

'They were only children when their parents died...'

Granny Merly interrupted, 'Yes, but they herd reindeer. They know all about the facts of life. They pretty certainly know all about inbreeding, too, if you think about it. They don't know our history yet, though. Plenty of time. For what it's worth, I think we should suggest we stay here for the winter. My only worry is whether we're fit enough to keep up with a reindeer herd on foot. I doubt whether we can follow them with the trucks, even if the road's good enough to follow them tomorrow. Odds are there are no roads at all most of the way wherever they go.'

'We're not unfit, and Gealbu manages.'

'But none of us can ski. We don't have any skis, either.'

Most of us had never even heard of skis and skiing.

'We'll have to find a sports shop, get some skis, and learn. Fast.'

'I wonder if Lieđđi knows where there's a sports shop? I get the impression they don't do any raiding at all. I wonder why?'

'We'll have to talk to them about that. They might not realize that that's how we've survived. They might not like it.'

'I doubt if it would bother them at all. They seem very down to earth. They've pretty much got to be to have survived. If they've not been raiding, it's only because they've not seen the need, or not realized that there's anything useful to be found. Maybe there isn't anything useful for their way of life.'

'Is there even any snow up in the mountains still? Or would we have to wait until winter before we could start to learn? And if we go looking for a sports shop, will we be able to find our friends again afterwards?'

'Do you think they have factory made skis, or do they make them themselves?'

There was so much we didn't know.

'There's another thing. They're pretty skinny. They called us fat, and by comparison with them, we are, but we're not fat by pre-war standards. I'm pretty sure that reindeer herders didn't used to be skinny. If they're living right on the limits, could their way of life support us all at all? Maybe they don't really have a big enough reindeer herd to support themselves, never mind fourteen of us as well.'

'We can ask them about it, but I suspect that's a very good point.'

Chapter 4

The grown-ups decided that only Grandad, the Grannies, Uncle Jake and the twins would go to meet our new friends near their new camp.

'We'd have to empty all the stuff out of the back of the Unimog to get us all in. We don't all need to go.'

I was so upset at the idea of being left behind that they decided to take me along too. Mum and Dad and Uncle Sid and Aunty Anna and the three little ones stayed with the trucks.

The road to the point where we hoped we'd meet up with them again was just a gravel track, but it wasn't in bad condition considering it hadn't been maintained for thirty-four years. The surface had gone completely in many places, but there was a rocky foundation that had survived pretty well – better than the foundation of the main road had in the washouts. It didn't give the Unimog any problems at all.

'The trucks would get through here, no problem, but it'd knock hell out of the tyres. The Unimog's light on its feet, I don't think its tyres are coming to much harm at all.'

'I wouldn't want to bring the trucks up here anyway. Imagine having to turn them round, if we had to go back.'

We found a prominent hill close to the road at about the right distance. Granny Persie even managed to drive the Unimog across country right onto the top of the hill, so we were confident they'd be able to find us easily.

We waited and waited. Grandad scanned the surrounding land with the binoculars, but couldn't see any sign of anyone, nor any reindeer. It began to get dark, and everyone began to think they'd decided against joining us. Eventually, after it was quite dark, Grandad and the Grannies decided to call it a day, and we set off back to the trucks, feeling very sad.

'I'd have thought Lieđđi would at least have come and let us know, so we wouldn't hang around waiting for them, if they've decided not to come.'

It was much slower driving back down the track in the dark. We couldn't really go much faster than walking pace. Then suddenly, about halfway back to the trucks, there was Lieđđi in the middle of the track, waving like mad.

It took the Grannies a little while to calm her down, and longer still to work out what she was saying. They didn't fully understand, but it was clear that something dreadful had happened, and that she desperately wanted us to come with her. Could the Unimog come across country, at least part of the way?

'We've no torches, so we'd find it pretty difficult on foot. We'll get the Unimog as far as we can, and then try to position it to give the best light we can with its headlights.'

'We'll probably do better without the headlights. We wouldn't be able to see a thing in the shadows with them on. Lieđđi's managed to get here, we'll manage with her to guide us.'

The Unimog didn't get very far before they decided it would be easier to walk. Lieđđi wanted Grandad and Uncle Jake to go with her, and one of the Grannies to translate, but she made it clear it would be better if I didn't go. Granny Merly and Aunty Dot stayed with me. The others disappeared very quickly into the night. We felt very alone, sitting there in the dark in the Unimog.

We'd no idea how long they would be gone. It began to get cold, and Granny Merly started the engine to get the heater working. 'They'll hear it, but they'll know I'm just keeping us warm. They won't think I'm driving off without them, don't worry, Mikey. They must be a lot colder than us, though. How Lieđđi manages I don't know, unless those reindeer skins are warmer than they look. What's it like here in winter? And them as skinny as they are, too.'

I snuggled down with my head on Granny Merly's lap and her arm around me. I was worried about what was going on, and couldn't sleep. But I did, whether I wanted to or not.

I didn't wake up until the Unimog started moving again, and even then I didn't wake up properly, and didn't think about whether everyone had come back or what was happening at all. Granny Merly had lifted me right onto her lap, and my head was on her shoulder, because the Unimog was so full, but I didn't know what had really been going on until the next morning.

Lieđđi and Suonjar understood Gealbu's gestures very well – their own private family sign language. He had told them in no uncertain terms that they should join our expedition, while he carried on living with the reindeer. They should forget about him.

'But how would you survive? You can't even put the lávvu up by yourself.'

'I'll manage. I can very quickly make a smaller lávvu that I can put up on my own. And the reindeer won't leave me behind, I know that. They only go on ahead with you two because they know you won't leave me behind.'

'You should come with us. We should all go. The reindeer will be okay, they're wild animals really. They're our friends, not our property.'

'The foreigners don't really want me, it's you two they want. Who would want me?'

'We do. And they do, too, they really do. I can tell that they see more than skin deep. They know you're intelligent and capable.'

'Do they? Or are you just saying that? They want you two because there aren't enough of them, they know they're too small a herd and will get inbred. They won't want to breed with me.'

'That's not the whole meaning of life. And anyway, who knows? They didn't just invite me and Suonjar, they invited all three of us.'

But Gealbu wouldn't believe them, and was determined to stay with the reindeer.

'If you're staying, we're staying too. We can't go without you.'

'You must. Things are getting worse here. Think about your old age.'

'Think about your old age, too. All alone.'

'Everyone dies sometime. I'll live until I die, just like everyone else. Now go and find them, and tell them you're going with them.'

'No.'

Gealbu set off walking as fast as he could. Lieđđi and Suonjar followed him. 'Where are you going?'

'I'm going to kill myself. Then you'll have to go with the foreigners.'

'You have to come with us!'

'No.'

'Then we're not going either.'

Between the two of them, they could stop him going anywhere. He'd seemed to accept that, but late that morning he'd found an opportunity to throw himself off a high rock.

He'd expected to die, but he didn't. How many bones were broken nobody knew, but he was alive and conscious and clearly in great pain. He tried to gesture to his cousins when they reached him, but his right arm and some ribs were broken, and he couldn't make himself understood. They guessed he was trying to tell them to leave him alone to die, but of course they couldn't do that. They made a makeshift stretcher out of their skis, lifted him onto it as gently as they could, and then started to carry him towards the road.

They didn't know this part of the country well – their normal route didn't meet the road for another half day's trek – so it was difficult. Lieđđi went ahead prospecting for a route they could manage carrying the stretcher with Gealbu on it. She saw the Unimog going up the road in the distance, and wished she'd realized they wouldn't have gone straight up there first thing in the morning. She could have been by the road and stopped them and got them to come and help.

She and Suonjar decided to use the best of the daylight getting Gealbu as far towards the road as they could, then at dusk Lieđđi would go and make sure she caught them coming down the road – or walk up the road in the dark to find them if they decided to stay late.

It was much harder in the dark. Luckily there was a moon, but it was only half a moon and not very high in the sky, and clouds kept on covering it. The foreigners weren't used to walking on rough country in the dark, so Lieđđi had to watch out for them, too. Eventually they reached Suonjar and Gealbu. Suonjar was very relieved to see them.

Grandad and Uncle Jake were amazed how light Gealbu was, even on a stretcher made out of six wooden skis. Lieđđi held onto Grandad's hand holding the front end of the stretcher, and helped make sure of his footing, while Suonjar did the same with Uncle Jake at the other end. At first, Granny Persie and Aunty Belle brought up the rear.

At this stage, none of us 'foreigners' knew what had really happened – all we knew was that Gealbu had had a terrible accident. Nobody had any proper medical training beyond basic first aid, but we did at least have a first aid kit with painkillers and bandaging, somewhere relatively comfortable for him to lie, and the means to feed him without him having to follow the reindeer.

They'd left me sleeping with my head on Granny Merly's lap. They emptied half the stuff out of the back of the Unimog, making a neat pile by the side of the road, to make space for the stretcher with Gealbu on it. Suonjar and Aunty Belle sat with him, half to try to keep him as comfortable as possible, and half to make sure he didn't try to get out of the back of the moving vehicle. Aunty Belle sought out his unhurt hand in the dark and held it gently.

Granny Persie dug out the first aid kit and found the pain killers, but Gealbu wouldn't take the tablets. 'There's morphine in the kit in the trucks, but I don't think I'd trust it after all this time. I don't know whether the tablets are still any good, but at least they wouldn't do any harm. I'm not at all sure about the safety of injecting ancient morphine.'

They wondered whether one of the Grannies should sit in the back with them to translate, but decided it wasn't necessary. Granny Persie was the best person to drive the Unimog on a rough road in the dark, and they didn't want to disturb me by moving Granny Merly.

Aunty Belle and Suonjar were fast asleep in each other's arms when we arrived back at the trucks. Aunty Belle's hand was still firmly in Gealbu's. Whether he was asleep or not nobody was quite sure, but he was breathing okay. The Grannies covered the three of them with blankets and left them where they were.

The next morning they very carefully moved Gealbu into the back of the sleeping truck. Lieđđi and Suonjar had a conversation with him – after a fashion. His usual animated gesturing was impossible for him; all he could do was nod almost imperceptibly. They had to phrase everything as questions he could nod yes or no to.

He was in pain, but had managed to sleep during the night. Could someone arrange something he could wee into? It was going to be harder when he had to empty his bowels, but with help he thought he'd manage. And yes, he felt a complete fool for landing everyone in this stupid situation and yes he was very sorry. But no-one gave him the option to say yes, he should have been left to die.

The Grannies felt him all over, trying to find out what was broken. There was nothing they could do to help his ribs to mend; only time would do that. They splinted his broken arm as best they could.

'It's a good job his back isn't broken.'

'We're going to have to reorganize ourselves a bit. We'd have had to anyway, but with Gealbu bedridden for at least three or four weeks it's going to be a bit more difficult. We won't all be able to sleep in the same truck, that's for sure.'

'Some of us can sleep in the cabs.'

'That's a possibility, but only two can lie down in a cab, and they can't snuggle up. It'll be hard to keep warm.'

'How on Earth those three have been keeping warm in their lávvu, I'll never know.'

'I think you might, really. You can ask them!'

The answer was 'reindeer skins,' and like us, 'snuggle up'. Then Lieđđi wanted to know where everyone would sleep, so Granny Persie translated the discussion we'd just been having into Swedish for her.

'Oh, we should retrieve our lávvu and our skins. We can put the lávvu up every night, it takes no time. If Gealbu's taking up a lot of room in the truck, two or three of you can come and sleep in the lávvu with us, there's plenty of room. We never bothered to make it smaller after our cousins died.'

It was only much later we learnt that they'd sometimes had one or two young reindeer snuggled up with them in the lávvu to help keep them warm. They laugh about it now, but they were embarrassed about it at first. But why? It was simply sensible.

Granny Persie, Uncle Sid and Lieđđi set off in the Unimog to go and pick up all the stuff that had been left beside the road, and to get the lávvu and the skins, and some of Lieđđi's, Suonjar's and Gealbu's other things. Lieđđi wanted to say goodbye to the reindeer, too. Uncle Sid started to load the stuff from the side of the road, while the other two headed off to where the lávvu and the rest of their things were.

Granny Persie saw that Lieđđi was about to catch a reindeer, and asked her why.

'I'll kill it when we get back to the vehicle. It wouldn't be happy riding, better to kill it first. But there's no sense carrying it to the road when it can walk.'

'We've got plenty of meat, and we can shoot wild animals whenever we need more. Why kill one of your beloved reindeer?'

'This is a young male, I'd normally let him get fat over the summer before killing him. There's plenty of buried meat near here, I could just dig some of that up. But fresh liver and intestines would be good for Gealbu. Well, good for all of us, but especially for Gealbu. And there's plenty of males in the herd, they won't miss one. Well, he's still young, his mother will miss him, but she'll get over it pretty quickly.'

That was the first time any of us foreigners had heard of burying meat. Granny Persie wanted to know how long they kept meat underground, and why it didn't go bad, and how long you could keep it after you'd dug it up.

'It depends. In a place where the ground stays frozen all year at the depth you bury it, it keeps for a year, no problem. We don't often leave anything much longer than that. Why would you dig it up and then not eat it straight away, though? Oh, I see, to take some more with us in the trucks. I hadn't thought about that. I don't know.'

'A few days, anyway, if we cook it thoroughly first. We'll not take a chance on keeping it any longer than that. One invalid is enough!'

So Lieđđi took one young reindeer, and dug one carcass up. 'Between seventeen of us, we can eat that much in a few days. I wonder if anyone will find the rest? It seems such a waste.'

'We could dig it up and leave it for the scavengers.'

'And help the wolves to breed? Our old neighbours wouldn't thank us for that. Anyway, it's far too much trouble. If our old neighbours weren't so far away, we could let them know where it is. That'd give them a surprise – the skinny outcasts giving the fatties presents like that!'

Granny Persie laughed. 'Do you want to let them know? Can they read?'

'I don't know. How would you leave them a message anyway?'

'We'd think of some way, but if you're not sure whether they can read, there's no point making much effort. Do you know where they are, though? If they're near a passable road, we could go and visit them.'

'I know roughly where they are, but I'm not sure you could get anywhere near there with a vehicle. More trouble than it's worth, anyway. They're quite fat enough, and their herds are healthy. I just thought it would be funny to offer them food, when they've never once offered to help us, even when we were pretty desperate. I'd rather not visit them anyway, to be honest. Especially not now we're leaving.'

On the way back to the Unimog, Granny Persie and Lieđđi met Sid coming to find them. He'd finished reloading the stuff that had been left at the side of the road. He was surprised to see them carrying meat and leading a reindeer. Lieđđi loaded him with what she was carrying, gave him the end of the rope she'd put round the reindeer's neck, and said she'd go back and fetch some more things. 'Just tie him to the truck, and you two come back and help me. The main thing I want to fetch is the lávvu, but there's some other stuff, too.'

'How on Earth do you move all this stuff? I can imagine pulling it along on a sledge in winter, but how do you manage when there's no snow?'

'Reindeer. There are several of them who don't mind carrying a load, as long as you don't overdo it. The biggest male is the only one who'll carry the lávvu. We don't normally move much once the snow's gone, anyway. This year's been hard. We've been getting used to the snow lasting quite late, then this year although it was very cold during the winter and there was a lot of snow, it went a bit early. Well, earlier than it's gone in recent years. Lots of rain. We'd normally be well up into the mountains by now, away from these damned mosquitoes.'

'Lucky for us. We'd have missed you completely.'

'Well, lucky for us, anyway. Another day and we'd have seen your lights and wondered what was going on, but been too far away to investigate. Two days the other way, and it would have been one of the other families you met, not us. Lucky for us either way.'

'Do you think the other families saw our lights? Then again, yesterday? Are they too far away to come and see what's going on?'

'I'm sure they saw the lights, but yes, they're quite a long way away. I'm not sure whether they'd want to investigate anyway. We weren't sure at first, but we decided at least to take a look. We thought we could watch you for a while without you seeing us. You had the fire in your eyes, and we were out in the dark. Then you just seemed like a cheerful family, and here we are.'

'It's probably just as well it was you three we've met, not one of the other families. We're very glad to increase our numbers by three, but more than that would be difficult for us. We could have brought more trucks, but we didn't think about finding more people when we decided just to bring these five. We just calculated that it was better to have two drivers for each truck, so we could keep going longer each day.'

'You had more trucks? How did you keep them going? Our parents used to have a truck and a couple of snowmobiles. Maybe they were still going when we were babies, I don't know. If we hadn't seen the rusting remains of them, we'd have only half believed the stories they told us.'

Then Granny Persie had to tell Lieđđi all about how we'd had loads of vehicles back at the old farm, and how we'd found the military depot. That led into lots of stories about our family history, and Lieđđi's. Lieđđi killed the reindeer and they all loaded the Unimog without a break in the storytelling, which was still going on when the three of them arrived back at our camp.

Lieđđi and Suonjar skinned and gutted the reindeer. To everyone's amazement, they washed out the intestines, cut them and the liver and heart up, and offered it all round – raw.

'Don't you worry about picking up parasites?'

Lieđđi didn't even know the word, and Granny Persie had to explain. Lieđđi wasn't worried at all.

'Everybody eats the innards raw, it's good for you.'

Grandad and the Grannies reckoned that if the locals ate reindeer innards raw, then they could too. In the end we all did.

Lieđđi was especially keen to feed plenty of liver to Gealbu, 'to help him heal quickly.'

Granny Persie reckoned she could see the sense in that, and if anybody knows about such things, it's Granny Persie.

Then Lieđđi wanted Granny Persie to show her how to use the stove.

'We usually cook the meat, the stomach, and the blood.'

She'd collected the blood in a skin when she'd killed the reindeer.

'You can eat it all raw if you have to, but most of it's better cooked. Maybe you really do need to cook wolves and foxes, I've never heard of anyone eating them at all before.'

She wanted to keep most of the meat for later, but cooked the stomach straight away, complete with all its contents. 'That's good stuff, too. You can't eat lichen like a reindeer does, but you can if a reindeer collects it and half digests it for you.'

She wanted to know how the devil we caught wolves. 'You couldn't snare them like you snare a hare.'

Granny Persie started to explain about guns, but Lieđđi stopped her. 'Oh, our parents told us about those. They used to shoot wolves in the old days, if they were bothering the reindeer. And they shot hares, too, for the pot. But that was before our time. I'd forgotten about those stories. So you still have guns?'

'Yes, but I don't know how much longer we'll have ammunition for them. If we don't find another gunsmith's to raid, we'll run out eventually. Who knows whether their ammunition will still be any good anyway? What we've got is okay so far, but for how much longer, who knows?'

'I wonder what the chances of finding another military vehicle depot are? One more truck would be no bad thing. We can teach you two to drive, anyway.'

I remember the first night I slept in the lávvu. It might have been the third or fourth night it was put up by the side of the road near the trucks. Granny Persie, Mum, Dad and Aunty Dot had moved into the lávvu the very first night, to make room for Suonjar and Gealbu in the truck. All us four little ones had stayed in the truck with Granny Merly. Well, we were with everyone else, too, but Little Liz and I were snuggled up with Granny Merly because we didn't have our Mum and Dad with us.

Then I decided I wanted to try sleeping in the lávvu. It was funny, being wrapped up in reindeer skins instead of a sleeping bag. Mum said I could bring my sleeping bag into the lávvu if I wanted to, but half the excitement was to be in the skins.

I slept in the lávvu every night after that. Little Liz came with me once or twice, but mostly she preferred to be with Granny Merly in the truck.

Over the next few weeks, lovingly nursed mainly by Suonjar and Aunty Belle, Gealbu's bones gradually mended, but he lost quite a bit of weight – and he hadn't had much in the first place. Somewhere in the north of Finland, Grandad shot a hare, thinking that if reindeer innards were okay to eat raw, then probably any herbivore innards would be, and the liver at least would be good for Gealbu's healing. But the liver was a funny colour, and had lots of little knots in it that Granny Persie said looked like some kind of encysted parasite. They chucked the whole animal away. They didn't want anyone to eat it, not even cooked.

'Some scavenger will get it, but there's no point burying it. We're not spreading the parasites any more than they'd spread naturally anyway.'

A couple of days later Uncle Sid got another one, and that one was fine, but nobody ate any of it raw. That didn't bother Lieđđi at all.

'We always used to cook hare meat when we snared one. I don't know why, it's just what we learned from our parents.'

Getting south through Finland was more difficult than going north through Sweden had been. The washouts weren't deep chasms like they sometimes had been in Sweden, but there were more places where there seemed to be bottomless mud, and often there was no way we could go across country to find an alternative ford – there'd be a lake or a massive bog in the way, and we had to backtrack and find a different road altogether. Turning the trucks round with trailers attached was often a real problem, but we couldn't detach them and manhandle them, they were much too heavy. Reversing them more than a few metres was very time consuming and tiring for whoever was driving, but a couple of times we had to reverse a kilometre or more before we found anywhere we could turn. After the second time, we took to following the Unimog at a good distance, and not proceeding until Granny Persie radioed to say she'd reached a place where the trucks would be able to turn. Progress was slow, but thank goodness for the intercom!

Somehow we kept getting finding we had to go further and further east, almost to the Russian border. Granny Persie didn't really want to cross into Russia until we absolutely had to.

'I'm less confident of finding the things we need once we cross into Russia. I just don't know enough about the place. And I rather hope we never meet any organized survivors in Russia. I don't know enough about what they might be like, either.'

Lieđđi and Suonjar had been very nervous about raiding at first, but had rapidly got used to the idea. They weren't quite sure what we were looking for. The skeletons that we found in the first couple of houses didn't bother them at all, but it was only when we were collecting tins and jars of food from a house that they realized that a lot of the food were were eating was well over thirty years old. They were amazed that it could possibly still be wholesome after so long. Tins, jars and packets of food were a new idea to them, but they they didn't mind. They took the same 'if you can eat it, so can we' attitude that our family took to the raw reindeer innards.

Lieđđi and Suonjar were learning English fast. Granny Persie was giving them some actual lessons, and teaching them reading and writing, but mainly they were just picking it up from all of us. We all picked up quite a few words of

Swedish from them – and some Sami too, for things like lávvu that we'd never known existed before we met our new friends. Grandad sometimes called it a tent, but that's a word no-one but the oldies knew before, so it was always a lávvu to the rest of us.

They were still 'new friends' then. They're family now. Two extra aunts and an uncle for me!

The oldies used to tell stories about dried meat and fish they used to find when they were raiding. By the time I was born, any dried food in any of the houses we raided was so old that no-one really trusted it.

'If we were desperate, I suppose we'd maybe boil it thoroughly and eat it, but we've always managed to find enough tins and jars not to think about dried food.'

Lieđđi said they'd never heard of it, and you can understand why when they could just bury raw meat and expect it still to be good a year or more later!

'If we'd known about it, we could have killed two or three more young male reindeer, and tried drying the meat.'

'A bit sad if we'd just ended up wasting the meat, though.'

I caught sight of Gealbu nodding agreement with that. It was the first time I'd realized how much English he was picking up.

Chapter 5

Close to the border on the Finnish side, but still well to the north of where Granny Persie wanted to cross into Russia, we did find another military depot. There was no hill overlooking it that we could study it from discreetly, but we'd reached its gates before we realized it was there anyway. It was pretty obvious that it was abandoned. Its gates were open, and there were small trees growing through the gates and along the foot and top of the boundary wall. As the road had been good and wide for some distance, all the trucks were close behind the Unimog. Granny Persie, Grandad, Uncle Sid and I went in to take a look around, while some of the other grown-ups prepared a meal.

The place had clearly been raided. Granny Persie and Grandad reckoned it must have been after the war, not in those terrible days while they'd been hidden away in the shelter and everybody else on the surface was dying.

'Well, *nearly* everybody else. Not Lieđđi's parents, for example.'

'It must have been after the war – long after. Someone's shoved those skeletons out of the way to move a vehicle. They surely wouldn't have got tangled up like that if they'd still been whole corpses when they were moved.'

'So somebody survived somewhere around here. It's the first sign we've seen of any survivors since Lieđđi and co. Do you think it's raiders from a camp like our old camp? Or another independent lot?'

'Who knows? Whoever it was, it was a long time ago, I'm pretty sure. They left the gates open, and the trees have grown through them since.'

'Unless the gates were left open during the war, and then the raiders came much later. Could have been yesterday.'

'Maybe, but the odds are it wasn't particularly recently. The odds of there being anyone around while we're here are minuscule. Let's take a good look around and see what they've left – if anything.'

Granny Persie and Grandad reckoned whoever it was had probably taken some vehicles, but they hadn't taken them all. There were a couple of trucks very similar to the ones we'd already got, a tanker, and several jeep-like vehicles.

There were also a couple of interesting looking vehicles, articulated in the middle, with broad rubber tracks on both halves instead of wheels. They had seats for lots of people in the rear half and half a dozen in the front half.

There was a room that looked as though it was probably a battery store, but there were no batteries in it.

'Hmm. Looks as though whoever raided this place took all the batteries. I bet there are none in the vehicles, either. I doubt they were expecting anyone else to come raiding, but they'd think they'd scuppered them anyway. But we only want one truck, and we've got batteries.'

'If they've taken the batteries, that probably means they weren't expecting to come back here at all, or not often anyway. Either they've got a camp a long way away, or they were moving out of the area. Very likely heading south, like us. But that wouldn't be a big group – a big group would have taken all the vehicles, I'm sure. Well, if they were moving away, anyway.'

'Not necessarily, not if they were worried about fuel supplies.'

'They've left a tanker.'

'True. So most likely it's either a small group like us – and one has to wonder how they survived – or a camp somewhere at a fairly considerable distance.'

'They could have survived like Lieđđi and co – just happened to be lucky with where they were. But only people born after the war survived long-term up in northern Sweden, and their parents died when they were quite young. It would have been hard to pass on the kind of technical competence that whoever raided this place seems to have had.'

Lieđđi and Suonjar had seen the tracked vehicles before.

'Bandvagn. There are a couple of those near where we spent the winter. All rotting away now, but I remember what they were like when we were children. We used to play in them sometimes. Mum told me they belonged to the soldiers, and the soldiers used to play games with them, driving them around on the snow, getting practice using them in case they ever needed to do serious work with them. But all they ever really did was play. But they can drive over deep snow. A damn nuisance they were, Mum said, because they crushed the snow and made it hard for the reindeer to dig. They can drive on water, too.'

'They're amphibious? That could be very handy. We should probably take one of those. Maybe even both.'

'We'd have to leave one of our trucks behind if we took both, though, unless we decided to manage with less than two drivers per vehicle.'

Lieđđi and Suonjar had started learning to drive, but they didn't drive for very long each day yet, partly because it slowed the whole convoy down when they were driving, and partly because Granny Persie and Uncle Sid found it very tiring being their co-drivers – more tiring than driving the vehicles themselves. Only Granny Persie and Uncle Sid felt confident enough to supervise them.

It turned out that the Bandvagns had petrol engines.

'That's hopeless. Fuel would be an awful problem. I bet their fuel consumption's terrible, and we can only carry five hundred litres of petrol in the jerry cans. And we can't refill them very fast, either.'

'We'll get a fair way on five hundred litres, even if the fuel consumption's really bad. I'd rather fill up every chance we get though. You never know when it might be an awful long way before the next chance to refuel. It's boring wiring up the generator and swapping pump innards in and out, but we can survive that. We're not that pressed for time, really.'

'I'm worried about crossing Russia and the other communist countries. I don't know how easy it'll be to find fuel. Diesel's likely to be easier to find than petrol, I think. And we can certainly go a lot further between refills if we stick to diesel.'

The grown-ups spent quite a long time working on one of the two trucks, but eventually decided it really wasn't going to start. The second one wouldn't either.

'This might be why they didn't take all the vehicles. Maybe they couldn't start them, either. I wonder if any of the jeep things will start?'

They had petrol engines.

'We might as well take a Bandvagn if we're going to take anything. If one of *them* will start.'

'It'd be fun to play with one for a while, anyway. But I can see us having to leave it behind sooner or later. And how useful would it really be to be able to go anywhere that we can't take all the trucks?'

'Who knows? I can imagine a few scenarios where it could be very useful, but how likely any of them are to actually occur, I don't know.'

'We're not actually running out of room in the vehicles we've got, really. How likely are we to find any more people?'

'We know – or we're pretty sure – there are more people around here somewhere. Whether they'd be friendly, who knows? My guess is it's a camp, and it's probably quite a long way away. The odds of actually bumping into them are pretty small, I reckon.'

'It could very easily be in Russia, not in Finland at all. We'd have no common language, unless some of the older ones knew a little English. At least if it's in Finland, they'd probably know Swedish.'

'If it's in Russia, it's probably near Leningrad, and we'll have to go through that area whether we like it or not – unless we go all the way round the other side of Lake Ladoga. Whichever way we go, we've got to hope the bridges have survived. There's no hope of fording the Neva or the Svir, and I don't know about some of the other rivers, either.'

'Don't. I can't bear the thought of having to go back now.'

'I suppose we could get across with the Bandvagn, if we take it, and then try to find some more trucks the other side.'

'That sounds like an awful palaver.'

'I hope we never have to do it, but I suppose it could come to that.'

'So we should take a Bandvagn. If one of them will start.'

'Or even both of them. I think we should.'

'But I don't think it's especially likely any camp will be particularly near Leningrad. Think where our camp was – right in the middle of nowhere.'

'Okay, maybe not. But we've no idea, really. Just because there was no camp anywhere around Oslo – or if there was, they'd got everything they needed and didn't bother going raiding – doesn't mean to say there couldn't be camps near other big cities.'

'No. But we've no reason to suppose there will be, either. They could be absolutely anywhere, although I guess somewhere farmable is more likely. We've just got to keep our eyes skinned everywhere, that's all.'

'Most of the time we can't see far enough. They'd hear us coming before we had a clue they were there. We've just got to hope they're friendly, or at least not unfriendly.'

'Why should anyone be unfriendly?'

That was a good question. It was a fear Grandad and the Grannies had had ever since they first escaped from their own camp, after Granny Persie had killed a soldier who'd been trying to rape Granny Merly. But that was a story none of the rest of us got to know until many years later. We just knew that the oldies were always afraid that people, particularly people running camps, might be unfriendly.

Grandad had become thoughtful, and considered for a while before answering.

'Your neighbours were unfriendly to you, weren't they?'

'Not really unfriendly, the way you seemed to be saying. Just not positively friendly. Anyway, they knew us already. No-one we meet now will know us.'

Granny Merly, usually the quiet one, spoke while Grandad was still thinking. 'That's true. We should stop being so paranoid. All that was donkeys' years ago and thousands of kilometres away. Nobody we meet now will know any of us.'

'True. But a camp with a military regime is still a camp with a military regime. They won't want their inmates to know there are independent survivors out here – not if they're operating the way we imagine our old camp probably is.'

'It'd be even worse for them if their inmates knew they were attacking independent survivors outside. They'd have to maintain a defensive force out of sight and earshot of their camp. We know our camp wasn't doing that.'

'I'm pretty sure any camp will be assuming there aren't any independent survivors. They won't know what to do about us. That's what I'm afraid of – that they might act first and think afterwards.'

'If we just get away again as soon as we see them, we'll be fine. They won't be armed and ready to fire because they won't anticipate there being anyone to fire on. They'll have some fun explaining our appearance and disappearance to their inmates if any of them spot us, but there'd be no sense in them coming after us. All they'll see is a convoy of military vehicles. They won't be heavily armed, and they'll be more scared of us than we are of them. They'll see these vehicles and think we very likely might be well armed.'

'Unless there are wars going on between rival groups. I can imagine camps like our old one spreading their raiding over wider and wider areas, and eventually coming into conflict with another lot.'

'Perish the thought. But that's one of those troubles that could have reached us where we were just as easily as us finding it elsewhere. We'll cross that bridge when we come to it. If we come to it. I hope we never do.'

'There's a fair bit of weaponry in this depot. We could be prepared.'

'I'd rather not. We're not experts in its use, and I certainly don't want to spend time practising. Playing with weapons is a risky game in itself, anyway. Add to that, the weapons would take up valuable space in the trucks. I'd rather carry as much food and fuel as we can.'

'That makes sense. It'd be worth seeing if there's any ammunition for the guns we've got, though, or any other suitable hunting weapons with ammunition.'

Most of this conversation was going on in English. Lieđđi and Suonjar were catching quite a lot, but not all of it. Sometimes the Grannies addressed them directly in Swedish, but then they had to translate for the rest of us – when they remembered. Granny Merly was pretty good about that. She also did some translation into Swedish, when she could see that Lieđđi and Suonjar were wondering what was going on.

But Lieđđi and Suonjar didn't immediately cotton on to the possibility of anyone actually shooting at us. Guns were strictly for hunting for food – and great care was required to make sure there weren't any accidents. They understood that very well.

None of the weaponry in the depot was suitable for hunting, and there wasn't any ammunition to fit our guns.

We did find some other useful things, though: a two thousand litre petrol bowser with its own electric pump and hoses, and another dozen jerry cans.

'That pretty much solves the fuel problem with the Bandvagns. We'd better see if they'll start. If the pump on the bowser still works, of course.'

'I bet it will. It's quite dry in here. Even if it doesn't, we can still use the bowser. It'll just be a lot less convenient.'

Both the Bandvagns started easily once all the preparatory work was done, and the pump on the bowser worked, too. There was even plenty of petrol in a big underground tank in the depot – but the diesel tank was almost completely empty.

'So whoever raided this place before either doesn't have any petrol vehicles, or they've not been back here much.'

'They could be keeping it for later. Maybe they've still got plenty of ordinary filling stations closer to home.'

The Bandvagns were actually very easy to drive. They took in their stride appalling road surfaces that were hard work for the drivers of the trucks, and they had automatic transmission. Lieđđi and Suonjar found them much less tiring than the trucks, and it wasn't long before Granny Persie and Uncle Sid let them take full shifts driving. The biggest disadvantage was that they had a different type of intercom operating on a different frequency, so the people in the Bandvagns could talk to each other, but not to the rest of us.

After that, the Bandvagn that wasn't towing the bowser went ahead with the Unimog. It could turn round almost anywhere. It didn't matter how soft the ground was, it could sink in a bog until it was floating and it'd still get through.

Uncle Sid and Dad removed all the seats from the rear half of one of the Bandvagns. Then we had two sleeping trucks, and Lieđđi and Suonjar didn't need to put the lávvu up any longer. They left the seats in the other Bandvagn, 'in case all of us ever need to travel in the Bandvagns.'

Grandad didn't want to say it, but I knew he was thinking that maybe there'd come a time when the trucks simply wouldn't be able to get through somewhere. The biggest worry then would be whether the Bandvagns would be able to pull the petrol trailer through – without it, we'd have thirty odd jerry cans in the back half of one of the Bandvagns, and not a lot of room for food.

We managed to avoid actually crossing into Russia until the end of the border, on the Baltic coast. Before we crossed, we made a detour into Helsinki in the hope of finding a gunsmiths. We topped up our diesel and petrol supplies at an ordinary filling station, and stocked up a huge quantity of food – for once, not by raiding dozens of houses, but at a warehouse on the outskirts of Helsinki that hadn't been ransacked.

'It looks as though there aren't any camps anywhere near here. They'd surely have emptied this place out.'

We did find a gunsmiths. Grandad tried a few samples of each sort of ammunition before loading several boxes into a trailer. 'No point loading ourselves down with dud stuff.' But he didn't find any duds.

Our family was still well supplied with clothes and footwear, but Granny Persie suggested to Lieđđi – there were just the two of them in the leading Bandvagn – that maybe she and Suonjar would like some clothes like ours.

'Oh, yes, that's a good idea. We'd feel more part of the family if we wore the same sort of things the rest of you wear. But you haven't got anything that would fit us. Maybe Gealbu could make clothes for all of you out of the old lávvu. It seems a shame to spoil the lávvu, but we don't need it any more now we've got the Bandvagn to sleep in.'

'That would be another option – but would there really be enough material in the lávvu to make so many clothes? I'm sure we can find a place to get clothes for you in Helsinki anyway.'

We could and we did. Lieđđi and Suonjar were very funny in the clothes shop, trying things on and looking at themselves in a big mirror that Uncle Jake dragged to the front of the shop where it was light for them. Granny Merly helped them find things that were actually practical.

Gealbu was still bedridden at that point, so he stayed in reindeer skins.

'We'll find somewhere to kit him out later, maybe in Poland or Germany.'

Helsinki was a bit of a shock to all of us. We were used to finding bodies – well, just clothed skeletons really – lying about every now and then, but in Helsinki we saw the first signs of physical violence. The first thing we noticed was burnt-out buildings, and at first we thought maybe they were simply fires that had happened accidentally – maybe lightning strikes. But after a while it became obvious that many of them were probably arson. There were overturned and burnt-out cars and a burnt-out police van rusting away. And then we found skeletons that had obviously been the victims of violent attacks.

'I suppose it's not surprising that things like that would happen in the complete breakdown that must have occurred in those last days. What an awful time that must have been.'

'This is where I was supposed to have been – where I would have been if our plane hadn't had a technical problem.'

'If it really did. Maybe from the very beginning the whole idea of the bargain basement holiday was to fill the shelter with slave class people. Same for our Lappland visit.'

'Yeah. That had occurred to me, too.'

But apparently it was the first time anyone had actually mentioned it.

The borders between Norway, Sweden and Finland hadn't impinged on my consciousness at all, but the Russian checkpoint certainly did. There was rusty barbed wire everywhere, and concrete blockhouses. The concrete was spalling off all over the place, revealing rusting reinforcement, and there were trees growing out of cracks in the buildings. There was an air of desolate foreboding about it all.

'Nobody's been through here since the war. We're going to have to break through the barriers.'

'Wait a minute. We'd better think how exactly to do this. They could be booby-trapped.'

'Good thinking. Just as well we didn't just drive straight at them. But how do we disarm any booby trap without knowing what it's like?'

'I wish we had a spare vehicle we could send at the barrier with a brick on the accelerator.'

'We could find one in that last village, but the odds of finding one we could start are pretty small.'

'We could spend a battery sending one through on its starter motor, as long as the engine's not seized. A Jeep has a low enough ratio for the starter motor to drive it.'

'That's a lot of hassle. Couldn't we just push a car through with one of the trucks?'

'I don't really want to be that close. I don't suppose they really have a huge bomb under their own barrier, or an automatic weapon that automatically sprays the whole area with bullets. But it's not a chance I'd like to take.'

'We could put a telegraph pole on the Unimog's trailer and push something with the Unimog in reverse. The trailer's disposable, really.'

It didn't take long to find a suitable vehicle, in a village just a few kilometres back up the road. They didn't even bother to break the steering lock – they just chose a big van whose wheels were pointing straight forwards already.

'Who cares what happens to its tyres? They'll last long enough for our purposes even if we drag them sideways!'

They towed it to a point from which they could push it straight forwards through the barriers.

Getting a telegraph pole was harder. They found they couldn't simply pull one over with one of the trucks' winches as the grown-ups had hoped. You could use a telegraph pole as an anchor point for a truck to haul itself along.

'If we could get far enough up the pole and attach the cable high up, we could do it.'

In the end they decided that the Unimog would be safe enough with just the trailer full of timbers between it and the car. Granny Persie backed the Unimog until the sacrificial van was well past the broken barrier and the trailer was halfway through before coming back, turning round and pushing the van forwards and out of the way.

If there had ever been a booby-trap, it wasn't working any longer. Most likely there'd never been one, and they'd relied on armed guards.

'There might well be landmines all along the fence. I wouldn't want to try crossing anywhere but a checkpoint.'

Chapter 6

The roads were in a worse state in Russia than they had been in Finland, but a bridge over the canal near Vyborg that Granny Persie had been worried about was okay.

'That's good. This map's not really good enough to be sure, but as far as I can see it might have been a really long detour inland if this bridge had been down, or unsafe looking. The route nearer the coast has so many bridges I really wouldn't be confident of them all being passable. One of them might even be only a railway bridge, I really can't tell from the map.'

'A railway bridge mightn't be a bad thing anyway. We could drive along it no problem, and it's more likely to be in reasonable condition, I'd have thought.'

'I wondered about that for one stretch in northern Sweden, where the railway was running more or less parallel with the road for a long way. Then at one point I got a good look at one of the bridges, and it didn't have a track bed at all, just a metal framework supporting the rails. You couldn't drive the trucks over it. Who knows which bridges might be like that?'

'It's going to get interesting when we get beyond the edge of the last decent map. I doubt if we'll be able to find a shop with maps in it in Russia.'

'I know. This map covers us as far as just past Leningrad, which is lucky because at least I can see where we're likely to be able to get across the Neva – plenty of bridges in the middle of Leningrad, and nothing else as far as I can see until you're practically at Lake Ladoga, where the M18 goes over. After Leningrad, we've only got the big atlas, and not much chance of getting a better map until West Germany.'

Granny Persie wanted to avoid going through the middle of Leningrad if she could. The map showed a bridge over the Neva where what looked like a ring road went to the east and south of the city. We followed the ring road. It was obvious that the Neva had flooded badly, probably many times, especially to the east of the road, but running right over the road in several places. Everywhere was covered in mud, and there was brushwood and other debris piled against every obstacle, even though we were actually surrounded by buildings. In some places the road was buried deeply in mud, and we couldn't tell whether the surface underneath the mud was intact – until our front wheels dropped into a deep hole. Both of them at once.

Suonjar was driving one of the Bandvagns just behind the Unimog. She got out of the way and let Dad bring the tanker up behind the Unimog. Dad winched us backwards out of the hole.

Then Granny Persie took over the Bandvagn from Suonjar, and went forward to investigate whether it was even worth trying to follow the ring road any further. Lucky little me got to go in the Bandvagn with Granny and Uncle Sid. Somehow I was almost always in the lead vehicle now – the advantage of being the oldest of my generation, the only child really taking a big interest in what was going on.

The Bandvagn half floated across the mud, but didn't have any trouble at all. There were several similar muddy stretches, and Granny Persie wasn't sure it was worth trying to get the trucks through.

'I've no idea how deep the mud is in some places. The Bandvagn just doesn't find the holes the way the wheeled vehicles do. There are other bridges in the middle of the city, and the roads might not be as bad. On the other hand, that might have been the deepest washout, where the main flow went through during the floods. But we really don't know how deep it is, under all that mud.'

Between the muddy stretches, the road wasn't too bad.

When we reached the bridge, we could see why the river had been flooding. There were two large ships and several smaller ones jammed against the piers of the bridge, completely blocking the river at surface level. From the fact that the river wasn't currently flooded, it was obvious that there was passage for the water underneath the mess, but much too restricted for the river's maximum flow. The water level was a metre or more higher on the upstream side of the bridge.

'There could be more boats under the water, and the ones we can see might simply be resting on top of a heap rather than floating. Who knows?'

Granny Persie didn't want to take the Bandvagn over the bridge until she'd had a good look at it, so we all got out and walked. I remember noticing that there was a lot of brushwood crammed into every gap amongst the wreckage under the bridge.

The first side span seemed to be okay. Concrete arches soared high above us on either side. The concrete had spalled off in many places, revealing rusting reinforcement, but Granny Persie reckoned the arches were still plenty strong enough for our convoy 'as long as we go over one at a time, not nose to tail putting the whole weight of the convoy on the bridge at once'. I think she was joking, and thought the span would carry the whole convoy, no problem.

The other side span was probably similar, but we never bothered to look, because the centre section, a bascule drawbridge, was so badly damaged that it obviously wouldn't be safe to take a vehicle across.

Back in the vehicle, Granny Persie tried to contact Lieđđi, but couldn't get any response.

'That's odd. I'd have thought someone would stay in the Bandvagn just to keep in contact with us. Not to worry, we'll be back with them in no time.'

The approach road to the bridge wasn't wide enough, and we had to reverse quite a way to a place we could turn round – the first time anyone had had to reverse one of the Bandvagns more than a few metres.

'It's not easy. Nastier than the trucks with trailers, in fact, which surprises me. Maybe it's just that I'm used to the trucks, but the visibility doesn't seem as good. And you've got to get used to steering it like a single vehicle, not like a vehicle with a trailer, even though you can see the trailer wiggling about in the mirrors.'

We found everyone in a bit of a panic when we got back. Granny Merly "wasn't feeling well" as she put it, but it was much worse than just not feeling well. She had bad pains in her chest and left arm. Suonjar had taken charge.

'Even when we were little, my aunty wanted to make sure I knew what to do if Gealbu had a heart attack, because she was afraid that he might.'

Gealbu's mother – Suonjar's aunty – had been a nurse, way back in the days when they'd herded the reindeer with snowmobiles and trucks, and some members of most reindeer herding families had had jobs as well.

Suonjar had got Granny Merly into a comfortable position, and Mum had gone through the first aid kit from one of the trucks, looking to see if there was anything that was any use. Reading all the labels – fortunately in English as well as Norwegian and several other languages – she'd decided that a nitroglycerin tablet there and then under Granny's tongue, and warfarin tablets regularly thereafter was the best she could do in the absence of proper medical advice, and definitely better than doing nothing*.

Granny Persie reckoned they'd done the best they possibly could in the circumstances. 'Whether there's still any active

---

* This probably really was the best thing they could do in the circumstances, with what was available to them – remember this military first aid kit was put together in 1990 at the latest, and was over thirty years old by this time. **Don't** take this as the best current medical advice!

ingredient left in any of our stuff is doubtful, but it won't do any harm.'

The nitroglycerine seemed to help a lot, and after a little while Granny Merly wanted to be put in the sleeping truck with Gealbu, who by this time was sitting up whenever the truck wasn't moving during daylight hours, but who was still bedridden. He was champing at the bit to be back on his feet, but was very concerned about Granny Merly – as we all were.

Most of us stayed with Granny Merly in the back of the truck, while Uncle Sid and Lieđđi took the Unimog – without its trailer – to go and investigate a possible route to one of the other bridges. Uncle Jake suggested that he follow them in a truck, in case the Unimog needed pulling backwards out of a hole again.

'Maybe the tanker. It's got plenty of weight to pull the Unimog, and it's easier to turn round if we need to.'

'I'll give you a call on the intercom if I need you. Just make sure someone's in one of the cabs! But the more people stay with Granny Merly at the moment, the better. Love is the best medicine we've got, really.'

For once, I didn't go with the exploring party – I wanted to stay with my beloved Granny. Grandad tried to persuade me to go, but I wouldn't.

Uncle Sid and Lieđđi didn't have much trouble finding a route to the bridge, and reckoned the bridge looked okay.

'Granny Persie'll have the last word, of course, but it looks okay to me. But if we thought Helsinki was in a mess, it's nothing to the state the centre of Leningrad's in. Half the buildings are burnt out, not just the odd one here and there. And there's burnt-out military vehicles all over the place. And bodies.'

He meant the usual clothed skeletons, of course. I'd never seen any other kind of body – apart from the occasional skeleton whose clothes had disappeared somehow – maybe rotted or been eaten by rats. What he didn't mention, but which I noticed myself when we all reached the city centre, was that one pile of skeletons had the charred, tattered remains of clothes, and several others looked as though a heavy vehicle had driven over them. Grandad noticed the same things, but it was a long time before he and I talked about it.

Granny Merly, meanwhile, was saying that she felt fine, and thought she was a complete fraud. Everyone else was telling her to take it easy. Granny Persie was trying to work out whether there was any possibility of getting hold of the means of making fresh supplies of drugs, and realizing that it really wasn't a practicable proposition at all.

'We can doubtless find old stocks of things, but whether they're still any good, who knows? How could we possibly find out? We can probably find laboratory equipment and glassware, and we can probably make it work. Some of the more basic raw materials will last okay, but actually making things requires knowledge we don't have and couldn't find out – unless we could find books on the subject in a language we knew well enough. And the whole operation would in most cases be too much for such a small team. The only exception might be nitroglycerine – that's relatively easy to synthesize. And our sample of that at least seems still to be active anyway.'

Granny Merly actually laughed, 'or it's still a perfectly good placebo.'

Little Liz snuggled up to her and smiled. She'd just turned four then.

Emma was three, and Dang eighteen months, but they both knew something was wrong with Granny Merly, and wanted to cuddle her too. Suonjar tried to stop them crowding her, but Granny Merly put her arms round all three of them and smiled at them. There were tears in her eyes.

'Love's the best medicine, Sid's right. We should get moving again, no point hanging around here. We're no nearer a hospital here than we are anywhere else, and a little bit of bouncing around won't make any difference, I'm sure. Anyway, I feel fine now. Next time, I'll take one of those magic pills at the first twinge.'

Granny Merly wasn't fine at all, we all knew that – apart maybe from the little ones – but there was nothing we could do except hope she'd be okay.

Granny Persie agreed with Uncle Sid's estimate of the safety of the next bridge.

'The other bridge caught the drifting ships and stopped them crashing into this one! And the general deterioration for lack of maintenance isn't nearly bad enough to weaken the bridges too much yet. But it's only a matter of time.'

We crossed without incident, and got out of Leningrad as quickly as we could. We didn't see the slightest sign of human life – in fact gulls were the only living creatures we saw – but the whole place was really creepy.

It was beginning to get dark by the time we'd cleared the south of the city, and we stopped for the night somewhere before Gatchina. In the morning, Granny Persie didn't want to start moving until Granny Merly had woken up, had something to eat, and got settled comfortably. She began preparing some breakfast, and Mum and Uncle Sid and Uncle Jake went for a short walk 'just to see what the world is like around here.'

Just a few minutes later they were back. 'Give us the guns, Dad!'

Grandad got the guns out for them, and they hurried off again. I say 'hurried', but they were moving as silently as they could. We heard three shots, almost simultaneously, then silence. Then one more shot, then silence again.

A little while later they were back.

'We missed. All three of us. Twice, in my case.'

'Well, if you will try to hit a fast moving target, at a distance where all three of us managed to miss an almost stationary one!'

'Sorry. Wasted ammunition.'

'Don't worry. We've got plenty, and I expect we'll be able to find more once we get to Germany. What was it?'

'Something like reindeer, but not reindeer. Smaller. Six or seven of them.'

'Some sort of deer then. There's lots of different sorts. I wonder what sort they have round here?'

The shots had woken Granny Merly, but she was quite perky and wanted to know why nobody had woken her before. 'Don't feed me too much though, Persie. Just a little for now, and maybe I'll want a bit more later.'

Aunty Belle and Suonjar would stay in the back of the truck with Granny Merly and Gealbu. I was worried that there was no intercom in the back of the truck, and Granny Persie would be driving the Unimog.

'No, but when Granny Merly wants anything, Aunty Belle can wave at the people in the truck behind, as long as they stay within a reasonable distance. They've got intercom.'

Granny Merly wanted the three little ones with her, but she told me that I should go in the Unimog 'to look after Granny Persie.' I think I actually understood what she meant – Granny Persie having me to look after would help her not to think and worry too much about Granny Merly.

Gatchina was confusing, and we somehow missed the route. We found ourselves on an increasingly minor road, that turned into a thickly overgrown farm track at the edge of the town. Our map wasn't good enough to give us the faintest clue where we might have gone wrong, or even which side of the main road we were. Fortunately the main convoy had waited quite a long way behind, and only the Unimog and one Bandvagn had to turn round. Granny Persie simply pushed through a rotten old fence and mowed down several saplings doing a U-turn completely off the road, Lieđđi following in the Bandvagn.

We explored along the edge of the town, first to the north west, and then to the south east, before we found what seemed to be the main road heading south west. We retraced our route, found the rest of the convoy, and led them onto the road – but after a long straggly village not far out of Gatchina, that road turned into a track as well. We were lost.

It took most of that day, first one way and then the other, to find what Granny Persie was fairly sure was the right road. 'I know the Russian alphabet, and I could read the signs if there were any that were still legible. But this road looks reasonable, and it's headed the right way.'

There weren't actually many signs at all.

The road did at least seem to keep on going on, it was two lanes wide, and it was generally heading in the right direction. It was badly potholed, and there were small trees breaking through the surface, but it didn't have major washouts like the roads in Finland, Sweden and Norway had had.

We'd had less than two drivers per vehicle ever since we got the Bandvagns, but the Bandvagns were so easy to drive that Lieđđi and Suonjar were quite happy doing long shifts driving them, and we'd been able to keep going almost as long each day as we had before. Now, with three drivers out of action, we were reduced to shorter days. But with a relatively good road, we mostly made reasonable progress.

Granny Merly seemed to be recovering nicely. She was taking the warfarin tablets regularly.

'Whether they're doing anything, who knows? They're long past their use-by date, but they were in well sealed packs and have probably never got more than vaguely warm. They might still have some potency. We're probably giving her less than the optimum dose, even if they're still 100% potent, but I don't want to risk overdosing her.'

We saw deer several times, and Grandad thought they looked like roe deer, but he wasn't sure. They'd always already heard the vehicles and started running by the time we saw them, so no-one even tried to shoot one. But then Grandad saw several rabbits – the first we'd seen since southern Norway – and they didn't run until we'd almost reached them.

'The co-driver in the Unimog should have a gun handy. Next time there's rabbits, you should stop before you reach them, Persie, and let them bag one. I fancy a bit of fresh meat. I bet everyone does.'

Even now that there weren't enough drivers to have a co-driver in every vehicle, there was always one in the Unimog, which led the convoy. But nobody managed to bag a rabbit.

The third evening after Leningrad, we stopped close to a river, and several of the grown ups went fishing. Fresh fish for supper and breakfast! What species they were nobody knew, and they were very bony – but what a treat. Gealbu in particular was almost bouncy.

Lieđđi and Suonjar were fascinated by the fishing rods, and said they'd never seen anyone fishing like that before. 'Our parents always used nets across a gap in a little dam in a stream, and then drove the fish into the net from upstream – or threw a net, weighted round the edge, over fish in a lake. But apart from your tinned and pickled fish, we've not eaten fish since our parents died.'

I wondered which method was actually more effective, but no-one knew. 'It'd be quite a challenge to make a dam across a river this size, though. Not the sort of thing you'd do for an evening's fishing in a place you'll never visit again.'

Grandad says we must have been very close to the border between Russia and Latvia at this point, but we never noticed anything marking the border at all.

Apart from Gatchina and a couple of other small towns, the road had been going through forest all the way since Leningrad. Much of it seemed to be old forest, but there were a lot of areas where the trees were all relatively small, on what Granny guessed had probably been farmland before the war. The old forest was mostly evergreens, rank after rank of similar trees, obviously originally deliberate plantations. The younger forests had many trees of the same species, but there were significant numbers of deciduous trees, especially birch, in amongst them.

Then, the evening after the fishing, just as we were thinking about stopping somewhere for the night, we saw a field with crops growing in it – the first field we'd seen since leaving our own farm in south Norway.

There was a fence around the field, but Granny Persie said it wasn't a high security fence like there'd been around the camp the oldies had escaped from. It was quite tall, made of the trunks of small trees interwoven with thinner branches, leaving quite large holes. Granny Persie thought it was probably to keep deer off the crops.

'It's certainly not to keep people out – or in. It must need a lot of maintenance just to keep deer out. So someone is living somewhere near here. I hope they're friendly!'

Our whole convoy had been together, because the road had been wide and we'd not worried that we might need to backtrack. Grandad came on the intercom from the tanker, just behind Lieđđi in the first Bandvagn. 'Why have you stopped, Persie?'

'Crops growing in a field, and a fence that's obviously regularly maintained. I wonder how far we are from wherever whoever it is lives? I wonder if they've heard the trucks? I hope they're friendly, and I hope we've not scared the living daylights out of them with these vehicles!'

The conversation had barely begun when I – yes, it was me – spotted a man, running away from us across a grassy area quite a distance away.

'Look! Granny! There's a man!'

Granny Persie spotted him just as he disappeared through a gap in a hedge.

'So he'd heard us coming, and now he's seen us. I think we should get down out of the trucks and walk slowly towards where he was going, so they can see we're no threat.'

Grandad was nervous. 'Maybe we should wait in the vehicles until we see whether he comes back with anyone else. If he comes back with people with guns, what do we do?'

'I think that's incredibly unlikely, and if they see a family group like ours, they won't shoot, even if they are scared and armed.'

Granny Persie and I went. 'An old woman and a little boy? Who's going to do us any harm – with a convoy of seven military vehicles behind us?'

'Just stay in our sight until we know what's going on.'

It wasn't long before the man reappeared with an old lady. They seemed as nervous as we were, and visibly relieved when they saw it was just Granny Persie and me walking towards them.

The woman was the first to speak – in Swedish.

'I'm sorry, I don't speak much Swedish, and no Finnish at all. Or do you know a little Russian, perhaps?'

Granny Persie replied in Swedish, 'I know Swedish, but not very well, and almost no Russian. Do you know English, perhaps?'

The woman's English was excellent. She'd assumed that Persie was more likely to speak Swedish, because she'd recognized the Finnish military Bandvagns. She thought, from our appearance, that we were probably Sami – or, in her word, Lapps. I'd never heard the word 'Lapp' before.

Granny explained that 'Lapp' is actually rather an insulting word for Sami folk, that Granny and I weren't Sami, but that three of our party were. The lady was quite happy to be corrected, and I warmed to her immediately – I'm sure Granny did too.

The lady's name was Laima, and the man was her son, Nikolai. Nikolai had a little English, but much less than Laima. Granny Persie was very interested to know how they'd survived, and whether they knew any other survivors; but was patient enough to let Laima ask all about us first, and tell her own story in her own good time.

After Laima and Granny Persie had been talking for some time, Granny sent me back to the trucks to fetch Grandad and some of the others. She explained to Laima, 'They can't all come out to meet you, because two of them are invalids, and at least one of the others ought to stay with Merly all the time.'

Then Laima wanted to know what was wrong with the invalids, and before I'd reached the Unimog, they were on their way to come and meet everyone at the truck where Granny Merly and Gealbu were.

'You're giving her warfarin? That's good. I hope it's still got some potency! We have some more here, but whether it's any better than yours I don't know.'

'Do you still have a refrigerator?'

'Not really, that packed up years and years ago. But Ivan – my husband – made an ice cellar, and we've managed to keep that stocked with ice ever since.'

'So things were out of refrigeration for a few months, or so?'

'No, he'd anticipated the fridge failing, and the ice cellar was ready already.'

'So yours is probably better than ours. Ours will have been relatively warm during the summer, thirty-four times at least. But the nitroglycerine seems still to be good.'

'Probably packaged in nitrogen rather than air, for a military first aid kit. They'll have expected poor storage conditions, even if they didn't expect a thirty year plus storage time! I don't know whether there's any way to improve the shelf life of warfarin, but they'll have done that too if they knew some way to do it.'

'Hmm. All the stuff has information leaflets in multiple languages, not just Norwegian – or Finnish and Swedish in the Bandvagn kits – so I'm not sure it's really special military issue stuff.'

'Oh, I expect it is. It'll have been manufactured in America or Britain or anywhere, for sale to multiple different military customers.'

Laima had a good look at both Granny Merly and Gealbu, and expressed her opinion that they were doing very well, considering the circumstances. Then Granny Merly wanted to know what Laima's background was, how she knew so much about medicine.

'Self taught, after the war. I was a meteorologist before that, but medicine seemed so much more useful when there were just the three of us.'

'Just three of you? How did you come to be survivors?'

'Ivan was a nuclear physicist. He was one of the very few people who was supposed to be given the warning, and get us all into the shelter, but he had suspicions about what would happen afterwards, and he understood the requirements for a proper shelter. As long as we weren't in an area that was actually hit by blast or heat, which was unlikely here, the important thing was to have a sealed space, with a microfiltered air supply, and plenty of food and water to last us a few months.'

Granny Persie nodded. 'We'd figured that out, too – but only afterwards, of course. None of us knew anything beforehand, we were just shepherded into the shelter without warning, but we realized that the people running the camp we were moved to from the shelter were bullshitting us when they said it wasn't safe outside the camp. Your man was right to be suspicious, if our camp was anything to go by.'

'Ivan knew from the design of the official shelter that three months was expected to be sufficient. The same design of shelter was equally good whether the danger came from nuclear, biological, or chemical agents – and in all three cases, our future depended on the agents, whatever they were, having limited lives in the environment. But since the future of anyone in any other shelter depended on that same issue, there wasn't much point working on any other assumption. Ivan made a simple shelter here at my old family home, and when the warning came, we sealed ourselves in here instead of going to the official shelter. They must think we simply failed to get the warning in time, but here we still are. Except that Ivan died thirteen years ago.'

'It must have been difficult, not telling your neighbours around here.'

'Very. But our own survival depended on it. Nobody knew we were here. It was just an old abandoned house in woodland, where my old family farm had been turned into state forest land when everything was collectivized. When we eventually came out, we went into the local village, and of course we found everybody dead – but many of the houses in the village had been looted before the last of them died. Thank goodness no-one thought there'd be anything worth looting here – if they remembered the house was here at all.'

Laima and Nikolai invited us all to a meal in the house. 'Nikolai caught a deer in one of his traps just yesterday, so we've plenty of meat for everyone. We'd invite you to stay in the house, but it really isn't big enough for so many!'

But they insisted we stay where we were at least one night. We'd been going to stop somewhere near there anyway.

Granny Merly was mobile enough to get to the house, walking slowly, leaning a little on Suonjar, and taking a breather every now and then. Gealbu's bones had healed enough that he wanted to walk, but Granny Persie insisted that he mustn't put too much strain on them yet, and Nikolai – who was much bigger than any of our men – just picked him up and carried him like a baby. Laima translated Granny Merly's instruction to be careful of his ribs for Nikolai, but Gealbu was already gesturing very clearly that they were fine.

I had my first taste of fresh milk. I wasn't sure I liked it. I'd only had condensed milk from tins and milk made from powdered milk before, and was used to that although I didn't get it very often. We'd not found any more since halfway up Sweden, and the grown-ups wanted to conserve supplies for the littlies.

Granny Merly took a sip of my milk, and told me that it was good goat's milk, that goat's milk tasted like that, and that I'd get used to it. 'You'll prefer it to cow's milk after a while. And fresh milk of any kind is better than condensed or powdered.'

But the littlies wouldn't drink the goat's milk. Little Liz said it was 'orrible'. I felt obliged to drink it to show them a good example.

Then Granny Merly realized that condensed milk tastes sweet, and suggested sweetening some goat's milk for the littlies. Problem solved! I decided I'd be big and grown-up and drink it without sugar.

'Do you want some sugar in yours, Mikey?'

'No thanks. I like it 'orrible!'

Nikolai caught the mood and laughed as much as everyone else.

The house had clearly been quite grand in an old fashioned sort of way, but that was long ago, and it was now rather shabby, with ramshackle repairs everywhere. 'We didn't do anything to the outside until after the war, because we didn't want anyone to know we were there. It was in a very bad state.'

They'd raided the neighbouring village, but hadn't raided as widely as we had, always returning home every evening. 'We didn't trust our car to get us home if we let the engine stop. And of course eventually the morning came when we couldn't start it. The tractor we stole in the village lasted a few years longer, but we never took that further than into the village and back. Mostly we just used it around the farm. But that died too, a long time ago.'

'Farming must be really hard, with no tractor and no animals.'

'We've got chickens and goats. Ivan bought some from a farmer the morning he got the warning, on the way here.'

'But nothing that can pull a plough for you, obviously.'

'No, we couldn't have kept a horse in the shelter! Never mind two, and one wouldn't have lasted any longer than the tractor did. It is hard, but at least we get plenty of meat since the deer and rabbits arrived. Getting enough vegetables is hard work though, and maybe we don't really get enough. How did you all manage?'

Granny Persie and Grandad did most of the talking from our side. They told Laima all about – well, everything, eventually. Laima translated for Nikolai, but I thought he must have missed a lot, because she said much less in Russian than she heard in English. Maybe he caught up on a lot later, after we'd all trooped back out to the trucks, late that night. The three littlies and I were fast asleep long before that.

I do remember that there was no electricity in the house. They did have a couple of good bright paraffin lanterns, though, and a beautiful warm stove that they burnt logs in.

Laima wished that we'd brought one or two tractors with us, but understood that there were more important things for us to bring, and that our little convoy could only carry a limited amount of stuff.

'I think our tractors were nearing the end of their lives really, anyway. We'd collected all kinds of vehicles from all around the area, but they were all pretty well finished. We were very lucky to find the military depot with all these vehicles almost unused and mothballed. With luck the Unimog will make a good workhorse for a good few years, wherever we end up.'

Laima wondered whether we could stick around for a while, and help them with a few jobs with the Unimog; and then they all got to discussing whether we ought all to stop right there, or whether to continue with the original plan to head further south.

'There'll be a lot more useful stuff to raid in western Europe than there is around here, and the weather's better.'

'There's everything we need around here, too, but you're right about the weather. But there's another worry about western Europe. Here, I'll get the map for you. This is something Ivan made, right after the war, as soon as he realized that survival rates really were very low indeed.'

It was a map of Europe's nuclear reactors. Ivan had realized that while many of the reactors would have been shut down safely even during the crisis, many of them would not have been. Either there'd have been no-one competent available to do it, or desperate people, desperate for their electricity supplies to continue, would have pressured the operators into keeping the stations running up to and beyond the last possible moment. The end result of which would have been the same anyway: no-one competent left to shut the reactor down safely.

'Didn't they have automatic safe shut down systems?'

'Not really. The nuclear chain reaction itself could be shut down automatically. All nuclear reactors have that built in, because sometimes it has to be done more rapidly than you can expect human beings to react. But reactors don't stop producing heat just because the nuclear chain reaction stops: the radioactive fission products and activation products keep on producing heat. A lot of heat – enough to boil all the water out of the reactor, and then melt the reactor completely and set it on fire. The end result is radioactive contamination everywhere – on a scale that makes the radioactive effects of nuclear weapons look trivial.'

'Did Ivan work on a nuclear reactor site? Was he supposed to be one of the people shutting it down?'

'He was a researcher at the Leningrad Nuclear Physics Institute in Gatchina, but most of his work in the years just before the war was actually at the Ignalina reactor, just forty-five kilometres from here. He was worried that Ignalina might not be shut down properly. He prepared this map so that we could move rapidly out of the area if necessary, avoiding going any closer than necessary to any other reactors that might also have contaminated large areas.'

'So Ignalina was shut down successfully?'

'It must have been, at least reasonably well, because the levels of radioactive contamination around here are quite small, and almost certainly come from further afield. Ivan was pretty sure that quite a lot of other reactors elsewhere must have made an awful mess. It might have been lucky for you that you moved out of southern Sweden into Norway. You said you came via Helsinki? There's one just east of there, Loviisa. You must have come right past it. I hope it was shut down properly, and that none of you got any significant dose. Hmm. Driving past once, about ten kilometres away, thirty-four years after the event? Unlikely to be significant, unless it was a really dreadful mess.'

'If it's close to Helsinki, to the east, we drove past twice. We spent a bit of time in Helsinki, too. How far is it from there?'

'I don't know. Maybe about eighty kilometres. Almost certainly nothing to worry about for a short visit like that. It might not be healthy living anywhere near there long term.'

'No point worrying about anything now anyway! What's done is done. But it looks as though it would definitely be worth studying Ivan's map carefully before we move on. While we've still got transport, it would be good to get somewhere with a better climate. Looking at that map, it doesn't look as though southern France or Spain would be such a good idea. That's where we originally thought we'd head.'

'Sadly, none of our monitoring equipment works any more, so we can't actually tell whether an area is contaminated or not. But no, it's pretty unlikely that France or Spain will be clean. And you'd have to get through Germany first, and that's probably pretty badly contaminated, too. In itself that might not matter much, as long as you take enough food and water, and don't have to live off the land on the way.'

'Tinned and bottled stuff would be okay anyway. We found plenty of that in Scandinavia, and I don't suppose Germany would be any different. We've not really tried raiding in Russia or Latvia yet.'

'Oh, houses are pretty good. People used to keep plenty of stuff in stock, because you never knew whether the shops would have anything in stock or not. If you're heading for Greece, which looks to me to be the best destination, I think you'll find the same all down through eastern Europe. There's a few nuclear sites to avoid – one in Hungary, a couple in the Ukraine, and one in Bulgaria – but you ought to be able to find a route okay. Western Europe looks pretty impossible to me.'

'You said that none of your monitoring equipment works any more. Is there any chance that we might be able to repair it, do you think?'

'Not since Ivan died. I don't know enough about it. I don't suppose any of you do, do you?'

Granny Persie thought it would be worth having a look. 'Tomorrow.'

Chapter 7

The next day, Uncle Sid went with Nikolai to look at some of the things Nikolai thought they could usefully do with the Unimog. Somehow they managed to understand each other – enough for the purposes in hand, anyway. Meanwhile, Laima showed Granny Persie all the old radiation monitoring equipment.

'The biggest problem is probably just batteries. I know Ivan managed to keep some of the stuff going for years with external power supplies driven from the tractor battery, and then from the dynamo after the battery failed.'

'How did he start the tractor? We used to start our vehicles using a generator, but I don't think you've got any electricity now, have you?'

'You could start the tractor with the crank handle. It was damned hard work. It's a good thing Nikolai's a big strong chap. He was already, even when he was quite young. It would have killed Ivan if he'd had to crank start the tractor.'

'What did Ivan die of? I hope you don't mind me asking.'

'No, I don't mind. It's a long time ago now. He got cancer – leukaemia – nothing we could do about it. He was seventy-two when he died, so not a bad age anyway. He was much older than me. I'd always known I was likely to be a widow for a long time.'

Lieđđi and Suonjar took us four children to find the goats.

The goats discovered that Lieđđi was approachable and friendly – or maybe Lieđđi had discovered that about the goats. 'They're not reindeer, but they've got surprisingly similar personalities. They're not as shy though!'

'We must fetch Gealbu. He'll be pleased. He misses the reindeer.'

But Gealbu found some of the goats a bit too boisterous, and wanted to be helped back to the house. I too found the younger goats too excitable, and went with him. Gealbu didn't put much weight on my shoulder as we walked. I think he was using me more to help him keep his balance than to support him.

Uncle Sid and Nikolai had taken the Unimog into the village to fetch some tiles and timber from one of the houses. The next easiest vehicle to manoeuvre was the tanker, so Granny Persie brought that up to the house to provide some electricity. Once she got power to the radiation monitoring equipment, she could see that it was basically working, but some small parts needed to be replaced before she could take any meaningful measurements.

'I wonder if they'd have them in a store at the nuclear power station?'

'I doubt it, they used different equipment there. This is from the Institute. Anyway, Ignalina pretty certainly never actually caught fire, but the site itself is probably pretty badly contaminated by now, just because of corrosion. I wouldn't want to go there. It's a lot further to Gatchina, but there's a much better chance of finding the bits you need there, and at least the site will be relatively clean. There's no power reactor there, just a low power research reactor and a synchrocyclotron. The decay heat from the reactor wouldn't be enough to boil all its water off, so that'll be fairly clean. Negligible contamination outside the reactor hall itself, as long as they didn't leave it running, and I think that's pretty unlikely. There were some power reactors at Sosnovy Bor, but that's seventy kilometres from Gatchina.'

'I think it's worth going back there then, if you can show us where the Institute is. There could be other useful stuff there, apart from the bits for this kit. It took us four days to get here from Leningrad, so the round trip will probably take us a week, but I think it would be worth it. I don't know whether I'll be able to get the instruments working properly, but they'll be so useful if I can.'

It was eventually decided that we'd all go except Nikolai, who would have to stay to look after the animals. Most of us wanted to stick together, Laima had to come to show us the way, and Nikolai said he didn't mind staying on his own at all. We wouldn't take all the vehicles. We took the Bandvagn with the bowser full of petrol, and the truck that we slept in with a trailer full of jerry cans of diesel.

Granny Persie was a bit doubtful about taking the Bandvagn at first, worried about our petrol stocks, but Laima was confident of finding a supply in Gatchina, 'and we can refill your jerry cans with diesel at almost any farm, I'm sure.'

'We'd get to Gatchina and back easily with what we're taking, and there's plenty in the tanker when we get back here, but you're right that it would be nice to keep topped up.'

There was one other thing that bothered Granny Persie. Was the Institute one of the places that would be in use by the people who actually made it into the shelter? Where were they now? Laima was pretty sure they wouldn't have wanted to revive the Institute, but didn't know where they were.

'I know where the shelter was, obviously, but we went and took a look there, and it's completely abandoned. We approached the area very circumspectly at first, but it was immediately clear that everybody had gone. Where they went, I don't know. We've never seen any sign of them.'

'Wouldn't they have included the reactor in their patch?'

'Ignalina? No, I'm pretty sure they wouldn't. The people who were left to shut it down would all be dead, and you can't leave a reactor unattended for three months, even if it had been shut down carefully, and expect to start it again safely. You've got to at least keep the cooling systems ticking over. The shelter wasn't close to the reactor – forty kilometres away from it – and where they went after they left the shelter, I don't know. I wouldn't be surprised if it was another forty kilometres further from the reactor, or more. A fair few of the people involved would understand the danger very well.'

With just one truck and a Bandvagn and plenty of drivers, we could get further in a day than we had coming south. We stopped for a late lunch somewhere near the place we'd stopped the night before we arrived at Laima and Nikolai's farm, and Uncle Sid managed to shoot a deer.

Laima encouraged us to try to get to Ostrov. 'It's only another fifty kilometres or so. We should stop by the river there, it's a really good spot for fishing early in the morning. Ivan and I used to stop there on the way to and from Gatchina.'

It was really nearly sixty kilometres, but we made good time and arrived before dark. Laima directed us off the main road, and we stopped just by the end of an old chain bridge over a big river.

'That bridge is only fit for pedestrians. You can't take vehicles over it. You might get away with it, but it might collapse. The best fishing is the other side, on the island, just downstream of the bridge. That's what Ivan always said, anyway.'

'Is that an island? You'd never know from here.'

'Yes, and there's another bridge just like this one over the other half of the river.'

Laima took charge of the deer. Everyone watched as she skinned and gutted it expertly, then butchered it carefully. She cut the bigger muscles into long thin strips. She said that she and Nikolai had both learned how to do that watching Ivan, but that she usually got Nikolai to do it.

'We'll have the offal tonight, and with a bit of luck there'll be fish for breakfast. But if we can find some string, I'll string all the good bits of meat up to dry for you for your journey. We can hang it underneath the bridge. It'll still be here when we get back in a few days' time, and it'll be nearly dried by then.'

'You dry meat even though you have an ice cellar?'

'Certainly. Dried meat keeps for years, wet meat only a few weeks in the ice cellar. We could make it colder using salt on the ice, but I don't know whether the ice would last all summer if we did that. Probably not.'

'You'd need a lot of salt, anyway.'

'There's plenty in the village. But you're right, we'd run out in the end if we used it too freely. We used to dry fish too, but we've had none since Ivan died. With no car it's too far to anywhere with good fishing.'

Grandad and Mum were up before dawn. They took the fishing gear over the bridge to the exact spot Laima had pointed out. By the time the rest of us were up and about, they'd caught several good sized fish. Laima knew the name of the species in Russian, but no-one knew what they were in English. It didn't matter: they made an excellent breakfast anyway.

Despite Mum and Aunty Anna carefully deboning the littlies' portions, Little Liz got a bone stuck in her throat and started to cry. Everyone was a bit surprised when Laima picked her up, turned her upside-down, and banged her on the back; then righted her, opened her mouth wide with one hand, and reached into her mouth with two fingers of the other – and produced the offending fishbone!

'It still hurts!' wailed little Liz, and Laima explained that the bone was out, but the bit of throat that had got poked would still be sore for a little while.

'Only a little while, though. Mouths and throats heal really quickly. But a bit of that potato would help it feel better quicker. A pity we don't have any bread, that's the best thing. But bread's history.'

Little Liz slowly came round to the idea of swallowing a bit of fried potato, and then smiled at Laima through her tears.

'Better now?'

Silent nod.

I wondered what 'bread' was. If it was history, it obviously wasn't the same stuff as the crispbread we'd got several cartons of.

Years later, probably about the same time that I found out what real bread was, I learnt that the fishbone Laima had produced had gone into Liz's mouth between Laima's fingers, and that swallowing the potato had really been the important part of the operation, to take the original bone down Liz's throat. It was all psychology, an act designed to stop Liz worrying. 'That was a trick Ivan used to play on Nikolai when he was small. I'm not sure Nikolai knows now that he was tricked. I doubt if he remembers anything about it.'

The main thing I remember about the rest of the trip back to Gatchina is that it rained and rained and rained. The worst thing was that we couldn't tell which of the puddles were deep potholes, and which were just puddles, so the ride was even bumpier in the truck than it was in the Bandvagn. After a little while, Granny Persie stopped for a consultation, and it was decided to try putting Granny Merly and Gealbu in the Bandvagn instead of the back of the truck. They decided they preferred it there, and stayed there from then on.

Getting through Gatchina, which had been so difficult the last time we'd been there, was no problem with Laima to guide us. She took us straight to the Institute. We arrived there in the early afternoon, and spent most of the afternoon breaking into various buildings on the site. Laima didn't know her way around the site, only how to get to where she used to meet Ivan.

Granny Persie eventually found a store containing not only the parts she knew she wanted for the instruments she'd already seen, but whole new instruments, and all sorts of other stuff. I have a clear picture of her in my mind to this day, standing there holding the pressure lantern high and gazing at the racks and racks of *things* with an expression of pure rapture on her face.

It didn't last long. 'I can't take all this stuff, we don't have room. And if I could take it, I could never use it all. There's loads of stuff here I could never make work, the infrastructure to support that kind of work just doesn't exist any more. I've got to think very carefully what's worth taking, and what's just so much junk now. And that's most of it, really.'

Grandad had one contribution to make to Granny Persie's thinking. 'It's not just what you can or can't use, Persie. It's what you can make use of to teach the children. Our grown-up children as well as the littlies.'

'Hmm. I'm not sure this is the best place for teaching materials, but I'll think about it. I'll have to spend a while exploring and thinking. This store won't be the only place with interesting stuff.'

It took Granny the whole of the next day to sort out the various things she eventually decided to take. I wasn't aware at the time what a lot of the stuff was, just that there was quite a pile.

One particular thing that did stick in my mind was a box full of drill bits, that Granny hummed and hawed over for quite a while. 'This is quite a set. Every size from 0.8mm to 10mm, in 0.1mm increments. With spares, plenty of them. But what would I ever need them for? I've already got a good set with 0.5mm increments. And I've only got a hand held power drill, no pillar drill. So I've no use for them really. But I'm so tempted.'

'There's a pillar drill here.'

'We can't take that. It'd be ridiculous to load ourselves down with that. There's a lathe and a milling machine, too. What are we going to do? Restart industry? Our little generator couldn't power those. It could run the pillar drill, but what for? Oh, I'd find a use, no doubt, but at what cost? Clogging the trucks up with junk...'

But she took the drill set.

'If we ever want a pillar drill, we'll find one in any machine shop. But we probably wouldn't find a drill bit set like this.'

That was just an excuse, and we all knew it. The set only weighs a couple of kilograms, so no-one really minded Granny Persie's little idiosyncrasy. We all love her to bits.

But Grandad quietly let me into a secret years later: Granny Merly had resisted the temptation to raid a jeweller's. 'Not that anyone has the slightest thought that there's anything wrong with raiding a jeweller's – but where would you stop? She could have filled the trucks with beautiful pieces, and weighed herself down like a princess, but what for?'

Granny Merly wore the necklace and earrings she already had before the war all her life. Grandad thinks she might have been given them by a boyfriend back in Hong Kong, but he never asked her and she never said. They might have been her mother's.

There were huge petrol and diesel tanks actually on the Institute campus, and we refilled the jerry cans and the bowser.

All the way in both directions, I was in the front of the truck with Granny Persie and Laima. Sometimes Granny was driving, sometimes it was Mum or Dad or Uncle Sid. Granny said it was quite a luxury to have so many drivers for so few vehicles!

But the best thing for me was listening to Granny and Laima talking. Laima understands things in the same sort of way that Granny does, and they've both got sharp minds as well as a scientific and technical education. A lot of their talk went right over my head, but I managed to pick up a few threads and I'm sure it's what got me started thinking the way I do.

One of the things they talked a lot about was the way the weather was getting worse every winter. They thrashed out a theory that it was a direct result of the collapse of industrial civilization.

'We'll never know whether we're right or not, but it seems very likely. Humanity is simply not burning fossil fuels like we used to, and we're not clearing forests any more – in fact, they're growing again. We've seen that for ourselves, in just the last thirty years.'

'The ice age that human agriculture has been forestalling for millennia is beginning to take hold now, you mean?'

'Exactly that, if I'm right. Human agriculture – clearing forests and burning biomass, wood and peat mostly – had been forestalling the beginning of an ice age that was otherwise long overdue by now. By sheer luck, agriculture had grown at just about the right rate to stabilize the climate when it should have been getting colder, to judge by the history of previous ice ages. Then fossil fuel burning, increasing carbon dioxide much faster than necessary to keep the cooling at bay, was beginning to threaten to bring in a new hot period. If humanity had carried on the way it was going, burning more and more coal and oil, faster and faster, it wouldn't have been an ice age, it would have turned the world into a hothouse. No ice caps, probably.'

'And that would have meant a huge sea level rise. I wonder how much?'

'I don't know. Tens of metres, anyway. Enough to flood a substantial percentage of the world's best farmland, and lots of big cities.'

'But we're headed the other way now.'

'Seems so, but there's nothing we can do about it, obviously.'

'So heading south seems like an even better idea than we realized – for our descendants sake if not for our own.'

Mum, who was driving at this point, had been listening too.

'Maybe you should come with us too, Laima? It can't be easy here with no tractor, and from what you say the winters are getting pretty bad here, too.'

'I was wondering that myself. I didn't know how to ask. I'm old, and I could live out my days here and be happy enough, but it'd be good for Nikolai to have someone after his old mother's gone.'

Mum laughed. 'Yes, and there are more women than men in our group!'

'I've not quite worked out who's already attached to whom, but my impression is that all the unattached women are a lot younger than Nikolai.'

'I don't suppose that would bother him, and I'm sure it wouldn't bother any of them. It didn't bother you, did it? How much older than you was Ivan?'

'Eighteen years. That's a good point. Funny, isn't it, how you don't think about your own history when you're thinking about your children's future!'

They worked out that the difference between Nikolai and the twins was actually slightly less than that, and Lieđđi and Suonjar would be even closer to Nikolai's age.

'But we'll have to let them all work these things out for themselves. I'm pretty sure that Suonjar's got her eyes on Jake, and I know that Belle's decided that Gealbu is something special. But what goes on in Lieđđi's or Dot's head I've not worked out. Belle and Dot always used to assume they'd have Jake's children, but it's not ideal because they're his half-sisters. Greg's my half-brother, too, but that's life.'

'I didn't feel able to ask about that. So all your generation are Pete's children?'

Mum started explaining all the relationships in our family. I knew all about that, and gave up listening. I stared out into the Russian countryside – or was it Latvian again by now? I wasn't sure. No, it must still have been Russia, because it wasn't long since we left Ostrov. We'd got more fish there again, as well as picking up the half-dried venison.

I spotted a rabbit, then lots of rabbits. I pointed them out to Granny Persie. She got Mum to stop, and climbed quietly out of the truck with the gun. Granny Persie is the best with the gun. She got a second rabbit, even though they'd all started running as soon as they heard the first shot. She'd got the first one in the head, which pleased Laima.

'That'll be a good rabbit skin! The other one won't be quite as good with a hole in its side. But I'll manage to do something with it anyway. We used to snare a lot of rabbits at one time, but we've got foxes now, and the rabbit population has plummeted. It's good for the crops, though. We can fence deer out, but it's hopeless trying to fence rabbits out.'

I saw several deer later on, but they'd heard us and were running before I saw them, and Granny Persie didn't even get Dad to stop the truck.

We arrived back at Laima's place after dark, but Nikolai had heard us coming, and came out to meet us with a pressure lantern. He looked relieved to see us. Apparently it was the longest he'd ever been separated from his mother – and he was thirty-five years old! But then, none of our family have been separated from each other for even that long, not since Grandad and the Grannies escaped from the camp. When there's no-one else in your world, you don't want to be separated for long.

Nikolai thought it was a wonderful idea that he and Laima should come south with us. 'We never thought moving was possible, not once the car was finished. And we couldn't have moved the goats even before that. It would have been difficult enough to move the chickens, although we could have taken fertilized eggs.'

'Incubating them without a hen would have been difficult. I don't think we could have done it reliably. We'd have managed to take a couple of hens, I think. But we didn't see any point moving in those days. We'd had a couple of bad winters, but I hadn't realized it was the start of a trend like this.'

'With all these trucks, we could take the goats as well, if we can find a bigger trailer for the Unimog.'

'Oh, there's plenty of them around here.'

'It's finding one that still rolls along, preferably one with the same wheels as something we've got already.'

Wheels were always a worry – well, tyres really, but as far as possible Granny Persie wanted to treat wheels and tyres as a unit. She'd managed to find reasonable looking spares for the trailer we'd got, which seemed to be a fairly standard size, and there'd been spares for everything else in the military depots where we'd found the vehicles. But thirty-four year old tyres are only any good if they've been stored properly. The original tyres on our trailer were still okay, but the rubber was cracked all over the place, and Granny Persie was always conscious that they could burst any time.

'If there'd been any weight in the trailer all those years, they'd have been completely flat and useless. There was no pressure in them to speak of. I was afraid they might burst when I first pumped them up.'

But they hadn't, and they were still okay three and a half thousand kilometres later, despite being dragged through potholes and over jagged rocks. 'We've been lucky. So far. But I wouldn't want to load that trailer too heavily. I wonder if we'll be able to find another one, big enough and with high sides, to carry the goats?'

'Another question is whether the hitch will match on the trailer and the Unimog. There's at least two different types of hitch around here, and they might be different from what they had in Norway.'

'Oh, I'm sure we can cobble something together. The Unimog's got quite a versatile arrangement, and if necessary I can unbolt the hitch it's got and bolt a different one on. Even if the bolt holes don't match, I can drill new ones. Tedious, but doable.'

It turned out that the hitch wasn't a problem. We found a suitable trailer in the village, and the hitch was a simple eye, very similar to the one on our old trailer. It was a bit loose on the Unimog's hitch pin, but Granny Persie wasn't worried about that. She moved the plate the jaw was mounted on down as far as it would go so the trailer was horizontal.

Tyres were more of a problem. We couldn't find wheels the right size with decent tyres on them anywhere. We found several more similar trailers, all with rotten tyres, before we eventually found a tyre store. For the first time, we had to change tyres.

Getting the old tyres off was the hardest part of the operation. The rubber had stuck firmly onto the rims, and the tyres came apart as Nikolai tried to lever them down into the well of the rim. Several of us, right down to me, spent a whole day scraping lumps of well-stuck-on rubber off rusty rims – and then scraping the worst of the rust off as well.

One of the wheels was so rusty that Granny Persie declared it unfit for use. She went off and got a couple more wheels the same size off another trailer. More scraping.

Then Nikolai had to lever new – thirty-odd year old – tyres onto all five wheels. Uncle Sid helped him.

'I'm glad we never had to do that before. I'm not sure we could have managed without you, Nikolai.'

Laima wasn't there to translate, but Nikolai somehow understood roughly what Uncle Sid had said. He looked towards the Unimog's wheels, which were a fair bit bigger, and laughed – the truck wheels are bigger still. Granny

Persie said that in other countries, a tyre store like this would have better equipment – a proper jig for taking tyres off wheels and putting new ones on. She was surprised they didn't have one here, but if Nikolai was a typical Latvian, she could understand why they didn't bother.

'Half Latvian, half Russian,' Nikolai said, pointing to his huge chest with a big grin. He knew more English than we'd realized. But the way he pronounced 'half' had an L in it, and there was an S not a Sh in the middle of Russian.

In fact, his parents had taught him to read and write English at the same time as they'd taught him to read and write Russian, because their large library contained more books in English than in Russian – and very few in Latvian, which Laima had never taught Nikolai at all. They'd initially taught him to say the English words, because that made it easier to teach the reading and writing, but once he was able to read the books quietly to himself, they never spoke English any more. So although he could read English quite well, he really wasn't used to speaking English – nor to following someone else speaking. But that background meant that, with people speaking it all around him, he was picking up the spoken language very fast.

The trailer had been designed for transporting cattle, so it was ideal for the goats. 'I'm sure they won't mind sharing it with the timbers, and the weight won't be a problem – goats are much lighter than cows!'

'If we'd had a trailer like this before, we could have brought the reindeer.'

'Yes, but they wouldn't have been happy, and anyway, they wouldn't like the heat where we're going. I wonder how the goats will take to the trailer?'

'Oh, goats are tough characters. They'll take it in their stride.'

The goats and the chickens were used to each other, and no-one expected any problems about them sharing the trailer.

The only difficulty was making the trailer chicken proof. The gaps in the sides weren't big enough for the chickens to get out, but the top was open. At first Granny Persie thought that what they wanted was some wire netting, but eventually she and Laima settled on making a solid roof, to keep the rain off a little, as well as keeping the chickens in.

They didn't want the weight of solid wood, and searched for and eventually found something suitable – the roof of an old van they found rusting away in a barn. The roof was the best bit of the van: it was aluminium. The roof of the barn had partly collapsed onto the van and dented its roof, but that didn't matter. They levered up the bit of the barn roof that had been resting on the van with a couple of bits of timber, and then propped it up so that could get the van roof off.

Uncle Sid drilled holes in the edges of the aluminium and the top of the sides of the trailer, and he and Nikolai tied the roof on with baling wire. Nikolai decided that it would be useful to have a box on the front of the trailer, where the chassis extended beyond the main body to the hitch, and in no time at all he'd knocked one up.

There were a few things that Laima and Nikolai wanted to bring with them, apart from the goats and chickens. Everybody was pleased with the pressure lanterns.

'We never saw any of these in Norway or on the way. All we saw were gas ones that screw onto disposable cartridges, and we never saw enough cartridges to make them worth bothering with. I think paraffin pressure lanterns had gone out of fashion in Scandinavia.'

The biggest thing Laima wanted to bring was all the books, but she knew that was too much. She spent a long time sorting through them to find the ones she thought were really worth taking. Nikolai picked out a few more.

Granny Persie started to look through the ones Laima was thinking to leave behind. The pile we were going to take grew. Grandad went to look too, and then he called me over.

There were some children's books in English, but the best ones were in Russian. Oh, the pictures! They were glorious.

How Laima laughed. We ended up taking about a quarter of their library altogether. At first we put them in the rear of the Bandvagn where half of us had been sleeping. They filled a substantial part of it.

'We'll bring the lávvu back into service. It's just as well we didn't leave it behind!'

Nikolai had a better suggestion: to keep the old farm trailer, and tow it behind the tanker. Granny Persie said the tanker didn't have a towing hitch, but the trailer would attach to the Bandvagn easily.

'We can clear out the back of another truck, partly onto that trailer, and partly into the Bandvagn. Then we've got two sleeping trucks. The truck is more comfortable to sleep in than the Bandvagn anyway.'

Nikolai and Uncle Sid decided that they would make another box on top of the trailer, to stop things bouncing out, and to keep the rain off everything. 'Then we don't have to worry about sorting out things that don't mind getting wet.'

They went off into the village in the Unimog to look for some suitable materials. They came back an hour or so later.

'All we've managed to find is a tarpaulin and some rope. There's plenty of wood to make something, but it'd take quite a while and be horribly heavy. We can put the spare wheels on the old trailer and free up some space in one of the truck trailers.'

'Don't even need a tarpaulin for that, all we need to do is rope them on. Spare wheels don't have to stay dry.'

'No, but you don't want rope damage on the tyres. Better just to put a tarp over them and tie it down round the edge.'

'We've got one spare wheel for the cattle trailer, and plenty for everything else. I wonder if we could find at least one spare wheel for the old farm trailer? Or at least some spare tyres.'

Back to the tyre store. But there weren't any tyres the right size. Granny Persie looked at wheels on a few vehicles to see if any of them might fit on the trailer in place of the wheels we'd got, but the wheel nut spacings were all different.

'Oh well. It'll last as long as it lasts, and they we'll have to think of something else. Maybe we'll find another trailer worth swapping it for sometime.'

'With tyres? We can't take a whole tyre store to make sure we've got the right ones.'

'True. Maybe it's worth trying to find another trailer here, while we've got a tyre store handy.'

Daft as it seems, I think people had become attached to our old farm trailer. It seemed sad to leave it behind, but there was a better one in the village. It was very similar, just a little bigger, with wheels the store had got three fairly decent tyres for. There was a small truck with a spare wheel the same size, too. The tyre on the spare was a bit worn, but unlike the wheels on the truck itself, otherwise in fair condition. It didn't have much pressure, but held air once it was pumped up. Nikolai changed the tyres on the trailer's own wheels. I helped with the scraping of the rims again.

Chapter 8

The morning we left, I noticed tears in Laima's eyes, and remembered how we'd all been like that when we left our own farm. I put my arms round her and looked up at her, and Little Liz came to her as well. Laima picked her up and gave her a big kiss, and then Emma and Dang wanted a cuddle and a kiss too. Laima laughed, but the tears kept on coming.

Nikolai wasn't crying, but you could see his feelings in his face. He busied himself loading the goats and chickens. He drove the big billy goat up the ramp, and then shut it. He lifted the other goats over it, but the younger billy jumped out while he was putting the last nanny in. Eventually he managed to get all the goats in and shut the top doors.

Then he put the chickens in one at a time, opening one of the top doors just a crack for each one.

'That's going to be even more of a palaver every time we stop. We'll have to let the goats out sometimes, and put them on tethers, to let them get some exercise and some grass. And we need a chicken run we can put down when we stop, too. At least a small one.'

Laima had to translate for the rest of us. Nikolai didn't say very much in English at first – especially when his mother was around to translate.

He found some strips of wood and cut some of the wire fencing from their old chicken run. Then he very rapidly put together four side panels and a roof that he could tie together to make a small chicken run, but which laid flat on top of the tarpaulin on the tyre trailer.

At that point, he realized that the box he'd made on the front of the trailer would make an ideal nesting box for the chickens. He got Uncle Sid and Aunty Anna to find somewhere else to put the things that had been secreted away in there, then dug out a drill and a padsaw from one of the boxes of tools, and cut a hole in the end panel of the trailer, through from the back of the box. Laima went and got some straw to put in the bottom.

Nikolai and Laima said that they'd like to do their share of driving eventually, but they'd rather just observe for a while first. Laima said she'd never driven anything bigger than a car, and that not for over twenty years – and that in those days the roads had still been in relatively good condition. Nikolai had only driven their small tractor, just a few times when he was in his teens.

We changed the order of the convoy around, putting the tanker right behind the Unimog at the front. That way, the people in the tanker could keep an eye on the trailer with the goats and chickens in it, and communicate if necessary with Granny Persie and Laima and me in the Unimog.

Granny Persie and Laima had worked out the route they wanted to take – subject to amendment in the light of road conditions, and possibly radiation measurements.

Laima had been rather concerned that the levels at their farm were significantly higher than they'd been a dozen years earlier. She said Ivan's measurements had shown the levels rising after they first came out of their shelter, peaking after a year or so, and then declining in much the way he'd expected based on what he knew about the most likely mix of isotopes involved. At first Laima wondered whether we'd picked up a significant quantity of contamination from Loviisa – the Finnish nuclear power station we'd come past – and brought it with us on the vehicles, but the readings were no higher near our vehicles than anywhere else.

'So Loviisa isn't responsible. Either it's a much more distant one that made a real mess that's only reached here in the last decade, or it's one that's started to leak much worse than it did originally – possibly even corrosion at Ignalina.'

'We should take readings once every ten or fifteen kilometres, to see whether we're moving into worse contaminated areas, or moving away from them. Then we can guess where the sources are, and avoid them.'

We headed away from Ignalina anyway, into Byelorussia, and the readings did indeed go down, so Granny Persie and Laima thought Ignalina was probably responsible. Then, once in Byelorussia, we headed south. Readings remained low, and roughly constant.

'I don't know what natural background levels are in this area. Ivan would have done. A fair bit lower than this, I'm pretty sure, but this level is certainly nothing to worry about. Ivan would have wanted to know what the particular isotopes producing the radiation were, because they have different probabilities of entering the body, and different pathways and residence times in the body once they get there, but I don't know enough about it – and I don't think we've got the means of finding out what they are anyway, have we, Persie?'

'Not really, although we could theoretically get some hints by comparing readings with different windows on the meter. But again, I don't know enough about it to interpret the results in detail. It's all there in Ivan's books, I saw them, but it would take me an age to get on top of it – and I'd need a lot of your help, because although a lot of it is language-independent, a lot of it isn't, too. But just trying to avoid areas where the readings are high should be good enough anyway.'

'True. Ivan was especially interested because he wanted to try to work out whether there'd been deliberate releases of short half-life materials as part of the war. He thought it was as much a deliberate cull as a war really...'

'Interesting. We'd wondered about that, too. In fact, we're pretty sure it was more like a cull, because of what the newspapers were saying after we went into the shelter.'

'You got newspapers in the shelter? That's really odd. I'd have been less surprised by television reception.'

'No, we found the papers after we came out, and not until after we escaped from the camp. I can see why they didn't want any televisions in the shelter either, whether it was war or a cull. The people who designed the shelter and the way it worked might not even have known it was going to be a cull rather than a real war.'

'What were the papers saying?'

'It's a bit hard for us to be sure, because we only ever saw Norwegian ones, and none of us know Norwegian. But we're pretty sure no war was ever mentioned, and that the deaths were being put down to a pandemic.'

It was quite late in the morning by the time we actually got going. There were nineteen of us now!

Late in the afternoon, Laima suggested we should stop for the night soon, because if we kept on going we'd reach Polotsk just about at dusk, and she wanted to be sure there was a good place for the goats and the chickens to get out onto the grass for at least an hour or two. 'We'll have to put them back in the trailer overnight, or the goats will chew through their tethers and get away, and a fox will very likely get the chickens.'

Laima and Suonjar milked the three nannies who were in milk. I watched, absolutely fascinated. Suonjar fed the three littlies straight from the goat's teat, which they seemed perfectly happy about. I thought that was funny, after the way they turned their noses up at goat's milk in a cup, but I didn't say anything.

There was an egg in the nesting box on the front of the trailer, too. Laima was disappointed. 'We've been getting two or three a day recently. Bumping about in the trailer with the goats must be upsetting them.'

I watched the chickens scratting about in their little run for a while, pecking up little titbits of something, but I couldn't see what. Then Nikolai took me to a patch of dandelions. We picked lots of leaves and took them back to the chicken run and poked them through the netting. The chickens came over to us and nibbled bits off the leaves. Nikolai was pleased. 'Good yellow egg yolks now!'

He got a small spade out of one of the trailers, and dug over a patch of grass. 'Not real work, no planting today. But chickens like these,' he said, and picked out several worms and grubs and threw them into the chicken run. The chickens almost fought over them.

Granny Merly seemed to be a lot better, pottering about and playing with the littlies pretty much like she always used to, but I could see that Grandad and Granny Persie were watching her worriedly all the time. She seemed paler and frailer and somehow old, older than Laima or Grandad or Granny Persie, who were all actually older than she was – thirteen years older in Laima's case.

I didn't know why we were divided between the two sleeping trucks the particular way we were that night, and I didn't think about it at the time. I was in one truck with Mum and Uncle Sid and Uncle Jake and all the littlies and Nikolai and Lieđđi and Gealbu; Grandad, the Grannies, Laima, Dad, Aunty Anna, the twins and Suonjar were in the other truck. I should have realized something was odd, with so many couples separated, but I didn't think about it. It was the first night we'd had Nikolai with us, so it was bound to be different.

None of us in our truck woke up during the night, or if anyone did, I never knew. But we all knew something was wrong in the morning. Everyone was very quiet, and there was no sign of Granny Merly. Nobody said anything at first, not in my hearing anyway, but I knew. I didn't say anything.

It was Little Liz who broke the silence. 'Where's G'anny?'

That's when I saw the tears in everybody's eyes. Laima spoke first, 'She's gone to Heaven, sweetheart. No more pain and troubles for Merly.'

'Where's heaven? Will she be back soon?'

Granny Persie didn't believe in beating about the bush. 'She died last night, darling. She won't be coming back. At least she died quietly in her sleep, cuddled up between me and Grandad the way she always liked to be.'

That was a lie of kindness, but none of us littlies knew that until years later. Granny Merly had in fact been horribly aware that she was dying, wide awake and in excruciating pain. Laima and Suonjar had tried their damnedest to save her, but couldn't.

Actually, it was only since her first heart attack that Granny Merly had slept in the middle; before that it had always been Grandad between the Grannies. Granny Merly had often had Grandad on one side and a huddle of littlies on the other.

Nikolai and Uncle Sid dug a grave in an open space in the woods a hundred metres or so away from the trucks, and buried Granny Merly's body there, but I didn't know that for years. I also didn't know then that Grandad and Dad and Nikolai spent several hours chiselling an epitaph into a substantial slab of concrete that they dug out of the road and placed on the grave. Laima drew a picture of the scene in her notebook, which I saw years later. The epitaph, clearly legible in Laima's picture, reads thus:

HERE LIES CHAN MEI MEI
11TH MAY 1970 – 29TH JUNE 2024
BELOVED OF
PETER SAMUEL COLLINS AND NGUYỄN THỊ PERSEVERANCE
MOTHER OF GREGORY, ANNA, BELLE AND DOROTHY
GRANDMOTHER OF MICHAEL, ELIZABETH, EMMA AND DANG
SORELY MISSED

Will anyone ever find it? If they do, what they will make of it? Grandad says it must be the roughest carving anyone's ever seen on a tombstone, but they did their best.

Some of the rest of us spent a lot of time fishing during the two days we spent at that spot, and caught quite a lot of fish. We feasted well, and Laima showed everybody how to prepare fish for drying. She rigged up a drying rack in the back of one of the trailers, in the clear space under the canvas and over the load. She was doing her best to keep people busy, but I knew that everyone was in a very sombre mood and I think the fishing suited them better.

The goats and chickens were happy, spending all day on the grass after a day in the trailer. Little Liz and I fed them dandelion leaves. At first we were just feeding the chickens, but the goats decided they wanted to be fed as well, even though the patch they were tethered in contained plenty of dandelions, as well as lots of other things they seemed to like. I'm sure that really they just liked attention. You could even say they were jealous of the attention the chickens had been getting.

All the goats and chickens went back into their trailer at dusk without any complaint.

'We should have loaded them in the evening before we left, rather than trying to load them in the morning.'

'Easy to be wise after the event, and it doesn't matter now anyway.'

'I wonder how they'll react when we don't let them out in the morning, and start bumping them around again?'

'They'll get used to it.'

There were four eggs both days, so us four littlies each had one.

We were still all very subdued when we eventually set off again.

Laima told Granny Persie that there was a military airfield a few kilometres before Polotsk, and Granny Persie thought we ought to visit it and see whether it was worth raiding.

'Assuming it's not become a camp of survivors like our old one.'

'I don't think that's particularly likely. Why there rather than anywhere else?'

Laima didn't actually know exactly where the airfield was, and we uncoupled the trailer from the Unimog to go scouting around for it. It didn't take long to find. Granny Persie was disappointed to discover it didn't actually have any aeroplanes – just a lot of helicopters.

'I was hoping to cut some aluminium panels off a plane. No, I'd no particular plans for anything to do with them, I just thought they'd be jolly useful material to have. I don't think there's anything useful here – apart from some fuel. We might as well top that up while we're here.'

But when we discovered the fuel tanks, Granny Persie wasn't sure it was really exactly the right fuel. 'We'll find some more somewhere else. I don't want to wreck any of our engines. I'm sure they'd run on this stuff, but they might overheat or burn the exhaust valves if it's not quite right.'

The only things we took from the airfield were a couple of paraffin stoves. 'We've got plenty of gas bottles for the gas stoves for the moment, but they won't last forever. We're much more likely to be able to get paraffin – or diesel, which will probably work in these almost equally well.'

I don't remember much else about Polotsk, apart from crossing a big river by a bridge that Granny Persie said didn't seem to have suffered the ravages of time at all. I remember that particularly because I had to get Grandad to explain to me what the 'ravages of time' were, and how to spell 'ravages' so I could write it in my diary.

The road from Polotsk to Minsk was in worse condition, and in two places we had to put down timbers to get through washouts. Oh, what a palaver! Each time, all the goats and chickens had to be taken out of the trailer to get at the timbers, and tethered or put in their run while all the vehicles got past the boggy bit, and then reloaded after as many timbers as could be rescued had been reloaded. Granny Persie wondered whether we should have come via Vitebsk and Orsha. The roads looked bigger in the atlas – the only map we'd got of the area – but it would have been a lot further. Laima wasn't sure the roads would really have been any better. 'And it's too late now. No point going back all that way.'

Three days to do just two hundred and forty kilometres.

We went right through the middle of Minsk. After our experiences in Helsinki and Leningrad, we weren't worried about cities any more. Minsk was in worse shape than Helsinki, but not as bad as Leningrad. Following our noses, the road went straight through the middle of the city, and we found ourselves at the airport.

Aeroplanes! I'd never seen an aeroplane before. I'd never seen helicopters until the airfield at Polotsk, either, but I'd not taken much notice of them. We were all still much too preoccupied after Granny Merly's death. But aeroplanes...a piece of family history.

And for Granny Persie, a source of aluminium sheet.

But for once in her life, Granny Persie was defeated. She found a set of moveable stairs that she could move up alongside a plane, got the little generator going, and found as she'd expected that she could cut aluminium easily with the circular saw. But she could only get quite small pieces of sheet out, because it was riveted to frames at frequent intervals.

She and Nikolai tried ripping a sheet off the rivets, but it just tore along the line of the rivets when they eventually managed to exert enough force using a chunk of timber as a lever. Nikolai hacksawed through a frame in a couple of places, and then tried to hacksaw the frame off the back of the panel. They tried all sorts of methods, but nothing worked, even after they got right inside the plane through an opening that the designers had never intended. Granny Persie managed to cut her hand quite badly, and at that point they gave up. Suonjar got out a first aid kit and bandaged her up.

I think Granny must have still been in a bad mental state. She's never as easily defeated as that – or maybe she normally works out more quickly what is and what isn't a feasible project. And she never normally hurts herself much.

Nikolai suggested that what they needed was a factory that made aeroplanes. 'They'd have big sheets in one piece with no holes in there.'

'Yes, but where are the aeroplane factories? I don't know. We just have to find what we find. We're out of reach of anywhere any of us know anything about now. All the information we've got is what's in the old atlas. Even if we find a bookshop, I don't suppose we'd find a book listing where all the different sorts of factories are.'

'Minsk is a big industrial town. We could spend some time just taking a look what factories there are here.'

'We could, but I think it would be better just to press on. We've got everything we need for the moment, and we'll have plenty of time to explore the area we eventually settle in and find whatever there is to find there.'

We found a Byelorussian-style filling station and filled up the tanker and the bowser. We'd probably never have noticed it without Laima's help. The jerry cans, which had been full of diesel for the trip to Gatchina, were at last full of petrol again. Granny rinsed each of them out with a bit of petrol before filling them.

'I'm pretty sure the amount of diesel there was left in them wouldn't matter in the petrol, but better safe than sorry.'

Finding our way out of Minsk was as bad as it had been getting out of Gatchina. There was a road to the west of the airport that seemed to head in the right direction at first, but very soon swung around to the south. We followed it a little way hoping it would swing west again, but it didn't and eventually we turned round and went back. Finally we got onto what seemed to be, and turned out to be, the right road.

Our next target was Brest, on the Polish border. Laima wanted to get to the west of a reactor at Rovno in the Ukraine before heading south in Poland. Radiation readings were fairly constant at a level that Laima and Granny were pretty sure was well above natural but not really worrying. 'Whether that's Ignalina still, or Rovno, or a bit of both, or somewhere else altogether, who knows?'

I wondered whether it was something left over from the cull, as we were all now calling it, rather than leaky nuclear reactors, but Laima said that it pretty certainly wasn't.

'If the cull involved radioactive materials, they were short half-life isotopes, pretty much all gone in just three months. There'd be none at all left by now, thirty-four years later. Of course they could have been contaminated with small quantities of longer half-life isotopes, not enough to be very serious in themselves, but still around for decades or longer. What we're seeing could be partly that, but I'm pretty sure most of it must be from reactors.'

How much of that sort of thing I understood at the time, I'm not sure. Laima and Granny Persie both used to explain things to me very patiently and in enough detail to make sense, so it's possible that I understood quite a bit even at six years old.

One of the consequences of Granny Merly's death was that Lieđđi and Suonjar didn't get conversations translated for them so much. It had nearly always been Granny Merly who did that. Laima knew English quite well, and some Swedish, but she found it difficult to translate between the two.

'I can cope with having Russian and English both in my head at once, or Russian and Swedish. But I really can't handle English and Swedish both at the same time.'

'What about Latvian?'

'Oh, that's there all the time. But it's so long since I used it that it's not the language I think in any longer.'

Granny Persie made valiant efforts to remember to translate for Lieđđi and Suonjar, but it didn't come as naturally to her as it had to Granny Merly – and really, in the long run, now they'd got the beginnings of a handle on the English language, they learnt more by just being immersed in the conversation without anyone translating for them. Gealbu was already understanding pretty much everything.

The funniest thing was hearing Nikolai and Lieđđi talking English together. Lieđđi was teaching him to drive a Bandvagn – or at least, she was driving and he was watching her. I was with them, instead of in my usual place with Granny Persie in the Unimog. Laima had insisted that she and Grandad should be in the Unimog with Granny Persie, and that we four littlies should be in the Bandvagns. I realized that Laima wanted to have a Serious Talk with our grown-ups, but I didn't say anything. I didn't want to let them know that I understood, even though it seemed pretty obvious, with the intercoms in the Norwegian trucks and the Unimog not connecting with the ones in the Finnish Bandvagns.

I could tell that there was a lot going on between Nikolai and Lieđđi that they couldn't have put into words even if they'd had a proper common language, and I was sure that all our grown-ups knew that too. But their talk was even funnier than that, because the way they each talked English was so very different. Nikolai had a huge vocabulary, much of it rather academic, that he built into ferociously complicated sentences, which he struggled to vocalize almost incomprehensibly. Lieđđi had a much smaller vocabulary, most of it words that we all used a lot, that tumbled out in short, haphazard utterances at considerable speed, with a strange but perfectly comprehensible accent.

Comprehensible to most of us, that is. I'm not sure how much Nikolai was understanding, and I'm pretty sure Lieđđi was missing an awful lot of what he was saying too. The conversation seemed to me to be two monologues, neatly interleaved with each other, but otherwise almost independent. But it didn't matter, they were hearing each other between the lines loud and clear anyway.

Nikolai managed to drive the Bandvagn perfectly well as soon as they decided it was his turn.

Uncle Jake was the only one of our family grown-ups who wasn't involved in the Serious Talk, whatever it was about. He was in the other Bandvagn with Suonjar, Gealbu, Emma and Dang. What was going on between him and Suonjar was no secret at all, not even officially.

Emma and Dang were learning Gealbu's language of gestures, smiles and nods as fast as they were learning English.

Little Liz was sitting on the knee of Nikolai or Lieđđi, whoever wasn't currently driving, soaking up the conversation like a sponge. Some of the things she comes out with are funny enough at the best of times, but her vocabulary of fancy words mispronounced in a strong Russian accent, all muddled up with ordinary words conventionally pronounced but in a Sami accent, had everyone in stitches when we stopped in the evening. Gales of laughter that stopped abruptly every time someone suddenly thought about Granny Merly.

The road from Minsk to Brest was in better shape, and we did it in two and a half days. Long stretches of it were incredibly straight and level, and for several kilometres we ran alongside an equally straight railway. The surface of the road was broken up and there were trees growing through it, but most of them were small enough that would could just drive through them, and it was no trouble to drive around the occasional stouter one. The road hadn't actually washed away completely anywhere, and all the bridges were still usable, although most of them had very visibly begun to deteriorate.

Not long before Brest, a tyre burst on one of the big trailers. Lieđđi's Bandvagn – I was back in my usual place with Granny Persie in the Unimog – was the next vehicle behind it and she saw it happen, but it seemed that Dad, driving the truck, hadn't noticed, and was just carrying on. Lieđđi stopped and climbed down and went and told Aunty Anna in the truck behind. Aunty Anna called Dad on the intercom to get him to stop, but by that time he'd realized there was something wrong and had stopped. We had several spare wheels with tyres already fitted, but it's still a big job. They'd driven so far on a completely flat tyre that the wheel itself was wrecked, but Granny Persie said that was a matter of no consequence: we'd got as many wheels as tyres, and whether we'd ever find any more tyres the right size was rather doubtful. The Soviet Union seemed to use different standards from Scandinavia.

'I just hope our tyres aren't reaching the end of their lives.'

The grown-ups inspected all the tyres carefully. Most of them weren't badly worn at all, but two had low pressure, and were duly pumped up, which took quite a while.

'We should have taken a decent size compressor from a garage in Norway, rather than this little motorist's one. We've got the mains voltage electricity to run one.'

'Yes, but a garage compressor's not a small item. What would you have left behind? What's an hour here or there to us?'

'I'm more worried about whether this little thing will stay the course.'

Which was prophetic. Moments later there was a loud bang and the sound of escaping air. The compressor was still working, but the connecting tube had burst. Fortunately that wasn't the kind of problem that held Granny Persie up for long. She cut the end of the longer piece of the tube off square, and reconnected everything a bit shorter. The clip that held the end of the tube onto the compressor wasn't reusable, but a bit of wire wound tightly round the connection a few times and then twisted up tight was just as good.

'The tube had overheated. It's still warm now. We've got to do it in stages. We shouldn't have been running it continuously for so long.'

'If I'd known we were going to be stopped here for so long, I'd have put the goats and chickens out on the grass, but I expect it's too late now.'

'Yes, I think so. I think it'd be difficult putting up the chicken run here though, anyway.'

'True. Mikey and Liz could find them some nice weeds though, anyway.'

We proceeded to do just that. Gealbu and Belle joined in. Liz was the right height to feed the chickens, while the rest of us fed the goats. I think one of the chickens ended up getting left out a bit, but I don't suppose it mattered much really. Mum had probably made the suggestion as much to keep Liz and me busy as for any other reason, but I'm sure it was good for the goats and chickens anyway, and definitely good for our relationship with them.

While we were stopped, Laima checked the radiation readings – which were up. Still not at a worrying level, but quite noticeably higher. She and Granny decided they ought to check them more frequently for a while, in case they went up even more.

They took to checking every ten kilometres. By the time we got to Brest, they were beginning to wonder whether we should turn back and try a different route.

'They've been rising more and more steeply as we approach Brest. There's some source right there, I'm pretty sure, but Ivan's map doesn't show any reactor there. They can't have put a waste repository or a reprocessing plant in a town, surely?'

'Ivan would have marked those too. He might not have known where they all were outside the communist bloc, and he might not have known where some of the military facilities were inside it, either. But I'm sure he'd have known about everything in Byelorussia or Poland. One thing does occur to me, though. There's a change of gauge on the railway here, and everything crossing the border in or out of Poland had to be unloaded and reloaded. I bet it's old contamination from loading and unloading radioactive materials. It'll be in the railway goods yards.'

'I don't suppose you know where they are, do you? It'd be good to skirt round them as wide as we can.'

'No, I've never been here. But we're only here for a few hours at most. People used to work right in the goods yards, year after year. Their life expectancy might have been reduced a bit, but if they'd been dying like flies someone would have noticed.'

'True. But unless we're very close to the yards now, the levels there must be pretty high. Maybe there were radioactive materials in transit during the cull, and they got damaged. Possibly by someone raiding goods wagons?'

'I doubt that. The containers would have been well marked up, and they wouldn't have looked like anything of interest to raiders.'

'Would they have been well marked up, though? Anything military might have been deliberately mis-labelled. Or some people might have been being destructive in sheer frustration.'

'All possible, I suppose. I was thinking of stuff just corroding and leaking where it was sitting in wagons, or in piles between unloading and loading again.'

'That could be, too. Whatever, if we don't know where the yards are, all we can do is keep monitoring and be ready to turn back.'

At that point we must have been close to the source of the contamination, whatever it was, because the levels began to decline again steeply from there on. We didn't do any raiding in Brest at all, we just got over the river Bug and into Poland and out of the area as quickly as we could.

We were really wanting to head south once we were in Poland, but for quite a way none of the roads southwards looked very promising. There was no road to the south marked on our map for about forty kilometres, and all the roads we saw looked as though they might not connect through. Even if they'd connected through before the cull, they looked like the kind of road that might have deteriorated to the point of impassibility by then. We stopped for the night rather late, having wanted to get as far away from Brest as possible before putting the goats and chickens out to grass, just before what we thought must be Biała Podlaska.

Radiation levels were well down again, but still a good bit higher than they'd been most of the way. Granny did some checks I'd not seen her do before. She changed the window on the meter, and put the meter down right close to the road, and again right close to the grass, then repeated it with yet a different window, and then did both measurements again close to the vehicle's tyres and under the wheel arches.

'There's quite a lot of an energetic alpha emitter in the grass. We shouldn't let the chickens and goats out tonight at all. The road surface and the tyres and wheel arches aren't bad though, so it's washed off the road long ago. It's really lucky we met you, Laima. I'd never have thought about this issue without, and wouldn't have known where to get the equipment, either.'

'It's lucky for us that you came by, too. Well, for Nikolai anyway. I'd have been okay, apart from worrying about his future.'

'Hmm. I wonder how many people there are around, really? In five thousand kilometres, we've encountered five of you, in two groups, know of a few more Sami families and seen evidence of one organized camp in addition to the one we escaped from, which we presume is still going.'

'We could have passed by a few others quite close without realizing. They might or might not have seen or at least heard us. Whether they'd have wanted to meet us, who knows? '

'They could have been put off by your military appearance. We were decidedly nervous. It was only when we realized you weren't Russian that we decided to risk meeting you.'

'That's something we've always been conscious of. But equally, we feel braver about coping with armed gangs or organized camps like this. And anyway, the expedition would have been impossible without these vehicles. But meeting a nuclear physicist's family, if not the nuclear physicist himself, is a miracle.'

'Probably not, really. You'd have thought it equally miraculous to meet a microbiologist or a chemical toxicologist, and I reckon those three types of people are the most likely people to have survived independently. Ivan reckoned that at least half the physicists at the Institute had probably made their own shelters, but obviously it wasn't something any of them talked about. There wasn't even any way of getting together afterwards. We wouldn't have dared try to contact anyone by radio for fear of our transmissions being picked up by the authorities. Even trying to go visiting could have been risky, but we did try to find a couple of his closest colleagues. They'd either gone into the official shelter like good little sheep, or, as Ivan thought more likely, they'd felt safer somewhere no-one would be likely to know about, like we did.'

Chapter 9

We arrived in Biała Podlaska soon after we set off in the morning. It was another confusing place, and it took us a while to find the road going south. A flooded area ran east-west through the middle of the town, but the road crossed it above the water level on a causeway, so presumably it had always been liable to flooding, if not actually permanently flooded, but mud on the road indicated that it had sometimes been flooded more deeply.

A few kilometres south of the town we reached another flood, and this time the road was completely submerged. Granny Persie detached the trailer from Lieđđi's Bandvagn, and she and Lieđđi went to explore, to see whether it would be possible to get through. They were back very quickly.

'Can't see where the road is, it's buried in mud. The water's not very deep, but we could be in real trouble if we put a wheel off the road with any of the trucks, or if there's a bridge missing somewhere in the middle.'

We had to go back to Biała Podlaska and keep going towards Warsaw another twenty-five kilometres before we reached the next road south that showed on our map.

I remember Biała Podlaska particularly because Laima told me about the aunt and uncle and cousins of one of Ivan's colleagues, who had lived there and were murdered by the Nazis during World War II. At least, they had lived there and never reappeared after the war, and Laima says everyone knew that the Nazis murdered lots of Jews from there.

I still don't really understand all about that. Who killed nearly everybody in the great cull? Was that the Nazis, too? Nobody knows who it was.

Someone decided to send Grandad and the Grannies into the shelter, and someone told Laima and Ivan and Nikolai to go into the shelter that they never did go to. Whoever they were must have known who was going to do the killing in the great cull. Where are those people?

I do know who the Jews were. Grandad says that one of his grannies was Jewish – the one who married his Jamaican grandad. So I'm one eighth Jewish. And one eighth Jamaican. And I know where Jamaica is. And I know where Israel is, but that isn't where my Jewish great-great-granny came from. She came from Whitechapel in London. She was still alive just before the great cull, but Grandad says it's very unlikely she'd still be alive by now, even if she survived the great cull. Which it's very unlikely she did anyway.

Grandad doesn't get all upset when he talks about his own granny, but he still gets upset when he thinks about his friends in Burnfield. Or about Granny Merly.

I still get upset when I think about Granny Merly. I wonder if I still will when I'm Grandad's age?

The next turn south was supposed to be at a place called Międzyrzec. Well, we found it easily enough, and were pretty sure it really was Międzyrzec, but finding the right road out of it was impossible. We ended up on a much smaller road than we thought it ought to be, heading consistently pretty much due south, when the road on the map was south-west. It was a narrow road, so we split up the convoy again, as we had all across Finland – except that now we had just the tanker on its own out in front, because everything else had a trailer and would have been difficult to turn or reverse.

Fortunately we didn't have to. The road kept on going, on and on. Sometimes it was several kilometres between places where turning would have been possible, so we were often that far ahead of the main convoy before they could catch up. Eventually we reached a bigger road running east-west, and we turned west, hoping to hit the road we should have come down in the first place. If we were on the road we thought we might be on, that would be at Radzyń Podlaski – but we were beginning to be very unsure that we really knew where we were at all.

'If this is the road that's marked in the atlas, and we really have been coming due south, Radzyń Podlaski should be about ten kilometres.'

Well, we reached a town after about twelve kilometres, so maybe Granny and Laima did know where we were after all. We found the road we wanted from there okay, or at least we think we did. It was heading in the right direction. Granny reckoned that we'd met the road we would have come down if it hadn't been flooded, in just the right place, and turned onto the road heading for Lublin – and reached another flooded section.

'Well, there is a river marked here. But we've crossed quite a few rivers, some marked on our map and some not. But whatever, there's no way we can get through here. We're just going to have to go back to Radzyń Podlaski and try the next road west.'

Granny had hoped to make it at least to Lublin by nightfall, but we stopped near Radzyń Podlaski. Granny checked the radiation levels, and decided it would be okay to put the chickens and goats out to grass for a while. Grandad and Mum and Aunty Anna went for a walk, and were thinking to take the guns and hope to shoot some rabbits or a deer – we'd seen quite a few during the day – but Granny said, 'No, it's one thing letting the goats and chickens eat here for the odd day, it'd be quite another for us to eat an animal that's lived in a contaminated area like this all its life.'

Laima emphatically agreed.

'If other animals can live in this contaminated area all their lives, why can't we? They're not getting food from somewhere else. Are humans more susceptible to radiation than other animals?'

Granny laughed for a moment, then stopped herself.

'That's a good question, Mikey. No, humans aren't more susceptible, and we could live here for a while. We might even live out a normal lifespan, although we'd probably die sooner than we otherwise might, quite likely a lot sooner. Other animals die sooner in a place like this than they would somewhere else, too.'

'But they still live here, because they don't know any better. I see.'

'Yes, that's right. It doesn't stop them breeding, either, although they might not produce as many young in their shorter lifetime. Some species might gradually die out here because of that, but others might do better because of reduced competition. It's quite likely worse for carnivores, or omnivores like humans, than it is for herbivores, because there's an extra stage of concentration. But that depends what the particular radioactive materials are, whether it ends up in the meat when a herbivore eats it, or in the poo. I don't know what the particular materials are here. Even if I did, I don't know which ones are concentrated in the food chain and which aren't.'

Whether anything uncomfortable had gone on between Nikolai and Lieđđi I don't know, but whatever the reason, the next morning Nikolai was driving the Unimog with Aunty Dot, and Lieđđi had Mum as her co-driver in the first Bandvagn. Maybe it was just to help Lieđđi and Nikolai with their English, but I had a funny feeling there was more to it than that. But what did I know? I was still only six.

Just a few kilometres down the next road we reached an impassable flood again.

'I can see us having to go back to the main road and go all the way into Warsaw, and then take the main road south from there!'

'There'd be no harm in that. In fact, we've probably already spent more time than that would have taken us. But the next road, via Łuków, only crosses one river that shows on the map, and that near its source where with any luck it'll be quite small. Let's hope.'

Laima's optimism was justified at last, and the road was quite straightforward. For a stretch the land was flooded each side of the road, but the road itself was on a good causeway and in relatively good condition. We reached the main Warsaw to Lublin road by midday.

Radiation levels were well down on what they'd been at Radzyń Podlaski, but still too high for Granny to let Grandad try shooting anything. They hadn't diminished any further when we reached Lublin late that afternoon – which Granny said wasn't surprising, since we weren't any further away from Brest than we'd been when we first reached the main road.

The goats and chickens got out onto the grass again that evening, but Granny and Laima hoped that we'd reach a less contaminated area soon.

'At least the different readings are in about the same ratios as they've been ever since Brest, which means it's probably all the same isotopes, so probably from the same place.'

'Well, mostly anyway. There's probably small contributions from all sorts of places.'

'Hmm. I suppose so. Just have to keep checking, that's all there is for it. I'm glad Ivan had rigged all these to work off twelve volts, so we don't have to start up the generator every time.'

The next morning we went right into Lublin, in the hope of finding some better maps of the area, and topping up the fuel. We weren't running low, but we never knew when we'd be able to find any.

We did find fuel and maps, and the maps were more detailed than our big atlas, and a bit easier to use in the cab – but they were just road maps, with no contours or anything.

Granny decided she needed the atlas as well. 'These will help, but they're not a complete substitute.'

We also found a lot of jars of pickles – and jam. Grandad laughed, and sang, 'Little bit of jam but NO bread!' I wondered why those particular words had a little tune, but I've never found out. Spoonfuls of jam became a regular feature of our breakfasts for quite a while after that. I remember how sad Little Liz was the day we ran out, but that day was still a long way off then.

There were more clothed skeletons lying around in the street in Lublin that we'd seen anywhere else, but we didn't see any sign of there having been any violence, vandalism or arson. There were saplings growing out of buildings everywhere, and in many places the streets were carpeted with grass and weeds with small trees here and there in a way I'd not seen before. Granny noticed the difference too, and thought it must be to do with the climate. 'Leningrad had plenty of trees, but most of them were conifers, and their needles don't get everywhere like the leaves of these deciduous trees. They were probably just heaped up under the trees, but I didn't take any notice. It's the leaves that have given all this vegetation a foothold, I'm sure.'

I found it all rather pretty and interesting, but Grandad and Granny and Laima found it a bit depressing, and wanted to get moving again. The real clincher was that the radiation levels were higher in the city than they'd been just outside it. Granny and Laima couldn't work out why that might be.

'It seems to be the same cocktail of isotopes, whatever it is – still the same ratio of all the various readings.'

It was only the vegetation that had high levels. Rain-washed surfaces and the interior of buildings were fine.

Our turning was actually a couple of kilometres before the middle of Lublin, so we went back to find it. The Lublin street map was really useful, and we got on the right road without difficulty. Happily we seemed to have got out of the area that was susceptible to flooding, and made good progress.

Using the big atlas and the road maps together, Granny's navigation improved a lot. The absence of floods undoubtedly helped, too! But we got the junctions at Kraśnik and Janów Lubelski right first time, which must mean something. And we were sure that's where we were.

Looking back, I wished that I'd been as conscious of our route in Sweden and Finland, and realized that my awareness of navigation had changed out of all recognition. Looking back again from much later, I realize that that's what being six is all about...becoming conscious of more and more things. Reading my diaries again now, I can see the changes in my six-year-old self.

At Lublin, Granny had thought that maybe we'd get to a place called Nisko that day. We actually got very close not long after midday – but then we reached the river San. Granny took one look at the bridge and decided that she needed to investigate it more closely. The more she looked at it the less she wanted to trust it with the weight of even one truck at a time.

We followed the river as close as we could, heading northwest, hoping for a reasonable bridge. This was the opposite direction from the one we eventually wanted to head, on the other side of the river, but it looked from the map as though we were more likely to find a bridge in that direction. We were on really minor roads now, little more than farm tracks in places, but Granny wasn't worried.

'We're close to the river, and it's quite a long way below us. The water table will be well below the surface. We shouldn't get anywhere flooded or boggy. If we have to, we can go straight across fields around here.'

It wasn't very far before a bridge came into sight. Granny thought it looked like a railway bridge, and that's what it turned out to be. We soon arrived at the railway, which was on an embankment. Our track went underneath, but Granny thought we'd be able to get up onto the embankment with the trucks without much difficulty.

'The question is whether the bridge has a proper track bed, or whether it's just an open structure supporting the rails.'

We got down out of the tanker, climbed up onto the embankment, and walked along until we could see the bridge properly. Granny was satisfied: we'd be able to get the trucks across this bridge quite safely.

'It's quite rusty, but this one was designed for trains, not just for lorries. The weight of our trucks is no more than a fleabite to it.'

Getting up onto the embankment was quite exciting. The front of the tanker seemed to be pointing right up into the sky, and Granny had to lean forward over the steering wheel to see where she was going as we reached the top of the slope. We stopped at the top. Grandad was shouting out of the intercom, but we hadn't heard him as we were climbing, because of the roar of the engine.

'It's all very well for you, in that tanker! Have you thought what's going to happen to all the stuff in the back of the trucks, and in the trailers? Will the Bandvagns and the Unimog be able to get up there at all, with undriven trailers hanging on their tails?'

Neither Granny nor Laima had thought about that at all. Neither had I, but I think I had a bit of an excuse.

So, to tell the truth, did Granny. She definitely was still not her normal self. I'm not sure what excuse Laima had, but obviously she'd not done anything wrong on purpose. Grandad reached the same conclusion very quickly, too.

'Okay, Persie, you're forgiven. What should we do now, though?'

'The bridge is a good one, and this is a big river with not many crossings marked on the map. How many of the bridges might be rusty wrecks like that last one, who knows?

I think we should explore along the track and try to find a gentler way up onto the embankment for the rest of you.'

'We'll do it along the bottom with the Unimog. Leave the tanker where it is. You three might as well come down here with the rest of us while we explore.'

It was actually Granny and Grandad and Laima who took the Unimog. They were only gone a few minutes when they called the rest of us to follow them.

'The railway's level with the fields here. It's a bit bumpy through the ditch to get onto the track, but it's no trouble. Just follow the track along the side of the railway and you'll catch up with us in no time.'

Driving along the railway was no trouble in the trucks or the Bandvagns, but we could see from the truck behind that it was a bit awkward for the Unimog. Our wheels straddled the track nicely, but the Unimog's wheels were just a little too close together to do that. Granny was managing to keep the wheels on one side running along the top of a rail most of the time, but every now and then they'd slip off and the wheels the other side would ride up onto the other rail. It must have been horribly uncomfortable in the cab.

The trailer was a little wider and just straddled the rails, but was being jerked this way and that every time the Unimog slipped off a rail. The goats were sensibly lying down, but the chickens were flapping about in a bit of a tizzy.

Uncle Sid, driving the truck I was in, was watching the tyres of the trailer, scuffing against the rail but not riding up onto it. 'I hope we don't end up with wrecked tyres on that trailer. We've only got one spare that size.'

When we reached the bridge, Laima got out of the Unimog and went to drive the tanker.

I could see it was easier for the Unimog on the bridge itself. There was a check rail on each side, obviously to reduce the risk of a derailment, and with a pair of rails to run on, Granny managed to keep the left side wheels up the whole way.

The other side of the bridge it was again a couple of kilometres before the track was level with the fields. Nisko was just another couple of kilometres across a field and down a farm track. By this time it was late afternoon, and we stopped there for the night.

The scuffing on the tyres was noticeable, but everyone reckoned they'd probably be okay.

Granny and Laima checked the radiation levels, going through all the window changing and waist-high and down-near-the-ground rigmarole again.

'That's a lot better. Another factor of thirty down from levels at Lublin. I feel a lot happier about letting the chickens and goats out to grass here.'

They checked the milk and the eggs, too, and pronounced them fit for human consumption.

'We'll check them every day for a while, even if levels in the environment remain good. We don't know how long things take to work their way through a goat or a chicken!'

The next day we reached Jarosław around midday, and found a street map of the town inside a little roadside kiosk, which was fortunate because otherwise we'd probably have ended up coming out on the wrong road. There were various other things in the kiosk, some of which caused some hilarity amongst the oldies. They explained what cigarettes were, but they never explained what prezerwatywy were. Laima said it was roughly the same in Latvian, and that although it sounded like the English word preservatives it didn't have the same meaning, but that made me none the wiser.

The other thing I remember about Jarosław was squirrels. I'd never seen a squirrel before, although I'd heard of them in Grandad's stories, and seen the pictures he'd drawn of them. Grandad's drawings aren't bad, actually.

Grandad and Granny and Laima were a bit surprised by the squirrels.

'I wonder if they survived near here, or whether they've spread from a population that survived somewhere else? We used to have them in Latvia, but they've not returned there yet. I wonder if they ever will?'

'Who knows? I don't suppose we'll ever know about what's happening anywhere except wherever we are ourselves. That's what life's like now.'

I'd never known it any different, so that comment stuck in my mind.

The only trouble we had anywhere on the road that day was at a place called Radymno, not long after we left Jarosław. Not one of the usual sorts of trouble at all – there was a train blocking a level crossing. We'd crossed level crossings here and there all the way, and we'd seen trains sitting abandoned on the track in a couple of places, but never a train blocking our way before. Half the train was in the station close to the crossing, but the line of wagons stretched right across the road. We eventually found a route across the line at the other end of the station, and then across a few fields and back onto the road. As usual, there were trees growing amongst the weeds in the fields, but most of them were small enough that we could simply push through them.

As we crossed the track, I looked towards the front of the train, which was in the middle of the station. The engine's windows were smashed. I pointed it out to Granny Persie, and she shook her head.

'I bet that happened while the driver was still in the train. Poor devil.'

Laima was driving, but she took a look as well.

'Poor devils whoever did it, too. Imagine how desperate they must have been. They probably wanted to stop the train to look to see what there was in the wagons. A lot of good it did them, any of them.'

'They could have stopped the train without hurting the driver. But you're right, poor devils all of them, and it all comes to the same thing in the end anyway.'

We were all so used to this kind of observation that we didn't dwell on it long, and curiosity got the better of Grandad. He climbed the footbridge in the station and looked down into the wagons. He didn't take long.

'Well, I've no idea what was in those wagons thirty four years ago, but whatever it was, grass and weeds grow in it quite nicely! But no trees. I wonder why that is?'

Granny and Laima wondered about that, too – trees seemed to be taking over every nook and corner elsewhere – but they didn't want to investigate any further.

At Przemyśl, Granny took radiation readings again. They were below those at Laima's old farm, and much to everyone's relief neither the milk nor the eggs showed any detectable sign of contamination. Granny and Laima reckoned that whatever the alpha emitter was, it was in the soil and not being taken up to a huge extent by the vegetation that the goats and chickens had been eating.

'You probably wouldn't want them to be out to grass there every day, but it's obvious that the odd occasion didn't do any harm.'

Going south from Przemyśl we were back on a fairly minor road, but there didn't seem to be any choice, as far as we could see from the atlas – and we'd run off the edge of our road maps again. The main road east didn't reach a major southbound route until it was uncomfortably close to a nuclear power station in the Ukraine, and to the west, there was one in Czechoslovakia, and one in Hungary.

A few kilometres south of Przemyśl there was a light barrier across the road, and a little blockhouse by the side.

'That'll have been the border post between Poland and the Ukraine – what a contrast between that and the one at the Finnish-Russian border!'

Laima was interested to hear about that, as she'd never been to Finland. Granny described the place in detail, and told her how we'd been nervous that there might have been a booby trap there.

'No, I don't think so. That's not the Russian style. Armed guards, twenty-four hours a day, every day of the year. It'll have been the same here, although very likely they were asleep half the time. They'd have woken up if anyone crashed through the barriers like this,' – exactly at the moment she did just that – 'but you could have slipped through quietly on foot without being noticed. Probably, but a bit risky – far safer to cross somewhere in the forest. Then if you do get spotted, you can just say you got lost. I doubt if the border's marked at all there.'

We stopped for the night immediately after a village just south of the border. Radiation levels were the lowest we'd seen, and the chickens and goats had a happy time out to grass. Little Liz and I had a happy time finding treats for the chickens, but the goats had plenty of interesting things within the limits imposed by their tethers, and seemed to have got over their jealousy.

Chapter 10

The following morning, not far from the village, there was an iron girder bridge across a small creek. When we first saw it, Granny was a little suspicious that the ironwork looked dreadfully rusty, but the real trouble was only apparent when we actually reached the bridge: the deck was wooden, and it was completely rotten. There were places where it had fallen right through, and the rest of the wood certainly didn't look fit to carry a truck.

The creek wasn't very deep, but the land each side of the road was so thickly wooded that we couldn't simply ford the creek alongside the bridge.

We'd left the rest of the convoy behind at the point where we entered the woods – old woodland that had obviously already been woodland before the cull, with big trees – because it was clear that we wouldn't be able to turn around at least until we got out of the woods. Granny reversed the tanker back to the edge of the old woods, then set off along the edge. We reached a place where we could get down to the water very quickly – but the trees were thick on the other side.

'Not to worry. We can go along the stream itself until we reach somewhere we can get up the other side. But we ought to hook ourselves together with the winch cables in case of difficulties.'

We changed the order of the convoy for the ford, putting the Bandvagn with the bowser first, then the tanker, and bringing up the rear with the Unimog and finally the other Bandvagn, all tied together with the winch cables apart from the final Bandvagn.

'Probably quite unnecessary, but better safe than sorry!'

We'd never had the whole convoy tied together, all moving at once before: they'd always either had just the front vehicle moving, pulling out the winch cable, or just the vehicle behind pulling the winch cable in as it moved. All the drivers said it was actually a bit tricky making sure that the cable in front of them stayed taut, or at least not so slack they ended up driving over it.

The water wasn't terribly deep anywhere, but when we reached a place where there were only little, young trees on the south bank, the bank was quite steep. The Bandvagn didn't have any trouble getting up it, but the bowser's chassis hit the ground a couple of times.

'Doesn't matter. That's only mud.'

Getting the tanker up would have been impossible without the Bandvagn in front for the winch cable. The worst bit was when the Unimog came up. The Unimog itself was no trouble, but the trailer got stuck – really stuck. All four wheels of the Unimog were just churning mud, and the winch was stalled.

The rear of the trailer was in the water, which the goats seemed to think was a special arrangement for them to have a muddy drink.

Granny turned the tanker round so she could attach the tanker's winch cable to the front of the Unimog and add another winch pull, but Laima stopped her.

'I think something will break before we pull that free, if the Unimog can't pull it with the winch as well as the wheels. We should back off and put some timbers down.'

But the Unimog just churned mud again when it tried to reverse. In the end, the only way they managed to get the trailer unstuck was to pull it backwards with one of the Bandvagns, minus its own trailer. The Bandvagns were the only vehicles they trusted to take back into the creek.

The trailer wheels were now almost completely immersed in the water, which by this time was really muddy. To get the timbers out of the trailer, we'd have had to get the goats out and tether them, and put the chickens in their pen – all while working waist deep in muddy water. Nikolai had another idea: pull up a few small trees with a winch cable, and use them instead of the timbers.

It took most of the day to get the trailer out of that creek, and when it finally emerged, we could see the extent of the damage it had suffered. Its front wheels were pointing inwards, pigeon-toed. Its front axle was bent, presumably where it had snagged on a rock hidden in the mud.

'Well, that's the end of that trailer,' Grandad opined, but Granny said, 'No, we'll just take its front wheels off and carry on until we can find a replacement. It's not too heavily loaded for two wheels. It means it's not properly balanced, but a bit more load on the hitch won't hurt the Unimog.'

They had to take the whole axle off after a few kilometres, because the brake drums kept on hitting the ground. That took quite a while, because none of the nuts would undo, and Uncle Sid had to cut the U-bolts with a hacksaw. It was an awkward place for him to work, underneath the trailer, and he broke two hacksaw blades before he'd finished. We'd got dozens in stock though, and nobody was bothered about a couple getting broken.

'Well, at least we've got plenty of spare wheels for that trailer again!'

'We've got no brakes on the trailer any more, though. There aren't any on the rear axle.'

'I really don't think that matters, with a Unimog in front of it! I'm not at all sure they were working anyway.'

With all the delay at the creek, the roads not in very good condition, and the rain, we only managed to do about forty or fifty kilometres that day. We got just a few kilometres past a place called Stary Sambor, and stopped just before a bridge over a biggish river, whose valley we'd been following since Stary Sambor. Between the road and the railway bridge there was a nice grassy meadow by the river, with better grass for the goats than we'd found in most places. Radiation levels were still close to what Granny thought natural levels ought to be.

Grandad and Mum and Dad sat on the bank of the river and fished, while Granny and Uncle Sid crossed the bridge and disappeared into the woods with the guns. Laima walked back up the road into the village we'd just come through with a spade and a bucket, without saying a word to anyone. Aunty Anna and Lieđđi started to cook, and the rest of us played on the grass with the goats.

We were, I think, all fairly happy. We'd come to terms with the loss of our beloved Granny Merly, or at least we weren't thinking about her the whole time any more. Life was easy, and the expotition was going okay – as well as could be expected.

Laima came back with a bucketful of potatoes and carrots. 'I thought I'd spotted potato plants in somebody's garden back there. It's amazing they've survived all these years though. And they're not a bad size considering the soil's not been broken for so long, and it's still only midsummer. The carrots were a complete surprise.'

They were little thin fingers of carrots compared to what I remembered from our farm and from Laima's, but there were lots of them. Nikolai wanted to know if one bucketful was all there was.

'I think there's quite a lot more, but it's getting dark. Time to put the animals away. We'll go back with both buckets tomorrow morning before we leave. There are onion plants and some other things, too, but apart from the carrots and potatoes everything else seems to have gone a bit wild and weedy.'

We weren't short of food, but fresh vegetables were a luxury while we were on the journey.

Granny and Uncle Sid had had no luck with the guns. 'Didn't see hair nor hide of so much as a squirrel.'

The fishing hadn't produced anything, either. 'We saw fish, nice big trout I think, but they weren't interested.'

Steamed potatoes and carrots made a good breakfast. Nikolai and Laima went and dug up several more bucketfuls. Granny and Uncle Sid had more luck fishing in the morning than the others had had the previous evening.

The hunting party still saw nothing to shoot at. 'Odd, considering how many deer and rabbits we've seen elsewhere. And this is ideal habitat for them.'

An oddity it remained. If it wasn't just chance, we never found out what the reason might have been.

That day we got into the hills – the first real hills since the mountains in Norway and Sweden. Up and down, up and down. I remember particularly descending a series of hairpin bends down into a valley with a big river. Then we began to climb more seriously, up, up, up. The state of the road got worse as we climbed, but it was still a lot better than it had been in many places in Sweden and Finland. Finally we reached the summit, and began to descend. The descent was steeper than the climb, and the road wiggled back and forth in a long series of hairpin bends.

Exactly what happened nobody knows. I was in the tanker at the front, and the first I knew that anything was wrong was hearing screams from the intercom, 'Stop, stop! Help them!'

Laima was driving, and stopped as quickly as she could. Even though we were going down slowly in a low gear, we couldn't stop very quickly because the hill was so steep. Granny leant forward to look in the rear view mirror, and was out of the cab before Laima had managed to stop the tanker completely, with the fire extinguisher from under her seat in her hand.

Grandad and Dad were already down from the Unimog and one of the trucks, also with the fire extinguishers.

The first Bandvagn was a ball of flame. The fire extinguishers were completely ineffective against such a fire.

Lieđđi and Mum and little Liz had been in the cab. They'd managed to get out, but Lieđđi's and Mum's clothes were ablaze. They rolled on the wet grass and managed to put out the flames, but they were both very badly burned.

Mum had managed to fold herself protectively around little Liz, and Liz wasn't very badly burned at all, but Mum herself was in agony.

I can't write much about the next few days, because the memory is too painful.

Somehow Granny Merly's death, while very sad, was manageable. She wasn't really old, but somehow it was her time to go. And of course I never saw her while she was dying. One evening she was there, and the next day she'd gone. That was the same for all us littlies.

But we experienced the whole of Mum's last few days. It wasn't her time to go at all. And we all knew she hadn't gone peacefully in her sleep.

Laima and Suonjar did all they could, but that wasn't really much. Even if they'd had the knowledge, they scarcely had anything useful, not even enough proper sterile dressings. Granny and Laima agonized over whether the ancient morphine in the first aid kits was usable, and in the end decided that it was most unlikely to do any good, and would very likely make things worse.

Lieđđi's condition was much less serious, but still bad. She insisted on her own idea of how she should be treated, and it worked – after a fashion. Whether any other treatment that was possible in the circumstances would have been any better, who knows?

She got Gealbu to cut some pieces of reindeer skin out of the lávvu, then made Suonjar boil them and use them to dress the burned areas, laced on with strips of reindeer leather.

'Of course it hurts like hell! What do you expect, when I've been burnt like this? But it'll heal.'

And it did. She's got fantastic scars now, and her left hand is a bit like a claw because the scar on her left palm doesn't stretch like skin should, but mostly she's fine.

Little Liz's burns really weren't very bad at all. They made her cry a lot, not surprisingly considering she was only four. But I think the fact that her Mum couldn't cuddle her was a bigger problem than the pain of the burns. Everyone else cuddled her; she was getting cuddles from someone or other most of the time. But she'd lost both her best cuddlers in less than two weeks.

The back of her right hand is the only place she's got a visible scar now.

Mum is buried in an actual cemetery on the outskirts of Uzhok, just at the foot of the hill we'd been descending. Grandad and Dad and Nikolai made her a gravestone very like the one they'd made for Granny Merly. We littlies saw this one being made, and laid. Since we'd all seen Mum's dying agonies, the grown-ups didn't see much point trying to shield us from her memorial.

HERE LIES FIONA JANE COLLINS

22ND SEPTEMBER 1993 – 9TH AUGUST 2024

BELOVED OF GREGORY PAUL COLLINS

FIRSTBORN OF

PETER SAMUEL COLLINS AND NGUYỄN THỊ PERSEVERANCE

SISTER OF SIDNEY PETER AND JACOB ANTHONY

MOTHER OF MICHAEL JOHN AND ELIZABETH ROSE

SORELY MISSED

We'd gone into the village in the hope of finding a hospital, a doctor's surgery, or a pharmacy where there might be more dressings. We found comfortable beds for a short stay, but no sign of a hospital, and if there was a doctor's surgery or a pharmacy, they must have simply been in ordinary houses and we didn't find them.

We also found sheets, water, and the means to boil it. Boiled strips of cloth were the best dressings we could make – apart from Lieđđi's boiled reindeer skins, of course.

Would Mum have been better off with boiled reindeer skins? She didn't want to try, and nobody wanted to force her. Lieđđi thinks it wouldn't have made any difference, but whether she just says that out of kindness only she knows.

Lieđđi was however firmly of the opinion that had they been wearing reindeer skins instead of nylon and polyester at the time of the fire, they'd have been much less badly burned, and Mum would almost certainly have survived. Granny and Laima thought she might very well be right. Gealbu set to work converting the lávvu into reindeer skin clothes for all of us.

'When we've arrived wherever it is we're going, we can all wear whatever we like most of the time. But while we're travelling in these trucks, who knows when we might have another fire like that?'

Granny and Laima both thought that the Unimog and the trucks were much less likely to have major fires, with diesel engines rather than petrol and steel bodies rather than fibreglass, but Lieđđi and Gealbu weren't moved. 'Unlikely isn't impossible. Gealbu says he'll make them for the Bandvagn crew first, but he'll make them for everybody.'

Lieđđi and Suonjar were still translating Gealbu's gestures for the rest of us, but we were all getting the gist of what he said most of the time anyway. Emma and Dang were already as fluent in Gealbu gestures as they were in English. They adored him, and he them.

Grandad, Nikolai and Laima took the Unimog back up the hill to where the fire had happened, to see what if anything could be salvaged from the wreckage. The worst material loss was all the spare wheels in the trailer. The tyres had all burnt completely, leaving nothing but a mess of steel wire, already going rusty.

The rear unit of the Bandvagn itself had also burned very badly, and a lot of jars of pickles, preserved fruit and jam had cracked in the heat. The seals had gone on a lot of the remainder, but there were a fair number Laima thought worth rescuing. 'We'll have to eat these first, because the lids are going rusty now. But no sense wasting them.'

A large number of the books had survived – more or less. Many of them were too badly damaged, either by the fire or by the rain, but in the middle of the stack they hadn't burned and had only got slightly damp if at all.

'The ones we can rescue, we can dry out overnight tonight, and leave tomorrow morning.'

Laima thought the nuclear physics and medical tomes worth taking, even though some of them were charred down one side and much damper than most of the books we were salvaging.

There was a woodstove in the house we were camping in, and plenty of dry wood, and the books did indeed dry out nicely overnight. A lot of them had slightly crinkly pages ever after.

We left Uzhok the next morning with heavy hearts. The weather was as sombre as we were. It was the beginning of August, yet the clouds were heavy and dark, and made Lieđđi and Suonjar think it was going to snow. Laima said that that really wasn't possible at that time of year.

'Maybe on the tops, but not down here in the valley bottom.'

The storm broke when we'd gone just a few kilometres. I didn't remember ever having seen hail like it. We actually had to stop, because Laima, who was driving the tanker, simply couldn't see.

The hail didn't last for very long, but the road was covered in big hailstones by the time it changed to rain. The rain didn't stop all morning. It just poured and poured. In some places the road was like a river, and sometimes there were torrents pouring out of the woods, spreading debris across the road.

I didn't remember ever seeing debris strewn across the road in such quantities anywhere before, and asked whether this was the first storm there'd ever been quite this bad.

Granny and Laima laughed.

'No! Some of this junk has been here for ages, since the last storm or the storm before that. It's the place that's different, not the storm. But I guess you don't remember southern Norway very well. There were places there just like this, where we had to drive over the top of piles of stuff in the road, or even sometimes dig it away before we could get through. It's worse when the streams wash the road away.'

I did remember the washouts – lots of them in Sweden.

Finally we had to stop again and wait for the downpour to stop, and for the torrent in front of us to diminish. Granny wasn't sure we'd be able to get past even when it had, but she was certain it wasn't safe with the stream in spate.

Suonjar and Nikolai and Gealbu were in the surviving Bandvagn, and so out of communication with the rest of us. Granny got out into the pouring rain and ran to tell them why we were stopped.

'I'll stay there with them until the rain stops, or at least calms down a bit.'

The rain stopped and the sun came out in the early afternoon, but the stream just kept rushing across the road. Some of the small trees and stones got washed off the road, but as fast as they went, more arrived to take their place.

We all gathered in the back of one truck and Aunty Anna and Uncle Sid cooked a meal.

By the time we'd finished, the torrent had subsided somewhat, and Granny decided it would be possible – and more importantly, safe – to drive over the top of the rubbish in the road.

'We'll have to shift that tree first. The trucks would get over it okay, but the bowser or the little trailer might get stuck.'

The winch on the front of the tanker, with its cable routed round a tree at the side of the road beyond the mess, pulled the tree out of the way easily. We were on our way again.

Granny had hoped to get at least as far as Uzhgorod that day, but by the time we reached Perechin she thought it was time to find a good patch to put the animals out to grass. It was hard to find a place with enough reasonably level space between trees to put up the chicken run – our usual method of finding a flood meadow by a river was no good, because the river was running high and they were all flooded. We did eventually find a patch of weeds in the middle of the town, with only a couple of very small trees in an area big enough for the run. Nikolai broke the tops off them so they fitted inside it.

The youngest nanny goat – the only nanny who wasn't giving milk – managed to knot her tether up round a tree some distance away from the tree she was tethered to so thoroughly that she couldn't get her head down to ground level to eat. She'd done such a good job of knotting the rope that Laima and Suonjar decided the best thing was to untie her and put her on a new rope while they disentangled the old one.

That night I dreamed about Mum, and the fire. I woke up everybody in the truck with my screams, and then little Liz started crying too. Granny Persie tried to cuddle us both, and little Liz went to sleep again, but I didn't want to be cuddled. I lay awake listening to the night.

There was the noise of the river, some distance away but very recognizable. Every now and then I could hear thunder, but it wasn't raining and the thunder sounded distant.

One of the chickens started squawking, and then all the others joined in, and the goats started bleating. That woke everyone up again, and Dad got up and looked out. With no moon, and heavy clouds again, he couldn't see anything, so he lit the pressure lantern.

'Can't see anything. Probably a fox, maybe a wolf, but whatever it was it's run off now. Didn't like the lantern. Wouldn't have been able to get into the trailer anyway.'

'Or a rat. That could have got into the trailer, and the chickens wouldn't have liked that a bit.'

Chapter 11

I was very late waking up the next morning, and everybody was just about ready to move on.

'Morning sleepyhead! You can eat your breakfast in the cab, we've all had ours.'

Steamed carrots and potatoes again, but us littlies were being spoilt again: a hard boiled egg and a mug of fresh milk. Little Liz confided in me that she'd had a spoonful of jam as well, which I'd already deduced just by looking at her face.

Pawprints had been found in the mud around the trailer, and muddy pawprints on the side of the trailer a metre and a half off the ground.

'That's a good size for a wolf. There must be plenty of prey of some sort around here.'

'That was no wolf. I don't know much about pawprints, but I'd have guessed that was more like a bear. Wolves don't have paws that big – at least, none of the wolves I've butchered did.'

'So we can add bears to our list of surviving mammals. Or was it some kind of big cat, perhaps?'

'Don't know. Just as well Greg didn't go out in the dark if it was a bear or a big cat. We'd better take to keeping a gun and a lantern handy at night.'

'There used to be bears in these parts, I believe, but no big cats for a very long time. Not in recorded history, I don't think.'

'No, but things have changed. I think the big death was pretty much total in most places, and things have re-established themselves from small pockets of survivors. The pattern of re-establishment probably isn't the same as the old ranges. For example, I'm pretty sure there were never any rabbits in southern Norway before the cull, but it was overrun with them just a few years after it.'

Laima spotted another overgrown allotment with potatoes and carrots run wild just as we were leaving Perechin, and she and Nikolai dug up several buckets full before we got moving again.

'We'll look like potatoes and carrots before long!' Granny said, but I know she was pleased really. Fresh stuff is better than tins and jars, even when it's all a bit samey. I know that Laima knew Granny was pleased really, too.

We reached Uzhgorod by late morning. The weather by then was glorious, and Grandad and Granny and Dad and Lieđđi settled down to fish from a bridge over the river, while the rest of us walked into the town to go raiding. The particular thing we really wanted was road maps, but as usual we were on the look out for anything useful.

We found road maps all right, but we found something else, too. There was a truck with its cab embedded in the front of a shop, and the driver still at the wheel. What was odd about it was that he wasn't a skeleton. He was long dead and decayed, but there was rotting flesh hanging off his face. Most of us had never seen anything like it, of course. Laima had – but not for over thirty years.

'He's in army uniform, too. There's a camp somewhere near here. We ought to be moving out of this area as quick as we can. We don't want to run into one of their raiding parties. I guess this happened on a raid. Lucky we found this chap!'

We hotfooted it back to the bridge, and told the others.

'A pity. This river's brimming with fish, and we've only caught a few so far. But needs must when the Devil drives.'

Even Granny had to get Grandad to explain that expression, so it really was an obscure one; but after the thorough explanation Grandad gave, it's stuck in my mind. It probably stuck even more thoroughly because we didn't get the explanation immediately. Everyone wanted to get moving as quickly as possible.

Once we'd got started, the first priority for Granny was working out our route, while Laima drove. With road maps and a street map of Uzhgorod as well as the atlas, Granny didn't find this difficult at all, but it still took a little time. Then Laima asked Granny what Grandad had been talking about, and Granny called Grandad up on the intercom. That's when we got the explanation.

A few kilometres out of Uzhgorod we got more recent, and worrying, evidence of the proximity of a camp. There was a stretch of road that evidently flooded from time to time, and the floods had left a lot of mud on the road. Fortunately the line of the road was still obvious, so there was no risk of ending up in a ditch. But there were tyre tracks in the mud.

They weren't absolutely fresh. In places they'd been buried under a new layer of mud in a more recent flood. Granny thought that even the most recent layer of mud had dried out before getting wet again in the previous day's rain.

'You can see how it's cracked and peeled, and then got soggy again.'

She reckoned that the tracks were at least a few weeks old, but almost certainly very much more recent than the crash in Uzhgorod.

'There's one reassuring thing. There's only one vehicle, that went first one way and then the other.'

'It's got self-cleaning tyres like ours, so you can see which way it's going. I can't tell which way it went first though.'

'We might be able to, if we look carefully. One set must be on top of the other in some places.'

Laima was right. Just a kilometre or so later there was a stretch of clear tyre tracks where the two sets merged for a short distance. Granny and Laima and I got down from the tanker to take a close look.

'Well, assuming they've not got their tyres on backwards, we're heading towards the camp. That's a blow.'

'It's worse than a blow. I think it's reason enough to alter our route. At least we've got a choice here. I think we should go back to Uzhgorod and then go via Chop instead of Mukachevo. I bet the camp's somewhere near Mukachevo.'

'You're the navigator.'

According to the map, there was a minor road not very far ahead, so we went to the junction to turn around. Theoretically, the minor road connected through to the Chop road, but Granny thought the risk that the minor road might be impassable wasn't worth taking.

'I wonder how often they come this way. I wonder what they'll make of our tyre tracks. They'll surely notice them.'

'Chances are it'll be a few days at least before they come this way again. We'll be a long way away. And it's not as though we leave tracks everywhere.'

The road south from Uzhgorod was very like the one to the east that we'd set out on – a good road, but almost level with the flood plain. It too had a coating of mud for long stretches. Reassuringly, there were no tyre tracks. I wondered what it looked like after we'd all been along there. Four big trucks, a Bandvagn and a Unimog, all but one of them with trailers. We didn't stop to look.

Laima was driving, and Granny was navigating. And cuddling me. Or maybe it was me cuddling her. She seemed to need it as much as I did.

Granny was thinking we ought to be reaching Chop very soon, when we reached a bridge that wasn't there. It looked as though it had been blown up. Granny got out to take a look, and came back looking worried.

'I wonder who did that, and why? That's definitely deliberate, and I don't reckon it was thirty-five years ago, either. Maybe three or four years ago, but probably not much more.'

'Competition between a camp here in the Ukraine, and one in Hungary?'

'Or one in Czechoslovakia. Not that I think national boundaries mean anything any more.'

'No. Natural boundaries like this mean much more, though this isn't a particularly big river. But are we stuck between two camps, wherever they are?'

'I don't know about stuck between, but I think there must be antagonistic groups in this area. But as far as I can tell from this map, Mukachevo is right on this river, further upstream. So which lot are on which side of the river, and where they are, who knows? As you say, it's not a very big river, but it'd be very hard to cross without a bridge. It'll be bottomless mud underneath.'

Not having any idea where the camps were, they thought it was as good a plan as any simply to press on the way we were going for the moment, and try and get as far away from the area as we could as quickly as possible. But could we get across the river anywhere near here at all?

We'd noticed a gravel track off to the left just before we found the missing bridge, running between big, old trees on the river side and small young trees on what had presumably been fields before the cull. Laima turned the tanker round and went back to it, leaving everyone else to turn round in their own good time.

'Don't follow us just yet. You've obviously got to turn round where you are, but no sense ending up all the rest of you having to turn round again.'

Just a few hundred metres down the gravel track, there was a turning towards the river again, and another bridge. It was smaller and older and not in very good condition, but Granny had a good look at it and reckoned it was still good enough to carry the trucks.

'But why is it still here, when the other one's been blown up?'

Some things are destined to remain a mystery. This was one of them. There might have been some clues in the jeeplike vehicle we saw almost hidden amongst the trees when we reached the other side, but Granny didn't want to investigate it closely. It clearly hadn't been there ever since the cull, but equally clearly it hadn't moved for several years, and that was good enough for Granny. She said she had an uncanny feeling there'd be skeletons inside it, or maybe more recent corpses than that.

'I wonder whether the chap in the truck in Uzhgorod had been shot? It never occurred to me to look whether there was bullet damage to the truck. I just assumed he'd died of a heart attack at the wheel or something, or died in the accident.'

'I think I'd have noticed if there'd been any bullet holes on the side we could see, but there could have been in the front, or the other side.'

We rejoined the main road very quickly, and Granny called the rest of the convoy to follow us.

We didn't have a roadmap for Chop, but we found our road without difficulty. There was a huge railway goods yard there, and a change of gauge, so goods wagons would have been unloaded and reloaded there; but Laima and Granny checked for radioactive contamination and found no sign of it. If radioactive materials had been handled there, maybe they'd been better handled than at Brest – and certainly there happened to have been none there at the time of the cull.

After Chop, the road was running on a causeway between flooded marshes. We were only just above the level of the water in most places. Here and there there were houses, in various states of decay, standing in the water. Five or six kilometres out of Chop the road climbed onto a dike, over a bridge over a drainage channel, over another dike, and then back down to just above marsh level. Granny pointed out an old pumping station just by the dike. It was half under water, and the level of water in the drainage channel was exactly the same as the level in the marshes either side of it.

I say, 'the level of the water', but there was no water visible in the drainage channel at all. It was the smoothest, greenest area of grass I ever remember seeing anywhere, but Granny said it probably wouldn't be safe to walk on.

'My guess is you'd sink without trace as soon as you put foot on it. In it.'

Laima wasn't so sure, but none of us wanted to try!

The causeway across the marshes went on and on. There were whole flooded villages. At this point, the road was heading towards Mukachevo. We wanted a right turn somewhere, but we hadn't picked up maps for this route in Uzhgorod, and the best map we had was the one in the big atlas.

We arrived in a bigger village at about the right distance from Chop, and there were several right turns in it, but they all looked like little roads just serving a few houses in the village. Then suddenly there was a signpost – the first legible signpost I ever remember seeing.

Legible? I couldn't read it, but Laima and Granny could. I didn't learn the Cyrillic alphabet until years later, studying Laima's books. Granny told me it said Mukachevo straight on and Beregovo to the right, and Beregovo was the place she was heading for.

The road didn't look too bad. The village continued for a few hundred metres – at least, it did on our left. There was a dense forest on our right, the first we'd seen since the river with the missing bridge. I was getting used to these different trees, too, with leaves rather than needles. I liked them, they seemed friendlier.

Then we were on a causeway between marshes again. Granny told me how she was sure they used to be fields.

'Long, long ago it would all have been marshes around here, but you can tell that the marshes had been drained to make farmland. But after the cull no-one was keeping the pumps going or the drainage channels cleared, so it's all turned back to marshland.'

Laima thought that threw an interesting light on the groups of survivors we knew there must be in the area.

'I wonder what the people around here are doing? They must be farming somewhere, and when it's drained, this must be some of the most productive land in the area.'

'There's probably not all that many of them. They've probably kept a few thousand hectares drained somewhere that we've just not seen. I hope we never do.'

What I did see, just at that moment, was a whole lot of big, white birds. I pointed them out to Granny.

'Swans! That's a great sight.'

'I wouldn't mind swan for dinner, but if we shoot one there, how will we go and retrieve it?'

'You're not thinking, Laima. The Bandvagn would have no trouble getting over there. But we'd have to detach the bowser, which is quite a palaver. We've got plenty of meat – and fish – at the moment.'

'Oh, it's not such a palaver! Let's do it!'

'I'd never get one from this distance, but they'll all take flight if you drive any closer.'

Laima stopped the tanker. Granny got down with the gun, and set off along the road on foot. Before she'd got close enough to feel confident of hitting them, the swans flew off. We watched them go. Granny never fired a shot.

'I reckon the people around here must shoot them. I don't remember swans being as nervous as that in the old days.'

'I don't know. Swans migrate over huge distances. I wouldn't have thought they'd come across people often at all nowadays. It could simply be unfamiliarity, or even just chance that they flew off at that moment.'

We reached another flooded village. The road, still just above the level of the water, wiggled its way between two rows of sorry looking houses, and finally ended at a major railway line, with several parallel tracks and no level crossing. We could have got across, but there was no sign of a road continuing on the other side.

'There were junctions in the village. We must have missed the main road.'

Turning the tanker was easy enough, but the rest of the convoy had the usual trouble. Back we went. We left the other vehicles at the first junction, and went exploring in the tanker. Eventually we found a level crossing with the road continuing beyond it. Granny gave Grandad instructions over the intercom about the route, and before long we were all together again.

By this time it was getting late, but Granny wanted to get as far away from any military camps as she could before stopping for the night.

'But for all we know, we could be going closer to them, rather than further away.'

'I don't think so. The best evidence we have of their existence is behind us. But another few kilometres won't make much difference, it's true.'

Nevertheless, we kept on going quite a long way, looking for a patch of grass to put the goats and chickens out on, but it was all marsh on both sides of the road. Eventually we gave up, because it was beginning to get dark, and we wouldn't have been able to put the animals out to grass anyway. We stopped by a patch of open water, and Grandad and Dad and Lieddi started fishing while Aunty Anna and Aunty Dot prepared supper.

Gealbu and Aunty Belle pulled up armfuls of weeds from the edge of the road and fed them to the goats and chickens.

Little Liz and I sat one each side of Granny, with her arms around our shoulders. We stared out into the evening. The moon was rising over the reeds at the far side of the water, its reflection a long stripe on the surface. Black shapes flapped across in front of it.

Granny laughed softly.

'Did you see that, my babies? The swans in front of the moon? That's such a cliché, but it's beautiful, isn't it? You know, Mikey, I don't think I could shoot a swan, not really. For one thing, I always try to shoot anything in the head if I can, so it dies quickly, and you've no chance of shooting a bird in the head. But anyway, a swan is such a wonderful creature. A deer is a wonderful creature too, but you've got to eat.'

Even at six I could see the inconsistencies in the things people say. Even Granny Persie. But I could still see her point, and I'm sure she could see the inconsistency too, and probably guessed that I could as well.

I wondered how she'd react another time if Laima or anyone shot a swan. She always tried to hit anything she shot in the head, but she never said anything when anyone else shot an animal anywhere else.

The fishing that evening was very successful, and Laima and Nikolai spent half the night preparing fish and hanging them up to dry in the trailer. We still had carrots and potatoes, too. When we'd set out on our expotition, we'd expected to be mostly eating stuff from tins and jars all the way, but it wasn't working out like that at all.

Chapter 12

Laima was too tired in the morning to feel up to driving, but Granny was the navigator, so there was a bit of a swap around. Grandad drove the tanker.

Granny and Laima got on really well, and had a lot to talk about – I learnt a tremendous lot just listening to them – but I think Grandad and Granny were glad to be together a bit more again. I know they were both missing Granny Merly and Mum dreadfully. We all were, of course, but Grandad and the Grannies had been together an awful long time. And Mum was their baby.

I noticed that whenever Grandad didn't need his right hand on the controls, it was either on Granny's knee under the atlas, or holding her hand. And when she wasn't too busy studying the atlas or the surroundings, her head was resting against his shoulder.

Holding the atlas on her knees all the time, she didn't have an arm free to put around me, but I understood that and didn't mind.

Laima and Granny always talked almost non-stop, but with Granny and Grandad it was different. Most of the time we drove in silence. Mostly the only time anyone said anything was when Granny pointed something interesting out to me – some particular plant growing in the road ahead, a tractor standing half-submerged in the marsh half a kilometre away, the remains of a house, or a patch of dead trees.

'They've drowned. They only lived here because people had drained the land, and now it's too wet for them again.'

At one point we got onto a minor road by mistake. It wasn't obvious which way was the main road in the middle of a village, but as soon as we got out of the village it was obvious we weren't on the main road. We could see where the road went, but the surface was below water. Not far below, but the main road had been above water level everywhere, and anyway, this road just didn't look the same. For one thing, it was narrower; for another, the surface was different. The whole convoy had to reverse about three hundred metres. Granny cursed herself for a fool, for not keeping the tanker a good distance ahead.

'Why do I have to learn the same lesson again and again?'

I knew why, but I didn't say anything. I'm sure Grandad knew too, and he didn't say anything either. We knew it wasn't only Granny who wasn't her normal self.

We found the junction, and Grandad drove the tanker to the edge of the village and made sure we were on the main road before calling the rest of the convoy.

Granny was sure we really were on the main road, but even the main road began to have standing water on it in a few places.

'I hope it doesn't get any deeper than this. We could drive through water a good deal deeper, but we might not be able to see the road, and it would be hell if we had to reverse out. It'll be a relief when we get into the hills again.'

'Pun intended?'

'Pete! You have to ask? How long have you known me?'

I know Granny too – have done all my life – but I had to have that one explained.

Happily the water never got very deep, and at no point were we unable to see a dry stretch of road beyond. Granny's biggest worry was that there'd be a collapsed culvert or something in the middle, but she thought it unlikely as the only water courses we crossed seemed to be those with levees and proper bridges.

It was another big relief to find a street map in Beregovo! We found a place to top up the bowser, too, and a road map that showed the route as far as the Romanian border.

Shortly after Beregovo the intercom came to life, but all we could hear was deep snoring and the noise of another truck's engine.

'That sounds like Nikolai to me.'

The gentle laughter sounded like either one of the twins, but we knew it was Aunty Dot. The intercom clicked off again.

We reached a little place called Vilok just before noon, where there was a bridge over the river Tissa. It was a steel braced girder bridge, and it was incredibly rusty, with holes right through the webs of the girders in places. But the road surface didn't look that bad to me, and it wasn't actually collapsing anywhere. Granny was a bit worried about it though, and the river was definitely too deep to ford.

'According to this map, there's another crossing at Vinogradov. It's twenty kilometres away, but I really don't trust this bridge.'

The road bridge at Vinogradov was even worse, but we could see a railway bridge just a couple of hundred metres upstream, and getting onto the railway was easy at a station we'd seen not long before we arrived at the bridges.

Getting back to the road the other side wasn't quite so easy, but Granny found a route in the end.

For the first time, we had trouble at the border crossing. There wasn't anyone there – no-one alive, that is, there were several skeletons – and it wasn't booby trapped or anything. The road was completely blocked with rusting trucks. We couldn't bypass them across the fields, because the border was a tangle of barbed wire. There was a railway line crossing the border parallel with the road, but that was blocked with a train.

We could, and did, bypass the queue to get to the actual crossing, but then we had to drag several trucks out of the way before we could get through. Granny tried to do it with the winch on the tanker at first, but didn't have enough traction to pull one end of a truck sideways, and Aunty Dot brought up one of the other trucks to help pull.

Then just the other side of the border, the train was blocking a level crossing. That didn't bother Granny much: she said we weren't far from Halmeu, and we'd be able to rejoin the road if we just followed the railway to Halmeu station. The going wasn't very good at first, with some rather soft ground alongside the track, and quite a lot of fairly stout trees, but we got through okay and very soon reached some sidings parallel to the main track, with firmer ground, and soon thereafter the station that Granny had promised us.

We were off the edge of the road map we'd found in Beregovo and wholly dependent on the big atlas again, but we reached the main road at Livada, and thought we were doing well. What the big atlas didn't reveal was that the route crosses the river Someşul by ferry.

'Maybe twice. It crosses the river again in about ten kilometres. We'll have to detour via Baia Mare. But I think this is a good spot to stop for the night. Good fishing and good grass.'

A few minutes after starting fishing, Grandad crept quietly back to the trucks, and took the gun. We heard a shot, then Grandad came back.

'Suonjar, bring the Bandvagn and come across the river. I got a deer on the other side.'

But Nikolai said, 'No, I'll swim over and get it. I was thinking of going for a swim anyway.'

Grandad thought it looked cold, but Nikolai laughed. 'Compared with the river back in Latvia? I don't think so!'

Suonjar and Gealbu didn't think so, either, and joined Nikolai in the river. Nikolai brought the deer over, and then the three of them stayed in the water for an hour or more. Gealbu's ungainliness on land didn't show in the water at all.

I remembered what Lieđđi had said about him skiing, and wished I could have seen that too.

Uncle Jake, Aunty Dot and Grandad gave up trying to fish, and sat and watched them playing. We'd got plenty of fish drying in the trailer, and now we'd got fresh venison, too. Lieđđi and I sat with them.

'Come and join us in the water!'

'Can't swim. Never learned.'

That was Uncle Jake. Grandad could swim, but hadn't, not in the last thirty-five years. He was astonished that Gealbu and Suonjar could swim, but when he asked them later that evening, they laughed. 'Obviously we wouldn't go in the water in winter back home, but in summer it's warmer than the river here was just now.'

Lieđđi would have loved to go swimming, her burns hadn't healed enough for her to feel comfortable with the idea.

Grandad had hit the deer in the head, which pleased both Granny and Laima, albeit for different reasons. Laima was quite happy that Nikolai was playing in the river, because Dad was keen to learn how to butcher the deer Laima's way, so that what wasn't eaten immediately could be conveniently dried. Nikolai tended to demonstrate things, but Laima wanted to instruct and supervise, so that Dad would actually learn.

They began by skinning and gutting it, and Laima said she'd teach Granny how to cure the skin later.

'We'll run out of reindeer skins eventually. I ought to find out how they cured them. I'm sure they can't have used alum, and I'll run out of that too in the end. It's not the kind of stuff you can find easily when raiding, I suspect.'

I could see Lieđđi squirming a little and not saying anything as Laima was talking, and wondered why. I think Laima was watching for her reaction out of the corner of her eye. She smiled at Lieđđi, and Lieđđi seemed to relax. She grinned back. It was a long time before I found out what that was all about. The other method of curing reindeer skins uses wee and poo...

Nikolai and Suonjar and Gealbu came up out of the river as the sun went down.

'This is a good spot. We could stay here. Why do we have to move on any further at all?'

'You're not thinking, my son. It's lovely just now, but what's it going to be like in winter?'

'True. Continental climate. We want to be on the coast. And further south, why not?'

'Short of going west – and you know why that's not such a great idea – the coast IS south. And there's nothing here at all, anyway. Fish, and deer while our ammunition lasts. Then what? And no buildings, and a hell of a distance to anywhere to find anything we might need. Not too bad while the trucks last, but after that?'

'There's coast to the east, too. Not many nuclear sites there, easily avoided.'

'True. But the Aegean is probably a better place to be than the Black Sea for other reasons. Not least that there's likely to be better pickings for raiding.'

The next day we backtracked and found what we hoped was the road to Baia Mare – it was in a village about the right distance back from the river, and was heading in roughly the right direction. The road was in better condition than most, and we arrived in the town in under an hour. Granny was desperate to find maps, and we spent a while finding some.

A large area of the town seemed to have been destroyed by a catastrophic flood, which Granny and Laima guessed had probably been caused by the collapse of a dam further up the valley. The river was little more than a trickle through the debris, and it didn't look as though it had ever been much more than that since the big flood, quite a few years earlier. Trees were colonizing the wreckage almost to the water's edge.

There was no hope of tracing the roads amongst the confusion and there were no surviving bridges as far as we could see, but the river bed was all stones and we found a route through the mess as best we could. There was enough of the town left on the other side for Granny to work out how it related to the map, and she found the right road south without any trouble.

We really did get into the hills for a while, but how much of a relief it was I'm not sure. The road didn't disappear under water here and there, but it did disappear under debris in some places, and in others it was washed away. But the washouts were stony not muddy, and none of them were at all problematic. Then there was a steep winding descent, and we were back on the plains beside the river. Granny said it was the same river, the Someşul. Now and then we saw it, then it would swing away from us in a great curve, or disappear behind a wall of trees.

The road surface was badly broken up, with weeds everywhere and small trees here and there, but none of it caused us any difficulty. We arrived at a bridge over the river late in the afternoon, and Granny said that according to the map there was a town, Dej, the other side.

We stopped for the night just before the bridge, where there was a grassy area by the river to put the goats and chickens out. We were so well stocked with drying venison and fish that Uncle Jake, Aunty Dot and Grandad gave up fishing once they'd got enough fresh for the evening meal and breakfast. Nikolai, Gealbu and Suonjar had another dip, but came out much more quickly than the day before.

'It's not as warm here!'

'No, but it was good. We don't know when we'll next get a chance.'

At Dej the next morning we found another military base. There were diesel and petrol tanks and we filled up, but nobody felt the need for any more vehicles and we didn't even investigate to see whether any of them were in a reasonable state of preservation. Dad and Uncle Jake did have a look for wheels, since we'd lost all our spares apart from one on each truck, but they didn't find any that would fit.

There was a trailer that looked a bit tougher than the Unimog's, but it would have needed a lot of work to make it suitable for the goats and chickens and Granny reckoned the one we'd got would probably make it to Greece all right.

Arriving at Cluj-Napoca later in the day, we found increased radioactive contamination again. It wasn't bad, but it was a bit worrying because we were a long way from any source marked on Ivan's map, or anything else Laima was aware of. It was a bit different from the contamination at Brest, too: Granny said that here it was mostly beta emitters rather than alpha. With the equipment she had, she couldn't identify specific isotopes, but the range of the radiation in air told her it was mostly beta.

'That means it's most likely from a reactor fire or nuclear waste, rather than nuclear materials in transit like it must have been at Brest. Most likely from Paks in Hungary, considering the prevailing winds. It's four hundred kilometres away, but there's nothing else marked any closer.'

'There's one on the Bulgarian border.'

'Kozloduy. It's just as far, and the prevailing wind isn't in this direction.'

'Winds don't blow in the prevailing direction all the time.'

'True. It could be from anywhere. We'll just have to keep monitoring. As we would anyway. We don't have to go close to either of them, so with luck it won't get much worse than this. And this is nothing to worry about for a few days, even for the animals.'

'Good that we've got plenty of fresh food at the moment, though. We shouldn't do any fishing or shooting or digging up vegetables around here.'

As at Brest, the contamination was in the soil or the vegetation, and had largely washed off the tarmac and concrete – where the tarmac and concrete wasn't buried in organic debris from the trees.

What was the determinant underlying which places burned during the cull, and which just calmly lay down and died? We couldn't figure it out. Cluj-Napoca, smaller than Lublin which seemed to have mostly stayed calm, had burned like Leningrad.

Maybe it was a matter of the local concentration of the lethal agent, and hence how long the process took? Or even possibly different lethal agents in different places, or differences between local cultures, or differing reactions of the local authorities. We'd no way of knowing.

South of Cluj-Napoca the road climbed into the hills again. Halfway up one hill, we had to detour completely off the road for a short way to get past the rusting remains of several vehicles that seem to have been involved in a major pile-up. Two of them looked as though they might have been army trucks, but it was hard to tell. All the tyres had disappeared, and Granny said they'd obviously all burned at the time of the accident. That was why the vehicles were all so completely rusty, even more so than most of the vehicles we saw littered around the place.

'Granny...'

'What is it, Mikey?'

'I've been looking at the maps, and the atlas, and Laima's reactor map...'

'You mean Ivan's map?'

'Yes, Ivan's map. You're taking us halfway between that reactor in Hungary, and that one in Bulgaria, is that right?'

'Yes, that's right. Very good, Mikey.'

'What's that funny Russian letter* on Ivan's map, right on our route, just before the border where we'll go into Yugoslavia?'

'I don't know. Do you know, Laima?'

'Let's take a look.'

She glanced at where Granny was pointing on the map.

'Oh, that's a uranium mine. Ciudanoviţa, or something like that, I think it's called. That won't be a problem. We won't want to shoot anything around there, or go fishing or digging vegetables, and we certainly wouldn't want to live in the area, but just driving through is nothing. We'll keep checking contamination levels, of course, but don't worry about it.'

'But people must have lived in the area in the old days!'

'Yes, and some of them got sick. Some of them died.'

'So why didn't everyone move away?'

That got us into a long discussion about the old days, and how many people there were, and how important having a job was, and how difficult it was to find a place to live – unless you were rich, then you could live wherever you fancied. And what rich meant, and what poor meant, and what money was. I said it didn't seem to make much sense, and Granny and Laima laughed.

'It doesn't seem to make much sense to me any more, but it did at the time. I remember how it just seemed the only possible way things could be. But I don't remember why it seemed like that. It just did.'

Then we got back to talking about the uranium mine, and how although it was a bad place in the old days, it was actually much worse now, because all the old mine workings must have flooded, and the tailings ponds must have failed. How, with all the rocks broken up because of the mining, the uranium – and even more importantly, all the other

---

* It was a Ч, but it's a C on Grandad Pete's English copy of Ivan's map at the back of the book.

radioactive stuff that the uranium turns into when it decays, in total nearly seven times as radioactive as the uranium itself – would get into the water that flooded the mine, and then into the streams and rivers in the area. How they used to store all the waste from the mining in tailings ponds – with all the radioactive daughter products of the uranium – and how when the tailings ponds eventually fail, everything from them gets into the streams and rivers, too.

'And then, when the streams flood, into the soil in the area. There's always some uranium – and its radioactive daughter products – in the soil, everywhere. Always has been. There's an awful lot more near an abandoned uranium mine, especially downstream from it. But it's nothing compared to what there is near an abandoned reactor, or even worse, an abandoned nuclear waste dump.'

Laima told me how they always said they planned to keep the water from the mines pumped out even after they'd finished mining, and keep maintaining the tailings ponds, too.

'How long they'd really have done it for, who knows? You couldn't keep doing it forever, and that's really how long you'd have to do it. But obviously whatever their plans, the cull changed all that. No-one left to look after anything. But as Persic says, even an abandoned uranium mine is nothing compared to a reactor or a waste dump.'

'Even while the mines were still working, they had accidents. Tailings dams burst, or parts of mines got flooded accidentally. These things happen. I don't know whether they ever happened at Ciudanoviţa, but things like that can happen anywhere.'

I dozed for a bit after that, but I was vaguely conscious of Laima asking Granny how old I was.

'He's just turned six.'

'Funny how different children are. Nikolai? Scientist parents – nuclear physicist Dad. Not interested in things like that at all. Anything mechanical, he'd have it to pieces, and back together again before his Dad found out he'd touched it. All working too, by the time he was about six. But intangibles? Forget it. Not until he was about fifteen.'

We stopped that night a couple of kilometres before Aiud. Radioactive contamination levels were down again. There was a lovely river and the fishing was good. On the other side of the river we saw deer coming down to drink again, but no-one felt like shooting one – Nikolai said it was too cold for swimming, and nobody mentioned crossing the river with the Bandvagn. We had plenty of meat anyway.

We saw swans on the river, too, and no-one felt like shooting one of them, either. I think Laima might have realized that Granny was more than a little reluctant to shoot a swan really.

I think it may have been at Aiud that Little Liz first recognized the remains of people. At any rate it was certainly there that she coined the phrase, 'rag and bone man'. Grandad was somewhat taken aback when she said she'd seen one, until he realized what she meant. Then he had to explain to the rest of us what 'rag and bone man' used to mean in the old days. Nobody else knew – not even Granny.

That involved a lot of talk about horses, which got us onto cows and cats and dogs. I think that was probably when I first understood what the oldies meant when they talked about 'draught animals' – but for a long time after that I thought that horses were as big as tractors, and that the rag and bone man's cart would have been as big as our trailers.

Chapter 13

The next day we had to use a railway bridge again at Alba Iulia. Granny Persie said she couldn't quite work out how the road used to cross the river – it just disappeared one side and reappeared the other, with no sign of a bridge or the remains of one, and no sign of any ramps for a ferry or anything.

Some days I used to write a lot in my diary; other days just a word or two. Sometimes I look at what I wrote, and wonder why I bothered to write it at all, or what on Earth the words meant; other times a single word brings the memories flooding back. Sometimes Ivan's map, or the atlas, or one of the other maps brings memories flooding back.

I know we stopped that night just after Hateg, but I don't remember a thing about the place, nor about Reşiţa that we went through just before we stopped the following day.

I do remember something about the day after that though. We passed Ciudanoviţa, the uranium mine. 'Passed' is the right word, though – we were never closer than about five kilometres from the mine, and we never saw it, nor did any of our frequent radiation measurements reveal it. We were in the next valley. Granny said she was glad the road didn't go down the valley where the mine was.

We did go right through Anina, and saw the remains of industry there. Huge rusting steel structures and a tall chimney kept appearing and then disappearing behind the trees again.

The road went steeply up and down and wiggled back and forth like crazy all that day. There were lots of places where it was covered in debris where streams ran across it, quite a few where it had washed away, and there were lots of small trees growing through its surface. Granny, Laima, and I were a long way ahead in the tanker most of the time, because we were never sure whether we were going to have to turn back and there was often nowhere to turn.

In one place we needed to move some big stones to fill a hole, and Nikolai and Uncle Sid walked about two kilometres to come and help – better a long walk than risk having to do a long reverse with a truck and trailer on that difficult road. After that, Nikolai and Uncle Sid rode with us in the tanker in case there was another big hole or a rock or tree trunk in the road, and Laima waited by the roadside for Grandad to pick her up. But we didn't actually find anywhere that was completely impassable.

With a lot of steep climbing, the engines all got very hot, and Suonjar insisted that no-one else should be in the Bandvagn. Jake wanted to stay with her, but she wouldn't let him.

'I know you're wearing reindeer skins now. Everybody is. But even so, if this thing catches fire, the fewer of us there are in it the better. I can get out damn quick if I have to, and all the quicker if I'm not thinking about anyone else.'

Happily, it didn't catch fire.

We did have to change two truck wheels though, because reinforcing rods in the broken concrete of a bridge went right through the tyres. Grandad didn't see the rods, probably because they were buried in debris.

That meant we only had two good spares left, for four trucks and three trailers. We kept the wheels, in case we ever found a tyre store with the right size of tyres.

That night we stopped near a place called Oraviţa. We'd only done about seventy kilometres, because the road had been so difficult.

The next day was very memorable – a turning point in our expotition. Literally.

Not long after breakfast, we reached Bela Crkva, having passed the border between Romania and Yugoslavia without even noticing it. From Bela Crkva, the plan was to go on to

Kovin, then over a bridge over the Danube to Smederevo. Granny was hoping to find more maps there, because from Smederevo onwards the only one we'd got was the big atlas. But just after Bela Crkva we reached the end of the road. A vast lake stretched in front of us. We'd caught sight of expanses of water through gaps in the trees for a while, and thought it was probably just flooded marshes, but it proved to be much more than that. We couldn't see the other side!

Far out in the water there were dead trees standing, but closer to the shore there were live trees. Granny said that meant that the trees further out had drowned, because the water had been up around them for a long time, but that the live trees showed that the water had only recently reached its present level.

Granny and Laima studied the atlas carefully. The only explanation they could come up with was that there was a large, well-organized outfit somewhere around who'd constructed a new dam on the Danube, or enlarged an existing one.

'Flooding a huge area of good farmland doesn't bother them an iota, there's no shortage of that now. But they presumably want more electricity, without using fossil fuels or nuclear power. If we're right, they've got the capability to build huge dams, and construct huge turbines and generators. They must be fantastically much better organized than our old camp – or for that matter the other two or three we've seen evidence of. With a much bigger population, and industrial capabilities.'

Bela Crkva was close to the one hundred metre contour, so they reckoned the water level probably wasn't very much below that, which implied an absolutely enormous lake. Exactly how big would depend on the exact level of the water, since the huge plain it was flooding had very little relief. The atlas simply didn't have enough information for them to be able to guess the limits of the lake, but they were pretty sure it would be an awful long way to go round it –

and almost certainly take us close to several abandoned nuclear reactors.

'If they're abandoned. If there are still organizations capable of building huge dams, maybe there are still organizations capable of running nuclear power stations.'

'Maybe, but I doubt it. I don't think it would have been feasible to maintain them for the duration of the cull.'

Everyone was just calling it 'the cull' by then.

The grown-ups had a big conference. It was clear that we weren't going to be able to follow the route we'd planned, and that this wasn't just going to be a minor diversion. Everyone was pretty sure that they wanted to avoid the Big Outfit, if at all possible – they were fairly sure it would be organized on autocratic lines, and very likely didn't speak English or Swedish. Laima thought that they very possibly did speak Russian, but she and Nikolai definitely preferred to be with our little group than any big, organized outfit.

'It's very possible that they're Romanian, Yugoslav or Bulgarian. If so, the older ones would probably speak Russian, but the younger ones probably wouldn't, and the older ones might not like to.'

'They could be from anywhere, though. An outfit with that kind of capability could take their pick of where to be, in today's world.'

'So how do we avoid them? And where are we heading, now?'

'Wherever we decide we're heading, we'll have to be ready to change our minds again if we encounter them – and we'll have to be ready to negotiate with them if they see us and don't just let us turn away.'

'That's always been the case. But we'd never before suspected that a group with this kind of capability might exist.'

'I wonder if the various groups are in touch with each other?'

'I don't think so. You'd expect long wave radio would be their method of communication, and there was never any of that kind of activity on long wave when we used to listen. We don't even have a working receiver any longer, but if they weren't doing it from the beginning, I don't suppose they've ever started.'

'They could have been using telephones.'

'No. The system relied on far too much infrastructure. It simply wouldn't have survived the cull.'

It was decided that we were still trying to get to Greece, to find somewhere on the Mediterranean coast if possible. The big question was how and where to cross the Danube. Granny was sure there must be some crossings downstream of Smederevo, but it wasn't at all obvious where they might be. The roads on the north side of the river didn't seem to match up with the roads on the south side in most places, probably meaning there weren't any bridges.

There was a dam marked near Turnu Severin and Kladovo. *Portile de Fier (Iron Gate)* was marked at roughly the same spot, all a bit tangled and confused on the map in the atlas. Everyone assumed there'd be a crossing there, but that there was most likely a hydroelectric power station.

'And if someone's either made that dam bigger, or built another one, the odds are very high that that power station is working. We're pretty certainly better off not going anywhere near it.'

But where the next crossing was, we really couldn't tell. It looked as though there might be one between Bechet and Orekhovo, but that was very close to the nuclear reactor at Kozloduy.

'I wonder whether there are any bridges downriver of here at all. It's a big river. It might be all ferries.'

'Well, if it comes to it, we could cross in the Bandvagn. If we can find a suitable small ferry, we might be able to tow a ferry with the Bandvagn, to get the trucks across.'

'Sounds like a dicey procedure to me. Anything big enough for the trucks to drive onto safely is going to be a bit big to tow with the Bandvagn, I reckon.'

'Oh, I don't know. As long as the river's pretty slow moving at the point we try to cross, you could tow something quite big. It'd just be slow, that's all.'

'I think there's probably a bridge at Giurgiu, look. The railway is marked as crossing the river there. Surely they'd have a bridge not a ferry for the railway?'

'It's an awful long way east. I wonder whether we can find out what's there without actually going there?'

'We can take a look at Bechet first, if the radiation levels aren't too high.'

'Look at the route to Bechet, though. It goes right past that dam. Do we want to go that way? It's an awful lot further to avoid it, and right up through the mountains. Who knows what the roads will be like up there?'

'You can't tell exactly how high the passes are from the atlas. As far as you can see, it's no higher than we've been in a few places before. But is it worth such a long detour to avoid the dam anyway? How likely are we to be noticed? There's a town on the north side, so I don't suppose we have to go right past the dam anyway. There quite likely won't be many people there – it's very likely a remote outpost from their point of view, and they won't see any need to guard it or anything.'

Going back through Anina was easier than it had been coming. The places where Nikolai and Uncle Sid had had to repair the road were still good, and since we knew it was passable everywhere we all stayed close together and kept moving, so it didn't take nearly as long as it had going the other way.

At Anina we turned off the road we'd come on, to head towards the dam. We had to leave everyone quite a long way behind again, because the road was narrow and in pretty rough condition. Rather than waiting at each possible turning point for everyone to catch up, Nikolai suggested we should describe the latest spot over the intercom, and just keep moving. This did speed us up quite a lot, but it was lucky it didn't end in disaster: after about the fourth turning point, Grandad caught us up in the Unimog while Nikolai and Uncle Sid were clearing a large tree that had fallen right across the road. He hadn't recognized the turning point Uncle Sid had described, and had driven straight past it! Luckily the road wasn't blocked, and before long we reached another place where it would have been possible to turn the trailers if we'd had to.

After that we reverted to our old procedure. We weren't in any terrible hurry really. We were well south, and we had plenty of food and fuel. What difference would a few days extra on our journey make?

Wherever it was we were going. The oldies were talking about a place in Greece called Thessaloníki. I knew they weren't particularly expecting to be exactly there – but maybe within reach of there for going raiding.

We reached a place called Mehadia late that afternoon. Fortunately, we were just on the maps that we'd found in Baia Mare, or we'd never have found our way in that area. It seemed such a long time ago that we'd been at Baia Mare, but we were forcefully reminded of it: Mehadia, like Baia Mare, had been devastated by a huge flood. This time the map showed no obvious big dam upstream that could have burst to cause the flood, and Granny thought that it must either have been a most terrible storm, or perhaps a dam had been built not long before the cull, after our maps had been made.

'It could even have been a dam still under construction at the time of the cull, that wasn't really finished and wasn't supposed to have filled – but the channel got blocked somehow after the cull.'

'Who knows? We won't go looking, that's for sure, so we'll never know.'*

The bridge or bridges had been destroyed in the flood, but it didn't take long to find a gravelly place where we could ford the river easily. Just the other side, there was a large grassy area, ideal for the goats and chickens. Radiation levels were low, and we had a lovely evening by the river. Lieđđi and Gealbu wished they'd got a net to try their parents' method of fishing, but we didn't have one, and they fished with the rods and lines as usual. By nightfall they'd caught three very small fish, which little Liz and Emma and I had as a side dish with our supper.

We were visited by a bear during the night. This time Dad was prepared, and had a gun with him when he went out with the lantern. The bear obviously didn't like the light and ran off, but Dad caught sight of its backside disappearing into the night.

'He was a big fellow. Or she was. Most likely a bear last time, too, I guess.'

In the morning we saw the bear's muddy paw marks even further up the side of the animals' trailer than the last ones had been, so we knew Dad wasn't exaggerating.

'Much bigger than that and he'd be able to smash the trailer. That'd be the end of our goats and chickens.'

'I reckon that one could have done if I'd not disturbed him. Maybe we should have taken that sturdier trailer when we had the chance.'

'No point going back for it now! But we should keep our eyes out for another, anyway.'

---

* Mehadia really does suffer from occasional catastrophic flooding due to the local topography and the occasional heavy rainstorms the area experiences, but obviously none of them had any way of knowing that.

'Another trailer, or another bear?'

Laughter. 'Both!'

'There'd be a lot of meat on a bear.'

'So far we've only come across them at night. Not so easy to shoot one in the dark. And we'd want to be sure of killing it with the first shot, if we do shoot one. Last thing we want is a really angry live bear. I reckon we should only shoot one if we can't scare it away.'

'Next time, it'd probably be better if two of us went out with a gun each if we think there's a bear, then.'

'And stick together. We don't want to end up shooting each other in the dark.'

'Hopefully the lanterns will always scare them away anyway.'

After breakfast, we set off down the valley towards the Danube. According to the map, the river was pretty wide at the point where our road met another one along the side of the river. Granny said it must be basically a reservoir, impounded by the dam at Portile de Fier. She was a bit nervous about what we were going to find when we reached the Danube. Had the existing dam been raised, and if it had, would the road be flooded?

And if it hadn't been raised? Presumably there was a new dam further upstream somewhere. Probably both would have functioning hydroelectric power stations, and there'd probably be traffic on the road between the two. The map showed a road on each side of the river. Which one would be being used? Or would they both be in use?

'How much traffic would you expect, though, Persie? I don't suppose they need very many personnel to run a hydroelectric power station, and it's very likely a long way away from the main centre of population. That could be almost anywhere. How often would people come and go? My guess is not often. There's obviously no traffic at all up this road, anyway.'

'If there's no-one about, maybe we can even cross by the dam itself.'

'We'll see what it looks like when we get there. It's very likely the crest of the dam is in full view of anyone working in the power station.'

'If they've even got windows looking in that direction.'

'Six big military vehicles is quite noticeable. And we make a fair bit of noise, so someone might come out to look even if they don't have a window in the right direction.'

'We make a lot less noise when the road's dead level, like the crest of a dam. And there'll be a lot of noise in the power station to cover it.'

'What are you so scared of, anyway? There won't be many people there. What will they do if they do see us? They'll be more scared of us than we'll be of them.'

'But they'll report our existence.'

'Nothing we can do about that. That can happen anywhere, any time. Once we get the other side, we just take the road that looks unused. Like last time, we'll be out of the area before anyone starts to follow us.'

'Hmm. There are two differences. Firstly, someone seeing our vehicles is a lot more immediate than someone seeing our tracks, quite likely not until days or weeks later. Secondly, as far as I can see there's only one road that goes anywhere the other side of the river around here. So if the organization is based that side, we don't have a choice but to head further downstream on this side.'

We didn't take long to reach the river. The road along the bank was clearly being well maintained, and presumably fairly regularly used, although there was nothing on it when we reached it. I'd never seen a road like it before. There wasn't a pothole in it, there was no debris strewn across it anywhere, and there wasn't so much as a weed growing through the surface, never mind the usual small saplings.

'Most roads used to be like this in the old days, Mikey.'

What wasn't obvious was whether the road was a completely new one, above a new, higher water level.

'Well, that's much as we expected.'

Taking our future in our hands and with our hearts athump, we headed downstream. It was about fifteen kilometres to the dam, and it took less than twenty minutes to reach it.

Looking at the atlas – we were off the edge of the road map at that point – Granny had expected to find a town by the dam, but it must have been a bit further downstream. The road continuing down the valley was as good as the road we'd just come along, which pleased Granny greatly.

'That probably means two things. Firstly, that there is probably a new dam further upstream, and that this one is still its original size. Secondly, and more importantly from our point of view, the organization who's running these two dams is most likely this side of the river, further to the east.'

'Interesting that there have been no fences. Very different from our old camp.'

'Dunno. The soldiers came and went outside the fenced area. It was only us serfs who were supposed to stay in the camp. There could be a fenced area full of serfs somewhere further east. I don't intend to find out if I can help it!'

There was a road along the crest of the dam, and that was in good condition, too.

I was puzzled by one detail that we saw as we crossed. At each end of the dam, there was a long, narrow stretch of water between tall parallel concrete walls. The water was well below the level in the river above the dam, but well above the level further downstream. I asked Granny about them.

'They're locks, Mikey. It doesn't look as though they've been used since the cull, but they used to use them to raise and lower ships between the upper and lower river. I've never seen such big ones before, but I've seen smaller ones often enough. Been in boats going up and down in them, in fact. Your grandad actually worked building some, before the cull. Much smaller ones than these, though.'

'You're right about the dam not having been raised, Persie. Even if they were still providing for shipping in the river, which I don't think they are, they wouldn't have bothered with one each side like that. Those were built in the days when this was a busy waterway.'

'Oh, look. Now we really know the outfit is on the Romanian side. Pylons with cables on that side, and pylons with no cables this side.'

On the south side of the river we passed some big buildings, notable from my point of view for not having plant life lodged in every nook and cranny. Immediately after the buildings, the road became the kind of road I was used to: potholes, gravel, and small trees.

'Well. I wonder if anyone saw or heard us? I didn't see any sign of life. Did anyone?'

A chorus of 'no' from the intercom.

Without any road maps, we were completely dependent on the big atlas again. The road followed the river, either upstream or downstream, but the downstream one appeared to go to a small town about twenty kilometres away and then stop. It might have continued to the next town, but it was impossible to tell. If it existed, it was so tangled up with the river and the border between Yugoslavia and Romania that we couldn't see it on the map. The topography was so rugged that Granny guessed that the upstream road was the only one that connected through.

'Well, I hope the new dam is further up the river than where our road turns away from the river, that's all. It'd be a sad shame to find our road disappearing under the dam.'

It was slow going, because the road was in particularly bad condition. In several places we had to fill huge holes in the road with rocks before we felt safe taking the vehicles across, and in several others we had to dig our way through landslides across the road. At least there were no bottomless mud holes. It was rocks and stones everywhere.

In many places we could see a line of white scars on the hills the other side of the river.

'That's the road the other side of the river, Mikey. Our side would have looked like that before the cull, too, but it's all overgrown now and wouldn't look so noticeable. But they're maintaining that road. Every time there's a new landslip, they come and tidy up the mess. They don't just dig a bit away so they can crawl over the mess like we do, they remake the road properly.'

The biggest relief of all was that the new dam was somewhere further upstream than our turning, and that our turning was obvious. It was the first side turning of any significance that we'd seen, and it was in pretty much the right place according to the atlas. It was up a flooded side valley. There was a lovely grassy area between the road and the water. We decided to stop there for the night, because Granny guessed the road was going to head straight up into the hills from there, and there probably wouldn't be another good place for the animals. Radiation levels were reassuringly low, too.

We could see a village just a little further up the road. Laima and Nikolai went to take a look, taking guns in case they saw deer or rabbits, and a bucket and spade in case there were any vegetables gone wild. Grandad and Dad and Lieđđi went down to the water and started fishing.

It wasn't me who saw the man first this time, it was little Liz. He was watching us from amongst the trees near the road. Little Liz was very good. She didn't jump and shout. She just very quietly told Granny, who was cooking with Aunty Anna. But she did point, and the man realized he'd been seen.

He came out into the open, with his hands spread wide. Granny told me later that he did that to show that he was unarmed, and not threatening us. He was wearing a one-piece suit, that Grandad later told me was called a boiler suit. I was a little confused by him at first, because I'd never seen a grown man without a beard before, but he didn't look like a woman.

He offered his hand to Uncle Sid, who shook it, and then he shook hands with all the other adults who were by the trucks. Then he spoke in a language I didn't recognize.

The only language I knew then was English, but I recognized Russian, Swedish and Sami. This didn't sound like any of them.

He quickly realized that none of us knew his language. Then he tried Russian. Laima and Nikolai weren't there, but at least we knew it was Russian he was speaking, and Granny had a few words. She explained, more by gestures than words, that two of our party spoke Russian and would be back soon.

'Do you speak English at all?'

The man looked blank.

'Chai?'

'Spasiba.'

Well, that's what it sounded like, anyway. And even I knew that much Russian. 'Tea?' 'Thanks.'

Sharing a pot of tea is a good way to start a conversation if you don't have much in the way of a common language, but the man seemed a bit anxious. He looked at his watch.

The man gestured in the direction we'd said Laima and Nikolai had gone, then pointed at his watch and make a questioning gesture. Not then knowing what a watch was, I didn't understand, but Granny did.

'Mikey, run and fetch Laima back. Quick as you can.'

I ran.

I didn't know where in the village they'd be, and wanted to shout, but I didn't have any breath left, so I just kept running up the road and eventually found them digging potatoes. As soon as she understood what I was saying between gasps, she left Nikolai to the work and came running back with me.

Considering that she was sixty-seven years old, she could fairly run!

The man was called Carol. He'd been working at the power station and had seen our convoy go over the dam, and wondered who on Earth we could possibly be. He'd followed us on his motorbike – another thing I'd known nothing about before then – far enough behind that he thought we probably wouldn't notice him.

He was right about that.

When we stopped, he stopped his engine so we wouldn't hear him, and crept up to take a closer look at us. He'd pretty much decided we were harmless, just a big family with old people and small children, and was just considering whether to introduce himself, when little Liz spotted him.

'Do you have to get back soon? Will anyone notice you're missing?'

'No, the place runs itself mostly. I'm the only person working there at the moment, but I ought to get back before it gets dark. My bike's got a reasonable headlight, but that's a terrible road. Not as bad on a bike as in a truck, of course – I saw how much trouble you were having – but still not funny in the dark. I don't think anyone's used that road since the war.'

Laima had to translate for the rest of us, and we probably missed a few things. Granny suggested that Laima should invite him to stay the night with us and go back in the morning, 'if he can stomach our food!'

'It'd be good to learn as much as we can about the outfit he's in. He seems relatively free. Maybe it's even possible we might want to join them.'

'And if he learns a bit more about us, that makes no difference now. He knows we exist. Either that matters or it doesn't.'

Everyone approved of the suggestion he should be invited to dinner and to stay, and Laima made the offer.

'Thank you very much! I'd be cooking for myself back at the power station. Something boring.'

The talking went on late into the night, and of course I went to sleep. But I caught quite a lot before I went to sleep, and more in the morning, and I know more or less what transpired, anyway.

Carol had been very, very surprised to see our convoy. Everyone he knew believed that the only other survivors were probably in communities similar to theirs, but a very long way away. The idea of a small group of independent survivors had never seemed possible to them at all.

Carol's community consisted of about twenty-five thousand people in and around Craiova, and about fifteen thousand in and around Bucharest – a tiny fraction of the former populations. About half of them were Romanians. Most of the rest were Russians, plus a few Ukrainians and Bulgarians.

Initially, there had been several closed camps similar to the one Grandad and the Grannies had been in in Sweden, each associated with one or a few shelters, scattered over a large area of Romania, Bulgaria and the Ukraine. Then, a couple of years after the war, the authorities had moved everyone to Craiova or Bucharest, where some of the old industrial units were being resurrected, and skilled labour was needed.

War? That was what Carol called it. He didn't know the details, but to him it was obvious that that was what had happened. None of us questioned that assumption that night.

Carol thought that for us to try to join the Craiova community wasn't really practical.

'The authorities say there aren't any independent survivors, so your arrival would immediately be a problem for them to explain. Language would be a problem, too. Everybody speaks Russian. We Romanians speak Romanian amongst ourselves, but we all speak Russian too.'

'That's a pity. We live comfortably enough for the immediate future, while we can find the things we need just there for the taking. But in the long run we'll need to trade with people with industrial facilities, or we'll be reduced to a very primitive way of life. Or our descendants will, anyway.'

'Certainly, in the long run – but at what cost in liberty in the short run? The regime here is pretty nasty. I've got to admit I'm very tempted to ask you to let me join you. I'd never before considered the possibility of living independently, it's never seemed realistic. But here you are, proving it's possible.'

'Your community has no fences, like the one three of us escaped from so many years ago.'

'But does it? Do you have to be approved to get a gate pass to come and work at the power station?'

'It doesn't need fences. Nobody even thinks of the possibility of an independent life.'

He said that if he told anyone he'd met us he'd just be making trouble for himself.

'Apart from Nina, my girlfriend, of course. I can trust her not to tell anyone else.'

It didn't take us long to decide to invite Carol to join us if he really was tempted. Nikolai was the only one who was a bit doubtful, and Laima reminded him that he was a recent addition himself.

'But what about your girlfriend? Would you really want to leave her behind?'

'I wouldn't leave her behind. If I'm welcome to join you, surely she is too? We wouldn't even need to slow you down. If you set off as planned tomorrow, I can go and pick her up on the motorbike and catch up with you very quickly. Your trail is easy enough to follow now you're off the decent road by the dam!'

'And what about the power station? We wouldn't want to cause problems for the Craiova community, however nasty the regime. And if you went missing, would someone come looking for you, and end up following our tracks?'

'Don't worry about the power station. I'm not a vital cog in the machine. Our disappearance will be a bit of a mystery, but people do disappear sometimes. Maybe some of them have headed off to live independently, but that's not what anybody would ever think. I wouldn't have until today. The authorities generally say suicide, and everybody else thinks, yeah, right, we believe you.'

'Will your girlfriend want to come?'

'I think she probably will, but I can't say for sure. Either we'll catch up with you in a couple of days, or we won't. Don't worry about us. If the worst comes to the worst and we try to catch you and can't find you, we won't have any difficulty getting back. People will just think we've been away for a little break. We'd get into a bit of trouble, but it wouldn't be serious. But anyway, your trail will be easy to follow. If we want to find you, we will.'

Nikolai wondered whether Carol and his girlfriend would learn English, or whether he and his mother would end up having to translate all the time.

'Or we could all learn Russian, or we'll all end up speaking a mixture of all our languages. Don't worry. You're learning English, aren't you?'

'Yes, but I could read English already. It's only the pronunciation I'm having to relearn, not the whole language.'

Carol didn't understand any of that, but Laima told him what was going on, and he said that of course he and Nina would learn English. Laima told us that they knew two very different languages already, and that she thought people with more than one language from childhood usually learnt new languages fairly easily.

'They're still young, too. A good deal younger than you, Nikolai. It's much easier to learn a new language when you're young.'

I wondered about the rest of Carol's and his girlfriend's families, and I'm sure we all did. But I think everybody was reluctant to ask about them. It was only months later that we found out about their families – or the lack of them.

Chapter 14

The next day Carol set off early. He didn't want to wait for a cooked breakfast. Aunty Anna opened a can of fish and a packet of crispbread for him. He'd never eaten anything like it before, but he said it was good.

When he set off, I wondered how we'd managed never to hear his motorbike while he was following us. The motorbike was pretty loud, and I didn't understand then about the inverse square law, but as soon as Granny pointed out that the truck was noisy and right in our ears and the motorbike was a long way behind us, I realized that distance makes a big difference.

'Another factor is that he's probably going quite a lot faster now, and I expect his bike makes a lot more noise when it's going fast.'

Our next destination was Zaječar, and we managed to find our way there using the big atlas and a big dose of Granny's common sense (which isn't common at all). We spent a little while lost in the town before we found a service station, where happily we found some road maps.

We'd taken most of the day just getting to Zaječar, and by the time we got out of the town it was late in the afternoon, so we made camp. We couldn't find a decent patch of grass. Nikolai had to break several small saplings to clear a place to put the chicken run, and the goats had the problem they sometimes had with their tethers getting tangled up.

Radiation levels were up – not enough to stop us putting the animals out to grass for one odd night, or refrain from drinking milk or eating eggs thereafter, but enough to make Granny want to take readings a bit more frequently again.

'That must be from Kozloduy. I wonder what levels in Craiova are like? Do the people there even think about it? Craiova's a lot closer to Kozloduy than we are here.'

'I'm not sure. We're still a long way from Kozloduy. Even Craiova must be sixty kilometres from it. I wonder if this is some industrial source nearer here. I don't know anything about this area at all.'

The next morning, we continued south to Niš. There was a town plan for Niš on the back of one of the maps we'd found in Zaječar, and we managed to get straight through the city without getting lost at all. Not long after Niš we reached the biggest road I'd ever seen.

There were the usual saplings growing through the surface, but only near the edges for most of the way. The middle of the road was clear almost everywhere, and were able to keep up a good speed most of the afternoon.

There didn't seen to be anywhere good to stop, but eventually the road crossed the river – and then immediately the railway – near a place called Grdelica*. We knew from the map that we'd been close to the river and the railway for a long way, but until the bridge we hadn't seen them at all because of all the trees. There was a lush green meadow between the river and the railway, but we were high above it on the bridge. By the time we were off the bridge on an embankment, we were the other side of the railway, and there was a long goods train blocking the path to the meadow.

Grandad said we could clamber between the wagons, over the tops of the buffers and couplings, or even crawl underneath, but it wouldn't be practical to take the goats or chicken run that way, and it was an awful long way to go around either end of the train. We pressed on, looking for somewhere else, but by then it was getting dusk and the animals wouldn't get long out on the grass anyway.

---

* In your leg of the trousers of time, this was the location of the Grdelica train bombing. But the NATO operation against Yugoslavia never occurred in this other leg of the trousers of time, the Big Death having already happened several years earlier.

We passed a village. We could only see it was there because the road went over a little side valley on an embankment, and there was a gap in the trees where we went over a bridge. The roofs of the village showed here and there between the trees far below us. We could see where the trees were old, and where they had grown since the cull, but even of the younger ones many were as tall as the houses.

Shortly after that the road went through a tunnel! I'd never seen nor heard of tunnels before. Granny told me that railways often went through tunnels, but that road tunnels like this were relatively unusual.

'I'm glad it's a short one that we can see right through, and can see that it's not got piles of debris in the road where parts of the tunnel have collapsed. It'd be pretty horrible having to reverse out of a tunnel. And there's an old road running parallel with this road here, but getting between this road and that would be impossible in most places, and the old road is probably mostly in worse condition.'

The tunnel was no problem. Where we came out, the road was high above the river, with a high wall down to the river on our right.

We stopped a little later in the middle of nowhere, as far as we could tell. The road was just a strip of tarmac through dense forest, and the forest was nibbling away at its edges – or, more accurately, slowly burying its edges under vegetation, dead and alive.

In the morning, Granny, Grandad, Laima and Aunty Anna took us four littlies for a walk through the woods and down to the river. Dang rode on Aunty Anna's shoulders and Emma on Grandad's.

I spotted something that confused me. 'The railway's on the other side of the river! I never saw where it crossed! It's shown this side all the way around here in the atlas.'

'It must have crossed before we went through the tunnel. The big atlas is too small scale to see detail like that, and the railway's not shown on the road maps at all.'

'But Granny, I could see the detail. The atlas is just wrong!'

The oldies all laughed.

There wasn't going to be any fishing or shooting, because the radiation levels were still up – not as high as they'd been near Zaječar, but still too high to think of eating any local wildlife. So it was just a walk for the pleasure of it.

We stared into the water for a while, and saw quite a lot of quite big fish, but nobody regretted not having the fishing rods.

'At these levels, once in a while wouldn't really do any harm, but we've got plenty of food in stock, so why use up our once-in-a-whiles?'

Little Liz and I agreed that the fish would be very pleased to hear that.

On the way back we saw a squirrel, the first we'd seen since Jarosław. It scampered up a tree and scolded at us from a safe height.

Breakfast was ready when we got back, so it wasn't until after breakfast that I got a chance to check the atlas. I was right! But I decided not to try to tell the oldies, not even Granny.

I could have told Granny Merly. She wouldn't have told the other oldies, either. She'd have said it was best to keep it 'our little secret.'

Thinking about Granny Merly started me crying, and of course then Grandad wanted to know what I was crying about. I should have just told him I was thinking about Granny Merly, but I didn't think, and it all came tumbling out. Then he looked in the atlas too, and saw that I was right, and gave me a big cuddle, and said that I was a clever boy, and that he'd tell Granny Persie, but I told him not to. She never said anything about it to me, but I think he must have said something to her really, because she never doubted my map reading again.

It's probably mostly because I've got young eyes. Granny's very good at map reading, but she finds tiny details hard to see, I think. She's got several pair of glasses, but she says, 'They're simple reading specs. They're not exactly right, but where could I get prescription spectacles nowadays?'

It was years later before I understood what *that* meant.

I'm good at reading what's there on the map to read, but Granny's incredibly good at guessing the things that aren't actually written on the map at all. What Grandad calls 'reading between the lines.'

The road was still in pretty good condition, and at first we made a good pace, but only about fifteen kilometres down the road we came to another tunnel. This one was too long to see through. Granny pointed out the lights in the roof of the tunnel, but of course they weren't lit. No electricity. Laima had brought the tanker right up to the mouth of the tunnel, and Granny got her to bring it just a little inside.

'It won't be any trouble reversing out this little bit.'

Then, with the headlights on main beam, Granny and I walked into the tunnel to see if we could get far enough to see through to the other end, and see whether the tunnel was safe.

It wasn't. The furthest point the headlights reached wasn't really much further than the daylight reached, but it was far enough that we could see light coming in from the other end. We couldn't actually see the other end of the tunnel yet, but we could see light filtering past an obstruction, which wasn't a pile of rocks, but the remains of several vehicles. Granny reckoned they were burnt out.

'Hard to tell in this light, but they just somehow look it.'

Granny reading between the lines again. I couldn't even see the lines. But I bet she was right.

Just before we reached the tunnel, we'd crossed a huge bridge high over the river. We reversed over the bridge to a junction only a couple of hundred metres back, which led us down onto another, smaller road that came under the bridge alongside the river, and then continued on the west of the river, while the bigger road went down the east.

'According to the road atlas, we ought to be able to rejoin the main road at Vladičin Han. I hope this old road is still passable!'

'It looks like about five or six kilometres on the map, but very wiggly, so it's probably a bit more.'

'I'm sure it will be, Mikey. Look, it's heading in exactly the wrong direction at the moment. It has to, because of the loop in the river.'

It was actually nine kilometres, and the road wasn't bad at all. The surface was more broken than the main road, and there was much more vegetation growing through it, but we'd been along very much worse.

We crossed the river right in the middle of Vladičin Han. From the bridge, I noticed a huge white building towering over the trees on a hillside, and pointed it out to Granny. She said she thought it was probably a church, and Laima said she was sure it was. It didn't look anything like the church in the village near our old farm.

Just after the bridge there was a service station – with a tyre store. It didn't take long to pull the big doors open with the tanker's winch. None of us cared that no-one would ever be able to shut them again. There were tyres to fit the animals' trailer, but not to fit anything else. We didn't have any extra wheels to put them on, but we took a couple of tyres and some inner tubes.

'Better than nothing. Much better than nothing, in fact. Nikolai is strong enough to fit them with the hand tools we've got.'

There was diesel and petrol, too. We still had plenty, but it was good to keep topped up.

Granny and Laima checked the radiation levels while we were stopped. They were lower again, now down to nothing to worry about at all, but still above what they thought was just natural background.

After Vladičin Han, the road just kept on and on. There were no more tunnels, and no other obstructions, all that day. Sometimes we got a good view when the road was high above the surrounding countryside on an embankment or a bridge, but most of the time all we could see was trees. Granny said she thought that after Vladičin Han they were almost all young trees that had grown in former fields since the cull, but I couldn't really see much difference. Maybe the trees weren't quite as big, the woods not quite as dark, there weren't any places where a big tree had fallen down and made a clearing, and no big dead branches lying rotting on the ground. So maybe I was seeing the difference after all. I just hadn't realized the significance of what I was seeing.

I'm glad I've got Granny. I wouldn't see or understand half as much if I hadn't. Oh – and I'm just glad I've got Granny anyway!

For a long way, we only saw the occasional building hidden in the trees. If they were part of large settlements, villages or towns, it wasn't obvious from the road. We passed a few turnings off the road, but it was very clear which was the main road.

In the middle of the afternoon, we reached Kumanovo. If the road after Niš had amazed me, it was nothing to the road around and after Kumanovo. In fact, it wasn't one road, it was two broad roads, side by side. Down the middle of each half it was so smooth and clear of vegetation that we could go faster than ever before. I thought the two roads were going to separate and go their different ways, but Granny said, 'No, they're two halves of the same road, this one for going in this direction, and the other one for going in the other direction.'

I tried to imagine it with enough vehicles going up and down it to need so much road.

Granny was driving the tanker at this point. I could see that she was enjoying herself. The trees flew past on each side, but the noise was incredible.

Then the intercom came to life. It was Uncle Sid, from the truck at the very rear of the convoy, behind the Bandvagn.

'Slow down, Mum. We're getting left behind. I think Suonjar's worried about the Bandvagn. She keeps flashing the rear lights. Now she's waving her arm out of the window and slowing down. We're stopping. She's jumping out.'

We heard him jump out of the cab.

We stopped and jumped out. The Unimog was right behind us, and two of the trucks, but the Bandvagn and the other truck were out of sight.

Grandad was still in the cab of the Unimog, so he heard what we didn't on the intercom. Aunty Anna was telling him not to worry, the Bandvagn hadn't caught fire or anything, but there was a warning light on the dashboard and Suonjar had turned the engine off and all seemed to be okay. Grandad opened his door, and we all crowded round to listen.

Uncle Sid came back on the intercom.

'I think you'd better come back here and have a look at the Bandvagn, Mum.'

'How far back are you? Should we walk, or turn something round?'

'How would I know? Oh, okay, Suonjar says you'd been out of sight for several minutes before she stopped. So a long way, anyway. You all shot off like rockets and we never went over about fifty.'

I heard Grandad calculating to himself, 'that's about thirty.' Granny heard him too, and laughed quietly. I caught them exchanging a little grin.

Granny had a look at the strip of vegetation up between the two halves of the road. There was a bit of a ditch in the middle of it, but nothing that would give the trucks any trouble.

'We can just do a U-turn across the central reservation. We'll take the sleeping truck and all go. We'll leave the rest here. We might end up staying the night back there, depends what's wrong with the Bandvagn. I hope it's something we can fix.'

It didn't take long to get back to the others. It would have taken a long time to walk it, though.

Uncle Sid already had the cover off the Bandvagn's engine, but hadn't gone any further.

'It's awfully hot. I wonder if it's got any water left.'

'Well thank goodness you didn't open the header tank!'

'I'm not that daft, Mum!'

Suonjar showed Granny which warning light had come on. Granny turned on the ignition, but didn't start the engine. The warning light didn't come back on.

'Overheated, but it's cooled down a bit now. Still damned hot, you can feel the heat from here. We'll have to wait until it's cooled down properly before we can top up the water. How long did you keep going after the warning light came on?'

'Just a few seconds.'

'Shouldn't be any damage then. When it's cold we'll check the oil and water, top up if necessary, and start it up and see what's what. We'll do it in the morning. This is as good a place to spend the night as anywhere.'

Granny and Laima checked the radiation levels, which were low, probably near enough whatever the natural background level had been around there. Several of us went off for a walk, carrying the fishing rods and the guns. We'd no reason to think there was anywhere to fish around there – we'd not seen a river for some time, and we weren't in an obvious valley – but who knows? There could have been a pond in the woods somewhere. Granny thought probably not, because the area was very flat, and she was sure it had all been under the plough before the cull. Grandad and Dad and Lieđđi were not to be deterred.

'Who knows? There can be ponds in amongst ploughed fields in the flattest country.'

We didn't find any, but there could easily have been some. We could have been just a few metres away from them without seeing them.

We tried to head consistently east, but constantly found ourselves being turned northwards, because in every other direction the undergrowth was too thick and tangled. Grandad thought we were probably being forced to follow an old minor road, now completely buried in vegetation, but restricting its growth somewhat.

He was probably exactly right, because after a little while we reached a small rocky hill sticking up out of the general flatness, with a definite recognizable track around the foot of it. The track ended in an area with distinctly different trees. They were smaller, with tangled, wiggly branches, and looked somehow much older than the rest.

Amongst the trees there were carved stones sticking up, and the broken remains of low walls and small buildings.

'It's an old graveyard,' Grandad said. 'What a contrast with the one we buried Fiona in, that looked as though it had only been abandoned quite recently.'

He was crying. He sat on a bit of wall that was still standing. Lieđđi put her arm around his shoulders, bent over and kissed him on the forehead, and then sat down beside him with her arm round him. I thought he suddenly looked old. I sat down the other side of him and held his hand.

Dad wandered off among the old graves. I thought he was probably crying too, but I didn't see.

We heard a shot. Lieđđi jumped up with a startled look and ran off in the direction Dad had gone. Then we heard Dad's voice.

'Sorry. I didn't think. I should have realized you might be worried. There was a deer, but I missed it. Can't see properly. Eyes watering.'

Lieđđi produced a bit of clean rag from her sleeve and wiped everybody's eyes before we set off back. We didn't say anything about the graveyard. Dad told them there'd been a deer, but he'd missed it.

I think Granny at least, and probably some of the others, could see we'd been crying, but they didn't say anything. Not in my hearing, anyway.

I woke in the night. I thought I'd heard a strange noise, but I listened hard and couldn't hear anything but wind in the trees. Then, just as I was nodding off again, I heard it again – and then it disappeared under the noise of the wind again.

The next time I woke, I could definitely hear voices. Talking – Russian? Then some English – ah, that was Laima – then a language I couldn't recognize. A voice I didn't know – a woman's voice.

I tried to jump up, but I was all tangled up in reindeer skins, and I woke little Liz. She started crying quietly, so I cuddled her to help her go back to sleep again. I realized Dad had got up, leaving me and Liz side by side.

Cuddling little Liz, I went back to sleep again myself.

I was all alone in the truck when I woke up, and it was quite light. I could smell frying meat. I thought, *someone must have shot a deer early this morning. And I didn't even hear the shot.*

It wasn't a deer, it was two rabbits. Only Granny can hit a second rabbit once they've started running because of the first shot, so I knew the second one was hers. But I was wrong, and there hadn't been a single shot.

We'd more or less concluded that Carol and his girlfriend had decided against joining us, but they'd arrived late at night. Carol had set several snares before going to sleep.

It had taken them longer to catch up with us than Carol had initially thought, because he decided to give his motorbike a thorough overhaul while he had access to spare parts. He wanted to make it last as long as possible. And then, with Nina on the back, he didn't travel as fast as he did when he was alone, especially on the rough roads.

By the time we were making camp near Zaječar, Carol had reached Craiova, and pretty much finished working on his motorbike, but of course we didn't know that. We had thought he was probably back at the power station by then, with Nina. We thought they'd probably catch up with us sometime the next day. If they were coming.

The next morning, Carol finished working on his motorbike, and the two of them set off. That night, they reached the place we'd stopped when Carol first came and met us. They spent the night in a house in the village. It was the first time they'd broken into an old abandoned house, and they felt very strange doing it – especially when they found skeletons. If Granny and Grandad hadn't talked with Carol about their own history, he and Nina might have been at a loss where to stay.

Or so they say. My impression is that they're more resourceful than they gives themselves credit for.

Carol had followed our trail as far as Zaječar without difficulty, but the tangle of our tracks in Zaječar proved more difficult. Eventually he realized that one truck – the tanker, of course – had wandered about all over the place while the rest of the convoy had stayed put until we worked out where we were going. In most places, the clearest evidence of our passage was broken down vegetation, but here and there he could see the Bandvagn tracks in muddy stretches – and the Bandvagn tracks didn't go wandering about all over the place at all. They were somewhat messed up by the truck and trailer coming along behind, but they gave him enough of the clues he needed.

Once he got onto the main road at Niš, he knew where we were headed, and just made the best speed he safely could. The odd bits of crushed and broken vegetation here and there in the road reassured him he was on our trail. His biggest worry was whether he'd got enough fuel to reach us before he ran out – and he certainly wouldn't have enough to get back to Craiova – so he was desperate to catch up with us before we moved on again. At least the road was good enough to go quite fast even after it got dark, but he had to concentrate hard because his headlight didn't reach all that far.

What Carol hadn't told us was that Nina was heavily pregnant.

Nobody minded that, though. Well, almost nobody.

'Three for the price of two!' Grandad said. He loves having children around him.

Nikolai was a bit annoyed at first, saying that Carol should have told us. Laima shushed him, and Granny said it wouldn't be him who had to be midwife, there were plenty of willing hands, and another little friend for the littlies would be a good thing.

Carol joined Granny and Nikolai looking at the Bandvagn engine. The oil was a bit low, but not worryingly so; but there was almost no water at all. They filled it up, and looked for leaks, but couldn't find any. The engine started okay and sounded sweet enough.

'There'll be a steam leak somewhere. It'll show up in a minute or two.'

Granny was right, of course.

'If we just had a spare hose, this would be an easy thing to fix. Without it, it's going to be quite a trick. There's no chance of finding exactly the right hose anywhere, but we could probably find one that we could twist into position somehow if we can find a parts store somewhere. It's only got to have roughly the right diameter at each end. I suppose we're not all that far from Skopje, but it'll take a day getting there and back, and a while searching. Worth it, though. We'll detach the animal trailer and take the Unimog.'

But Carol had a better idea, and he and Granny set off on the motorbike. Grandad laughed.

'They'll have fun! Persie has about fifteen words of Russian!'

'And no Romanian at all. But she's got a lot more than fifteen words of Russian, Pete. She doesn't say much, but she understands a lot. I was watching her last night.'

I wished I could have gone too.

The goats and chickens were very glad of a whole day out to grass – well, out to weeds and saplings, really. Nikolai moved the chicken run a couple of times to let them have fresh weeds.

'When we finally settle somewhere, I'll make them a couple of nice big runs like we had back at home, so they won't run out of fresh stuff so quickly, and one run can recover while they're in the other one. But this arrangement isn't bad for now.'

Nikolai and Laima and Nina talked Russian all day. Laima translated for the rest of us from time to time, but we knew we'd have to catch up slowly later too.

Grandad and Dad and I walked all the way to the other trucks and back, just for the walk really. Grandad said he wanted to check they were okay, but of course they were. We saw lots of rabbits, a couple of squirrels and we heard rustling in the undergrowth that Grandad thought might be a deer, but we didn't see it. We saw various small birds, too, but none of us knew what sort they were. We were halfway back when we heard the motorbike in the distance, and I realized that was the sound I'd heard in the night. Carol and Granny arrived back at just the same time we did.

'I feel a complete fool,' Granny said. 'If I'd measured all the other hoses on all the vehicles before we left, we could have brought spares for all of them. This one's not an exact replacement for the busted one, but it's pretty close and it's flexible with this bellows section in the middle.'

'Sure, but we can't carry every possible spare for every vehicle. And I'm sure that Thessaloníki will be at least as good a place for raiding. It's not so far now.'

'True. If this road is as good as this all the way, we could get there tomorrow.'

'Don't go too fast, Persie. We don't want to kill the Bandvagn.'

'I'm sure it ought to be able to do more than fifty. Once we've fitted this hose, I'm going to take it for a spin myself, and see if I can spot anything wrong with it. We could spend another day here, or more, rather than risk killing it.'

'It's only got sixty on its speedo, so I wouldn't be surprised if its maximum is about fifty.'

'Oh, fair enough. I'd still like to ride in it for a bit, just to get the feel of it. Perhaps I should come with you tomorrow, Suonjar? I'm sure Laima doesn't need me to navigate. The route is just straight down this main road all the way to Thessaloníki now. According to the map it's a dual carriageway all the way, and there aren't any others.'

'We could lead the convoy anyway, Persie. On a road like this, we can all turn anywhere, it doesn't matter who leads.'

'Hmm. I'm not sure. I don't really like to put the Bandvagn first or last, because of not having intercom between it and the others.'

'True. It's a pity you got so far ahead yesterday. It would have been awful if we hadn't been able to communicate.'

Chapter 15

Carol set snares again that night. Grandad and he were up at dawn preparing the four rabbits they'd caught. We four littlies had rabbit liver for breakfast. And an egg each. Nina said she wished she'd thought to bring some bread with her, it would have rounded our breakfasts off nicely, but we didn't know what bread was then. I thought she meant crispbread, but I knew our oldies didn't want to use up our stocks of that too quickly, so I didn't say anything.

The oldies had the last of the potatoes with their rabbit.

Laima hoped to find another village where people had had vegetable gardens that had gone wild. We hadn't seen any since the night Carol found us. The trouble with the good road was that it didn't go through the villages, it avoided them. And now the road was even better.

The new hose was quite tricky to fit. Granny ended up cutting a few millimetres off each end to get it in, and she wasn't a hundred percent satisfied with it even then.

'I'm pretty sure it'll hold for the moment, but it'll wear through eventually where it's kinked. Depends partly how much movement there is between the radiator and the cylinder head. We'll look out for a better one in Thessaloníki. We might even be able to get the right one there. This engine is probably used in other vehicles – just not here in the communist bloc – and the radiator might be in the same relative position in at least some of them.'

Nikolai and Carol decided between them that it would be better to carry the motorbike than for Carol to ride it. They eventually decided that the best place would be on top of the nesting box, roped onto the front of the animal trailer.

'A bit of a nuisance when we want to get the eggs, but better than anywhere else.'

Because of the trouble fitting the hose, we were quite late setting off. In the end Suonjar had decided that she'd still rather be alone in the Bandvagn, and Granny came in her usual place in the tanker with Laima and me.

After just a few kilometres, the two halves of the road – that Granny had so firmly said were just the two halves of one road, one half for each direction – went their separate ways.

'Are you sure this is the right way?'

'Take a look at the map, Mikey!'

The road we were on joined up with the other road after a while. They just wiggled differently. Reality on the ground didn't quite match the map, though. It showed our road as a minor road, and the other road as the main one. I told Granny.

'I know. I looked earlier on. But it's obvious what happened. They decided to upgrade the old road to be an extra half for the new one.'

The map didn't show the tunnels, either. There were three of them, but they weren't very long. We could see right through before we went into them, and they were clear.

The countryside changed a lot. Instead of dense woodland, it was much more open. Instead of flatness, there were hills – big hills, but nowhere near as big as the mountains we'd seen a few days earlier. There were trees, but far fewer of them, and they were smaller, with much less foliage. What leaves there were were small and pale, instead of lush and dark green. There was no undergrowth to speak of, and in many places there was just bare rock or gravel. Every now and then a flock of small birds would take to the air as we approached. Granny hoped she might see wild goats or ibex, but little birds and insects were the only animal life we saw. Granny tried to tell me what ibex were, but I didn't really understand until later, when Grandad drew a picture for me.

We went through another patch of young, lush forest – perhaps not quite as lush as further north – and then more bare hills. We crossed a big river several times, on big bridges that were in pretty good condition. Then we were in a valley between huge, wooded hills again.

We stopped for lunch somewhere there, and Grandad, Dad and Lieđđi went fishing while Aunty Anna and Uncle Sid cooked. Nikolai and little Liz and I pulled up armfuls of weeds and fed the animals.

Granny and Carol checked the Bandvagn's radiator hose, which seemed to be okay so far. Granny thought the engine was running a bit hot, but that it was probably just that it wasn't designed to do a steady fifty kilometres an hour for hours on hard roads in hot weather. It hadn't actually reached the temperature where the warning light came on.

Then Granny and Laima checked the radiation levels again, which were pretty near what she thought background ought to be.

All was right with the world.

Except that Granny Merly and Mum weren't there. Suonjar spotted me crying again, and came and gave me a big cuddle. Gealbu hobbled over and held my hand too. I smiled at them through my tears. How can anyone be sad when they've got such good friends?

Like that.

The fishers hadn't caught anything by the time lunch was ready. They'd seen lots of big fish, and Grandad made his favourite joke about the one that got away. Maybe they really had seen one as long as his outstretched arms, but it was funny how often they were exactly that big. The biggest one I can remember them ever actually catching was about as big as Grandad's forearm. I've seen a few in rivers that might have been a bit bigger, but not as big as Grandad says.

Maybe he spends more time staring into rivers than I do. Maybe. Well, to be fair, he definitely does.

A tyre burst on the Unimog's trailer shortly after we set off again. Suonjar was driving the Bandvagn just behind and saw it happen, but Uncle Jake driving the Unimog was unaware that his trailer was running on a flat tyre. Suonjar stopped, got out, and ran to tell Grandad in the truck behind what had happened. Grandad called Uncle Jake on the intercom and everyone stopped, but by that time the trailer had done a couple of kilometres on the flat tyre.

'Lucky we got those spare tyres yesterday! I hope the wheel's not too badly damaged.'

Uncle Sid and Nikolai had the trailer jacked up and the wheel off in no time. Getting the tyre changed took longer.

'It's a good job it's a tubed tyre. That rim's not too bad, but it wouldn't make an airtight seal to a tyre.'

'It wouldn't have anyway, with all that rust.'

By the time the wheel was back on the trailer it was getting late, and we decided to stay the night where we were. It was handy for the river, and there was a reasonable place to put the chickens and goats out for a while.

It was a lovely warm evening, and we all sat on rocks by the river after supper, Dad and Lieđđi sort of fishing, but not really concentrating on their lines. The sun went down and the stars came out and there was no moon, but there was just enough starlight to make our way back to the trucks. We'd seen on the way down to the river that the ground wasn't too rough.

Then in the south, the stars began to disappear, and we could see the tops of big clouds illuminated in the starlight.

'We'd better get back to the trucks while it's still light enough to see!'

Dad and Lieđđi packed up the fishing gear, and we all trooped back to the trucks. Granny and I were the last to climb into the trucks, holding hands and enjoying watching the stars and the clouds. The clouds were getting higher up the sky. Just before I climbed into the back of the truck, I noticed that, right down on the horizon, the underside of the clouds was glowing orange. I thought maybe it was a trick of the light, the light of the setting sun getting down there somehow. I pointed it out to Granny.

I couldn't really see her face in the dark, but I heard her intake of breath.

'Pete! Look south, down on the horizon!'

Grandad climbed back out of the truck.

'Good God!'

It wasn't the setting sun; the sun had set long before. Grandad said it was Sodium Vapour Lamps. Lots of them.

'Well spotted, Mikey! We could so easily have missed that, and gone blundering down there all unprepared.'

I wondered what on Earth he was talking about.

'Don't light the lamp yet, Dot! Come out here everybody and look what Mikey's seen!'

Everybody climbed out the trucks again. Most of us wondered what all the fuss was about, but Laima and Carol and Nina understood.

'That must be just about where Thessaloníki is. Thank goodness Mikey saw it. Now what? I don't see any point heading for Thessaloníki now.'

Laima was talking Russian with Carol and Nina. Then she turned to Granny.

'I don't suppose any of you know Greek? I doubt if we want to introduce ourselves anyway, do we? Carol was saying that if we want to take a look, rather than driving down with the whole convoy, maybe the best thing would be to take the motorbike down there. Just Carol and maybe you, Persie, unless there is anyone who knows any Greek. The motorbike wouldn't be so noticeable, and much better for making a quick getaway.'

'It makes quite a lot of noise, especially if we were making a quick getaway. And no, none of us know any Greek at all. Who's to say they're Greeks anyway? They could be Americans or Chinese for all we know. Or more likely still, Russians. Or Turks. Or a mixture. Could be anyone, really. We'll never know unless we go and ask, and I don't fancy doing that, personally.'

'I wouldn't mind taking a peek, but from a good distance. But it's not like peering through binoculars at a probably-abandoned military base from the top of a hill overlooking it. We don't even know how far their territory extends.'

'That's my feeling too, Pete. My guess is that they're farming the lowlands between the foot of the hills and the sea. You can see the likely area in the atlas. But the scale's too small to know where might be a good place to look down on it from, and it's off the edge of any other maps we've got. They don't show relief anyway.'

'They've certainly got electricity aplenty.'

'Most likely hydroelectricity, like Craiova.'

'They can't have anything like as much as Craiova has. Craiova has the Danube, and a huge head of water.'

'No, probably not. But Craiova has a superabundance of power there. I don't know what they use it for – much less why they thought they needed another big dam. I'm looking forward to asking Carol about that, but maybe now isn't the time. Unless the population down at Thessaloníki is a lot more than Carol says there is at Craiova and Bucharest, they'd be well supplied with a fairly modest hydroelectric scheme. I don't know anything about what Greece had before the cull, but it's got the mountains so I bet it had a few schemes already.'

Carol whispered something to Laima, and they had a whispered conversation.

'Carol wants to know what we're going to do. I told him we don't know yet, we're still thinking about it. He feels very sure we don't want them to know we exist, but he says we need to know how far their territory extends, and in which directions. Otherwise how will we know where we should head for?'

We all climbed into the back of one of the trucks and Dot lit the pressure lantern.

'Well, we know their territory doesn't extend this far. Nothing's been up or down this road for ages. We could stay here a couple of nights and see if we can see lights anywhere other than in the Thessaloníki direction. Then we could head in any direction we've not seen lights. Mikey, go and get the atlas. You can put the cab light on, but don't forget to turn it off again. We don't want a flat battery in the morning!'

I went to get the atlas. The clouds had completely hidden the stars overhead. I could still see the orange glow in the sky to the south, but there were flashes of white light off to the south-east, too. I could hear the grown-ups talking in the back of the truck, but in a gap in the talk I could hear crashings and rumblings in the distance.

Going back with the atlas, I tripped over a stone I hadn't noticed. I did my best to stop the atlas getting damaged, and ended up whacking my elbow on the ground. I yelped.

'What's the matter, Mikey?'

'I tripped up. Couldn't see properly. Didn't drop the atlas, it's all right. I've whacked my elbow a bit though.'

Suonjar came out to find me, carrying the pressure lantern.

'I don't know why you didn't take this in the first place. They don't need it in there. They're just talking.'

'I don't carry that. I'm too little.'

'One of us big people should have gone for the atlas then.'

'Easy to be wise after the event.'

I was so proud to use one of Grandad's expressions. Suonjar laughed. She knew it was one of Grandad's, too.

'How's your elbow?'

'It hurts, but I'll survive.'

'Take your top off and let's have a look.'

There wasn't any blood, and the bruise wasn't showing yet.

'Thank goodness for reindeer skins! You'll be fine in no time.'

It was lucky I was wearing them. We were all beginning to feel hot in them during the day, and were wondering about changing into something cooler. Lieđđi and Suonjar wouldn't let us.

'Reindeer skins give you good protection from fire!'

'Cotton doesn't burn like nylon.'

'No, but a thin layer of it wouldn't give you much protection, either.'

Nobody wanted to argue with them.

Granny was pleased that I'd managed not to damage the atlas. She wanted to have a look at my elbow too, but Suonjar assured her it was okay.

'Don't make him take his top off again!'

Looking at the atlas, the grown-ups decided between them that we should skirt round Thessaloníki at a good distance. They hoped that maybe we could settle somewhere on the coast east of Thessaloníki.

'There are a couple of towns out that way. Probably not such good places to raid as Thessaloníki would have been, but beggars can't be choosers.'

We were near the bottom of a valley, and I suggested that if we moved the trucks to the top of the hill, we'd get a better view of any glow there might be in the sky in other directions.

Laima was telling Carol and Nina what was going on. She relayed a suggestion of Carol's to the rest of us.

'Carol wonders whether we should act on Mikey's suggestion, and then stay camped at the top of the hill for a few days. He can explore the roads skirting Thessaloníki to the east on the motorbike. He wants to know if it's possible to take one of the intercoms on the motorbike.'

'No, the intercoms are built into the vehicles pretty thoroughly, and they run on twenty-four volts. But if we know where he's going on the map, and we know when he's expected back, we could come looking for him in the Unimog if he's late. Actually, I'd like to go with him anyway.'

I said I'd love to go, too. Granny didn't think that would be a good idea even if it was possible, which she didn't think it would be, but Suonjar sided with me and got Laima to tell Carol what I'd said. Carol laughed and told Laima that I could ride on the petrol tank between his arms; he'd seen whole families on motorbikes around Craiova.

'He'll be useful, too. He's an observant lad, and he won't have to be concentrating on the road like Carol will. He'll get a better view than Persie will from behind Carol.'

The rain hit us while we were talking. It absolutely bucketed down. Uncle Jake and Uncle Sid rolled down the canvas at the back of the truck, but not before we'd seen a flash that lit left me seeing afterimages for ages. The crash of thunder arrived only a second or so later.

We all spent the night together in the one truck, apart from Uncle Jake who slipped out to go and shut the back of the other truck so it didn't get too wet inside, and didn't come back. He shouted from the other truck to tell us that he was okay, and that he'd stay there, rather than get even wetter. It was pretty cosy with eighteen of us in one truck, and we couldn't all lie down properly, but everybody slept somehow, I think. I certainly did, and everybody else said they did, but how much sleep they really got I'm not sure.

The next morning was bright and clear. There wasn't a cloud in the sky. Carol and Granny and I had a crispbread and tinned fish breakfast before anyone had cooked anything, and loaded a good lunch of similar fare into the luggage box on the back of the motorbike. Grandad, Dad and Lieđđi had gone fishing as usual. Uncle Sid helped Carol fill the motorbike's fuel tank, and we set off.

We headed north back up the road we'd come down for fifteen or twenty kilometres, then turned right onto a minor road. We were back on the Yugoslavia road atlas territory at that point, but we weren't carrying either the road atlas or the big atlas. Granny had memorized the map as far as Sérrai, but didn't expect to get that far. Carol didn't want to go more than about a hundred and fifty kilometres before turning back.

'The last thing we want to do is risk running out of fuel!'

He'd scared himself quite enough being too far away from Craiova to get back, long before they caught up with us.

I felt very important, because I could see much better than Granny could, and I kept telling her what I was seeing. Then she was telling me what she wanted Carol to do, and I was showing him in gestures. It all worked very well.

This road was in much worse condition than the main road, but the motorbike coped with bad roads a lot better than the trucks did. Carol weaved in and out around the potholes and all the little trees that were growing in the road. We could go straight over piles of mud and rocks that might have tipped the trucks over sideways, and would have had to be at least partially cleared.

Granny was heading for a place called Strumica, where she wanted to turn right again to head down the valley towards Petrich. There was another, shorter, route to the south of a ridge of mountains, but that involved going closer to Thessaloníki than she really wanted to be.

We never reached Strumica. We came over the top of the pass just a few kilometres before it, and the road disappeared into a huge lake. We stopped and all got off the bike. The whole valley ahead of us was flooded. We could see where our little valley joined the much bigger valley that the town was supposed to be in – but that much bigger valley was flooded, too.

'Well! That's that. We can't go east. There's only one possible explanation, and it explains why Thessaloníki has plenty of electricity. They must've built a dam across the Struma. It must be a huge one. It probably means they're farming the Struma valley below the dam, as well as the Axiós valley near Thessaloniki. We'll have to head west, that's all there is for it. We'll have a look at the atlas when we get back. I hope we're not going to find ourselves blocked in every direction around here.'

We were back at the camp in time for lunch. They hadn't even started to move the trucks to the top of the hill, but they had caught some beautiful big fish, and the goats and chickens looked to be having a good time.

Carol got Laima to say that he thought we could probably find a minor road south of the new lake, and cross the road between the dam and the populated area, if we wanted to go further east.

'It's not as far as going right across to the sea westwards, and it's very unlikely anyone would see us, unless the populated area spreads right up to the dam. It was pure chance I happened to see you crossing our dam. We could at least go on the motorbike and spy out the land. Very unlikely to be spotted. And if we are spotted, it's likely to be by one serf or a small group, who'll prefer to say nothing rather than make trouble for themselves. There won't be guards patrolling the borders or anything like that, it's simply more trouble than it's worth when you don't believe there's anyone out there to guard against.'

'Tell him he's generalizing from his own experience at Craiova. Things could be completely different here. For all we know they might have a security fence all round the whole of their territory, and armed patrols to keep people *in*, even if they don't believe there's anyone outside.'

Granny looked carefully at the atlas. She reckoned it was unlikely there were any passable roads in the mountains between the two marked in the atlas, having seen the condition of the one they'd been along. According to the atlas, the next road south ran along the foot of the mountains, where she thought it was very likely people were farming the land.

'We'll take a look westwards tomorrow. I wonder if we'll be able to see anything tonight? There's no sign of clouds yet. If there aren't any tonight, we probably won't be able to see the glow of the street lighting at all. It was really lucky you saw that last night, Mikey. But with luck, from up there we might even have a line-of-sight view of the lights themselves.'

She nodded in the direction of the top of the hill we were planning to camp on that night.

I say, 'the top of the hill', but we only took the trucks up to the highest point of the road. The hillside continued up on the right. A lot of it was bare rock, hard dry soil, and gravel, but there was some vegetation, and even a few small trees. Some of us walked up quite a long way just to see the view, but we didn't get anywhere near the top. It just kept on going up and up.

We didn't get any view to the west at all, but to the south and south-east we could see an incredibly long way. Even from up there, in daylight we couldn't see anything anywhere to indicate the existence of continued human life, not even with the binoculars. We walked back down to the trucks long before dark.

The clouds had boiled up again in the late afternoon, and after dark we could see the glow of the streetlights on their undersides again, but we still didn't have line of sight to the lights themselves. We could see the glow very clearly in the Thessaloníki direction, and I thought that maybe I could see a very faint glow further east, too. Granny and Laima couldn't see it, but the twins thought they could.

Granny laughed. 'You've got younger eyes than we have!'

I was used to the idea that the oldies couldn't see detail, but I'd never before thought that they had any trouble with dim light. One lives and one learns, as Grandad says.

Or maybe I'd imagined that very faint glow in the south-east, and the twins were just being nice to me. I wasn't sure I could see it any more, but I didn't say anything. Granny was very happy to have confirmation of her theory, and I wasn't going to disappoint her.

What she wasn't sure about, and we couldn't possibly determine, was whether the populated area extended to the west as well. Looking at the atlas, there didn't seem to be any roads west without going almost down to Thessaloníki first, or a long way back into Yugoslavia. Everybody agreed that the latter was the only option.

It didn't rain at all where we were that night, but we could see flashes and hear thunder in the distance in the east.

Chapter 16

The next morning we drove back to Gradsko, where the turn was to go west across southern Yugoslavia. We'd driven down that road just a couple of days earlier, so we were confident it was a straightforward drive. We kept up a good pace – the fifty kilometres an hour that was the maximum the Bandvagn seemed able to do.

For the first few kilometres the road to Bitola, our next destination, was in fair condition, running through fairly level countryside, young forest that Granny didn't need to tell me had grown on former farmland. I could even spot where the field boundaries had been in some places. Sometimes there were gaps in the trees through which we could see wooded hills.

Gradually the hills got bigger and closer, and then suddenly we were climbing. The road was narrower, and the surface was in worse condition. Granny clicked on the intercom, and told Uncle Sid, in the truck just behind us, to stop and wait until we'd checked that the road was passable.

'It looks as though it'd be pretty hard to turn on the next stretch, if we have to.'

Nikolai came on the intercom. He had Carol and Nina with him.

'Carol says why doesn't he go on the motorbike to check the road ahead? It's a pity he doesn't have intercom, but he can go and find the next turning point, and come back in the time it would take the tanker to get there. And then once we're on the move, he can go and find the next one as well. We should be able to keep moving continuously like that. The motorbike will end up doing between two and three times the distance, but that doesn't matter.'

'Good idea!'

So we all stopped, and Nikolai helped Carol get the motorbike off the trailer. Carol set off, and was back in just a few minutes.

'There's a long stretch where you'll be able to turn easily after just a couple of kilometres like this. Stop again when you reach the next narrow bit. I'll go on and check the next section, and come back and find you there.'

Laima translated for us. I could see Granny really wanted to go on the motorbike, but she wasn't saying anything. So I did.

Granny shushed me. 'He'll be quicker on his own. And use less petrol.'

Laima laughed. 'You and Mikey weigh nearly nothing, Persie. You wouldn't make any difference at all.'

So we went with Carol. It's true that he must have weighed a good deal more than Granny and me put together, but I don't believe we really made no difference at all.

The 'long stretch' where the trucks would have been able to turn if they'd needed to was only a few kilometres, and then the road got pretty rough and narrow again amongst steep, rocky hills, with narrow bridges over little gorges. In a couple of places we stopped for Granny to check a bridge, but once she'd looked at them she was confident that they were good enough for the trucks.

We went a long, long way without finding anywhere where the trucks would be able to turn. We were getting pretty high in the mountains. Eventually we reached the summit of the pass. Right at the highest point there was a wide area of gravel that Granny said was a parking place, for people to stop and admire the view. It was big enough to turn the trucks, and that's what we cared about.

We stopped to stretch our legs – and admire the view. The way we'd come up, the valley was narrow and steep and winding, and we couldn't see very far that way, but the other way the valley was broad and the slope was relatively gentle. There were the remains of a village just below the summit, but Granny reckoned that most, maybe all, of the houses must have been abandoned for a lot more than thirty odd years.

Carol was trying to tell Granny something. Granny tried a few words of Russian, trying to get him to say what he was trying to say in different words, and slowly, and maybe she'd understand. Eventually he managed to get his point across, more in mime than in words.

Would Granny like to drive the motorbike? She'd be able to see better if Carol rode behind her.

Granny wasn't sure about that, but Carol showed her the controls, and she had a go on her own around the car park. But she didn't want to ride back to the trucks. She didn't feel confident at all.

By the time we got back to the trucks, they were beginning to be a bit worried about us. Laima and Grandad were just beginning to think about setting off in the tanker to look for us, hoping we'd not had an accident. They thought maybe we'd broken down. They couldn't believe it was really so far to the next place the trucks would be able to turn.

'I wish there was some way you could rig up an intercom on the bike, Persie.'

'I very much doubt the intercoms would have worked between here and where we've been. Not more than the first two or three kilometres, anyway. Too many hills in the way.'

The three of us set off again, to investigate the next stretch of road while the main convoy headed for the car park at the top of the pass. It wasn't very far beyond the summit of the pass before we could see a town in the middle distance, and it seemed no time at all before we were in it. There were plenty of places to turn, and plenty of places to raid – in particular, a petrol station.

'It'll be ages before the trucks get to the top of the pass. We should take a look around.'

It was all very well telling me that, but she couldn't get it across to Carol. We set off back to the top of the pass. When we got there, Carol turned the engine off and we could hear the trucks labouring up a hill in the distance. The sound varied as they progressed. Sometimes we could hear the engines working hard, other times they were obviously running fairly level or even downhill. Sometimes the sound was very clear, other times it faded away almost to nothing. Granny said it was the shape of the valley, sometimes funnelling the sound towards us, other times reflecting most of it off somewhere else entirely.

'If we knew that road better, we'd probably be able to work out exactly where they were.'

I felt as though I did know that road pretty well. There weren't many stretches of road I'd been along three times! But I didn't have any idea how to work out where the trucks were.

Then suddenly we could see them moving in the distance. We couldn't really see the road, just the trucks. If they'd been stationary I don't think we'd have been able to spot them – and even though they were in direct line of sight, the sound was only reaching us very thinly.

They disappeared around a shoulder of the hill. Strangely, the sound got much louder at the same moment.

I mentioned that to Granny that evening, and she explained about the difference between the speeds of sound and light. She also showed me how to take my own pulse, and use it to time the interval between a lightning flash and the beginning, and the end, of the thunder, and so get a rough estimate of the distance to the nearest and furthest parts of the thunderbolt – or how far away a moving vehicle was.

By the time the trucks arrived at the summit it was getting late, and we stopped there for the night. Radiation levels were slightly up. Granny and Laima wondered why, but couldn't figure it out. As usual, it was stronger the closer to the ground you took the readings, so Granny said a large proportion of it was probably alpha.

'So it could just be natural for this area, or maybe there was a uranium mine somewhere around here. Ivan wouldn't necessarily have known about it. It's nothing to worry about at this level, but we'd better keep an eye on it in case we're heading into a contaminated area.'

We always kept an eye on it anyway.

There wasn't much vegetation, but the chickens seemed happy scrabbling in the dirt, and Nikolai tied extra rope onto the goats' tethers so they could each reach a few stunted shrubs. Little Liz and I went on a long expotition to find some weeds for the chickens, and saw several little lizards. We'd never seen lizards before, but I knew what they were from Grandad's stories and the pictures he'd drawn for us.

I don't think any of the grown-ups believed we'd really seen them – until Aunty Dot saw one herself. Even then I'm not sure. I'm never quite sure whether Aunty Dot, or Aunty Belle for that matter, say things like that just to be nice to me or little Liz, and I suspect that some of the other grown ups might wonder about that, too.

Granny and Laima studied the Yugoslavian road map and the atlas. The town we'd visited was Prilep, and we *were* on the road Granny had intended us to be on.

The next morning we did a bit of raiding in Prilep, and found a truck depot. There were two trucks full of cardboard boxes of food. There were jars of various sorts of pickles, some of which I'd never seen before – such as pickled carrots and pickled aubergines. There were cartons and cartons of crispbread, and something else I'd never seen before – rusks. Some of the cartons had got damp, but most

were fine and there was more stuff there than we'd got room
to take anyway.

The petrol station had plenty of diesel, and we topped the
tanker up although we weren't low at all – but the petrol
tanks were both completely dry. Granny wondered whether
perhaps the tanks had a leak, but Laima thought it was quite
likely they'd simply sold out during the cull, or even before
it.

'There'll be more as soon as we get back into Greece.'

From Prilep to Bitola the road wasn't bad at all, although
it had obviously been flooded pretty badly a few times, and
in places it was hidden under dry mud. Granny was a bit
worried that the mud might only be dry on the surface, and
the trucks might drop a wheel into a hole, but it didn't
happen – not deeply enough to be a problem, anyway.

What did happen was that a wheel bearing failed in one of
the big trailers. Unfortunately it was the last vehicle in the
convoy, so there was no-one behind to notice that something
was wrong, and the first Uncle Sid knew was that his truck
suddenly stopped with a bang and a loud graunching sound.
The trailer wheel had come off completely, and the end of
the axle casing had dug itself into the road.

Uncle Sid called everyone on the intercom, and we all
stopped. Granny took one look at the mess and realized that
that was the end of that trailer.

'If we'd spotted that as soon as the wheel started to
wobble, we might have been able to find a bearing that fitted.
Even that's a long shot, really, though. There's no chance at
all now. There won't be any trailers like that one anywhere
around here, and no parts to fit.'

We loaded all the stuff out of the trailer into one of the
sleeping trucks, and detached the trailer. It was the first time
any of those trailers had been detached since Norway.

'Let's hope we can find an ordinary farm trailer
somewhere. Obviously there's no hope of finding a trailer

with a driven axle, but with luck we won't really need that again. We can always winch, and we've not had to do even that for ages. But if we all have to sleep in one truck for a night or two, we know we can manage if we have to.'

'There were big trailers in that truck depot in Prilep. It's not that far to go back to fetch one.'

'I didn't look at their hitches. I wonder if they'd fit? I dare say we could cobble something together, if necessary by nicking the necessary fittings off the back of one of their lorries. I wonder what the tyres are like though?'

'That's going to be a problem with any trailer anywhere. There's a better chance of finding some decent tyres at that depot than in most places.'

It was decided. Granny and Nikolai and Uncle Sid set off back to Prilep in the trailer-less truck, with all the tools and the little petrol generator. The rest of us waited. We put the chickens and goats out for an unscheduled feast. We were in the middle of new-growth forest, and it was very lush.

"It's a pity we don't have a duplicate set of tools. We can't even get the wheels off the dead trailer until they get back. There might be other bits we should salvage, too."

Carol set off on the motorbike to go and investigate the road at least as far as Bitola, and maybe a bit further. He knew it would take them a long time to fix up a trailer.

He arrived back long before them. He looked tired and drawn. Laima got some rags and a bowl of water, and Nina helped Carol wash his hands and face. She gradually got the story out of him. Laima relayed it to the rest of us.

Granny and Laima had forewarned Carol and Nina about skeletons in abandoned houses, and they'd taken it in their stride when they found them. What Carol had not been ready for was piles of skeletons, in the tattered remains of their clothes, in the street. There had been a military vehicle resting on the top of one of the piles. We'd seen things like that a few times, but we'd sort of worked up to it gradually, and we'd not been alone.

'There's probably a lot of raiding could be done in Bitola, but I haven't got the stomach for it. I'd rather get through there as quick as we can.'

That was Laima's translation of what he said, anyway. Nobody was going to argue with him.

It took Granny and Nikolai and Uncle Sid all day, but late that evening they turned up with a huge box trailer behind the truck. To hitch it up, they'd had to grind off part of the back end of the chassis of a lorry, and bolt it onto our truck. It hadn't been possible to connect the new trailer's brakes, so Uncle Sid was under strict orders to be very careful, especially going down steep hills.

They'd half filled the trailer with food, but there was still room for us to empty the sleeping truck into it.

'A pity we ever transferred everything out of the old trailer in the first place. Unnecessary double handling. Never mind. Such is life.'

Laima told them about Carol's experience in Bitola.

'There's no need for us to do any raiding there. We're very well supplied now anyway. I'd like to try to find a road map of Greece, but we wouldn't find one of those in Bitola anyway. Oh, and petrol. We've probably got enough to get down to the west coast of Greece anyway, but I always prefer to be well topped up.'

Carol had been right through Bitola and a good way beyond. He hadn't reached any obstructions and there were plenty of places to turn round, so they put the motorbike back on the front of the animal trailer. Carol could ride in the truck with Nikolai and Nina again.

Carol and Nina decided they were ready to start learning English in earnest. Granny wanted Grandad to teach them, but it ended up being a big co-operative effort between all the grown-ups. Lieđđi and Suonjar and Nikolai weren't sure whether they were teachers or pupils, and the truth is they were a bit of both. There was much hilarity all round, and we ended the evening with a big sing-song, singing all the family songs Grandad had taught Mum and Dad and all the aunts and uncles when they were children, and everybody else joining in on the choruses by the time each song was finished. Gealbu kept time thumping the side of a truck with his stick.

In the morning, Carol didn't ride with Nina and Nikolai, he came in the tanker with Laima and Granny and me instead. He'd explored Bitola enough to be able to guide us along a route that avoided the piles of skeletons. He didn't want to see them again, and even more, he didn't want Nina to see them. He knew there was a risk she'd come across things like that in some other town, but Laima reassured him that it wasn't very common.

'Next time, I want someone who's used to these things to come with me, though.'

'That'll usually be Persie. She likes to be in the forefront of everything!'

Granny laughed. She'd understood that much Russian.

When we reached the place Carol had turned back, he got Laima to stop, and he and Nikolai got the motorbike down again. Nina moved into the tanker with Laima. She said she wanted to be able to see Carol as much as possible, but I think she was actually finding Nikolai a bit too intense. I think everybody knew Lieđđi had felt that after a while.

Another advantage was that Laima would teach her some English, while being able to talk in Russian as well.

Carol hadn't quite reached the Greek border the previous day. We arrived there very soon after we set off on the motorbike. Carol was quite surprised, but Granny had been expecting it. It wasn't nearly as forbidding as the border between Russia and Finland had been, but it was a lot more impressive than any of the others. There was plenty of room for the trucks to turn round on the Yugoslav side of the border, so we went back to tell Laima to follow us.

There would have been plenty of room for the trucks to turn around on the Greek side, too, if it hadn't been completely clogged up with trucks. They were all facing towards the border. They'd presumably been waiting to cross into Yugoslavia at the time of the cull.

We still hadn't talked with Carol and Nina about the difference between a war and a cull.

We left the rest of the convoy on the Yugoslav side, and headed into Greece. The road wasn't very wide, but there were lots of minor side roads the trucks could have turned in, and the road didn't look as though it was going to be blocked. However, Granny thought it would be better to move the trucks a reasonable distance at a time, so we pressed on to Flórina, which didn't take long at all. The road was fine all the way – potholed and growing small trees amongst the weeds as usual, but no problem at all. We went back to call everybody to join us.

Granny and I got back into the tanker, because Granny wanted to study the atlas carefully. She was almost sure the Thessaloníki people's stamping ground wouldn't extend as far as Kozáni, but she said she didn't see the point in taking even a tiny chance of bumping into them.

'There's a minor road big enough to show on the atlas that we can take westwards from Flórina, and join the main road twenty-five kilometres west of Kozáni. I think I'd rather do that.'

Laima wasn't so sure.

'That road goes right through the mountains, really high, look. I bet that's a hell of a road. I think there's a fair chance it's blocked somewhere or other. Landslip, bridge washed away, something. I know you've coped with such things before, when you had to, but do we really need to take the chance?'

'Okay, you win. We'll just make sure we always spy out the land on the motorbike first, and be ready to make a quick retreat if we see any sign of civilization.'

'Kozáni's a lot further from Thessaloníki than we were when Mikey first saw the city lights. You're worrying about nothing, Persie.'

'You're probably right. But now we've got Carol and the motorbike, it's always worth spying out the land anyway.'

We didn't actually take the convoy into Flórina, because the road to Kozáni turned off a few kilometres before it. The first day, Carol and Granny and I went back and forth, back and forth, spying out the land, but the road was passable everywhere, and there was no sign of human life at Kozáni. We got a road atlas of Greece there, and petrol. And engine oil. We'd brought plenty all the way from Norway, but Granny was happy to top up our supply and we'd got so much more room now we'd got that huge trailer.

We stopped that night just west of Kozáni, and had another long evening of laughter and song. Carol and Nina were managing to join in on the choruses almost straight away. Well, so were Laima and Nikolai and Lieđđi and Suonjar, and they'd only started to learn the songs the previous evening – but at least they had a big head start in the language.

The next day, Granny decided that we really didn't need to go ahead on the motorbike any longer: the road seemed good, and we were heading away from Thessaloníki. The motorbike went back onto the front of the animal trailer.

That night we stopped near Kalabáka. Granny and Carol went on the motorbike to have a look at the town, but I didn't go with them because I wasn't feeling very well. The rest of us never saw the town, because we turned right at a junction before we got there, to keep on heading towards the coast.

The next day we were on an exceptionally wiggly winding road that climbed up and down, up and down, and went through lots of old villages in the mountains. I remember especially the fantastic rocks that looked as though they were carvings done by a mad giant.

Remembering what the road was like where the other Bandvagn caught fire, everybody was a bit worried about Suonjar, but there was no trouble.

We camped that night by a huge lake near Ioánnina. The grown-ups discussed possibly staying there. It wasn't the coast, but it did have that big lake, and Ioánnina itself seemed like a good place for raiding – a much bigger town, according to the atlas, than anywhere actually on the coast in that area. Some of the land looked as though we'd be able to farm it all right, once we'd removed a few trees.

That was one regret our grown-ups had. They'd never let trees get a hold on our fields in Norway and Latvia, but they knew they'd have to clear trees before they could make any fields anywhere else. But with the winches on the trucks nobody anticipated any problems pulling small trees out.

We spent two days having a good look around Ioánnina, and eventually decided that we'd carry on down to the coast. Ioánnina was – just – within raiding distance of the coast, and the grown ups thought being right on the coast was worth it.

Granny and Laima reckoned that it probably got pretty cold in winter at Ioánnina, although it was nice and warm there that September. I think the real attraction was the sea itself – seaweed, shellfish, and probably better fishing than the lake.

We've got a really nice farm right on the coast now, not far from Igoumenítsa. Radiation levels are low – Granny thinks they're probably just natural background. We don't often go to Ioánnina, because there's almost everything we need in Igoumenítsa. We found several houses in reasonably good condition, and plenty of materials to fix them up and make them just how we want them.

Nina's baby, Tatiana, was born just a couple of weeks after we arrived. She was adorable. She still is – or maybe I

should say she is again. We fell out a bit when she was in her
early teens.

Liz and I have a half-brother, Oaván, and a half-sister,
Erica. Dad and Lieđđi say they're going to get married.
They've been saying it for years. Nikolai and Dot, Jake and
Suonjar, and Belle and Gealbu think the whole idea is funny.
'What does it mean?'

Carol and Granny found several motorbikes in a
showroom, and got a couple of them working in no time.
'Much easier than fixing cars and trucks that have been
standing idle for thirty-odd years!'

Carol said he really liked his original bike best, but
couldn't get spares for it, whereas there were spares for the
ones they found in Igoumenítsa. Granny quickly got pretty
good at riding her bike, but she could never persuade
Grandad to ride with her. 'Give me four wheels,' he says.

Nikolai says Grandad's got sense. He won't ride the bikes,
either. I know that Laima's secretly pleased about that – she
was worried that he might go a bit mad on one.

I often rode in front of Granny when I was little, but now
I've got my own bike, and Tatiana usually rides behind me. I
love the feeling of her arms wrapped around my tummy and
the rest of her snuggled against my back. She can ride the
bike on her own, but doesn't like to have a pillion passenger.
I'm a lot heavier than she is, and she says it's hard to control
with me on the back. She sometimes takes Zuza – Nikolai
and Dot's youngest – on the petrol tank between her arms.
Zuza loves it, but it makes her Dad very nervous!

Carol and Uncle Sid fixed up some little sailing dinghies.
Carol said – in English! – that he and Nina used to go sailing
on the new Danube reservoir. 'Fishing from a boat is better
than fishing from the shore.'

At first Granny thought Carol was just saying that because
he wanted an excuse to go out in the boat, but she said she

didn't blame him. 'I'd quite like to learn to sail myself. I wouldn't mind going over and having a look around Corfu, for one thing.'

Grandad was doubtful. 'We could go over in the Bandvagn.'

'I don't think I fancy taking the Bandvagn out to sea. I don't trust it that much. I'd do it in an emergency – to rescue someone who got into trouble sailing, for example!'

Most of us go sailing now. Gealbu and Belle are the undisputed champions.

There have had to be a couple of rescues, but nothing serious. We've always managed it with the dinghies. Some of them have outboard motors, and we make sure they're always working in case we need them, but we very rarely use them.

We've explored Corfu thoroughly – and one by one we're raiding all the fancy millionaires' houses. We've found shelters in several of them, but they'd never been used. Well stocked with all kinds of goodies! Granny jokes about moving into one of the posh houses, but really we all like the farm on the mainland better.

Grandad's not very keen on sailing, and Nikolai won't go sailing at all – although his mother loves it, partnering with Granny. Grandad's been over to Corfu a couple of times, but really doesn't like being in little boats – and no-one's fixed up a big one yet. Carol and Granny had a go at getting the engine working on one, but couldn't manage. 'Motorbikes and outboards are much easier!'

We did eventually hear about Carol and Nina's family histories. Both their mothers had been working in factories before the cull, and had been shepherded into shelters without any forewarning. When they came out, most of the survivors were Romanian women factory workers, with a much smaller number of men, more than half of them Russian and Ukrainian soldiers. Very few of the women's husbands had survived, and the military were very much in charge.

Carol's and Nina's mothers had each had several successive liaisons with soldiers, who had deserted them as soon as they got pregnant. Their babies were forcibly taken away to be fostered as soon as they were weaned. Not until the two women were in their mid-thirties were they finally allowed to keep their last child.

Apparently during the first decade or so after the cull this pattern was not at all unusual in Craiova and Bucharest. Not universal, but very common.

Carol and Nina were raised by their single mothers, but orphaned in their late teens. They knew they'd each had several half-siblings, but had never met them. Not knowingly, anyway – they knew lots of people who'd been fostered, but which if any of the people they knew were their half-siblings they'd no idea.

Most of the foster mothers were military officers' wives, fostering huge families. Nina and Carol were especially angry about the way any child who was the least bit 'difficult' then somehow ended up in an institution. They'd known several people who'd been through that – and heard about more who'd ended up completely deranged.

Carol said his mother had told dark stories of similar institutions before the cull. She'd always said it wasn't human to do such things, and that she was disgusted that the authorities organized things that way. Carol and Nina were especially angry that the authorities had continued the policy after the cull.

Grandad had known people who'd grown up 'in care' in England. 'We used to hear about terrible conditions in orphanages in Romania, but some of the people I knew had had a pretty bad time in England, too. Maybe not as bad as in Romania, but it's hard to know without seeing both at first hand. You couldn't really go by the reports. Comparing the worst of one country with a random selection of another doesn't give a clear picture of the norm in either. It sounds as though the sheer number in institutions in Craiova after the cull was rather large, but who knows what's happened in England since the cull?'

Everybody knows English very well now, and most of the talk is in English most of the time, but sometimes I hear Carol and Nina talking Romanian, and Tatiana knows Romanian too. Lieđđi and Suonjar talk together in Sami from time to time, and of course Gealbu joins in in his mute fashion – but I've noticed how much English creeps in, even when they're talking Sami. Laima and Nikolai talk Russian if there's just the two of them, or just them and Carol and Nina.

Granny and all us young ones know Russian too. Laima has taught us, so we can read our fabulous Russian library. We've discussed trying to teach ourselves Greek, because there's an even bigger selection of Greek books to be had in Igoumenítsa – and more still in Ioánnina – but no-one's taken the plunge yet. (There's another of Grandad's expressions!)

There's probably nothing as good on the science and technology front as Laima's collection anyway, and Tatiana and I adore the pictures in the Russian children's books, and haven't seen anything in the Greek books to compare with them. But we're sure there must be some very interesting stuff to read, if only we could read it.

Grandad and Granny often say how pleased they are that we've all grown up 'thoroughly literate'. They tell tales of televisions and the 'telly generation', and how they don't regret the loss of television 'one little bit'. I've seen tellies, gathering dust, but of course I've never seen one working.

Granny still makes the most gorgeous seaweed stew. It's always got bits of all sorts of things in it, but it's mainly seaweed.

And Grandad says I have to mention that he STILL owes Mike seventy quid. And now he's gone all nostalgic and sad again.

Ivan's Map

Redrawn and relabelled in English by
Peter S. Collins. With a few extras of his own.

·········· Our expotition

● Reactor site operating in 1990

○ Reactor site shut down by 1990

N.B. Many sites have more than one reactor
Low power research reactors not shown

Norway

Ireland

UK

East Germany

West Germany

France

Spain

Portugal

Italy

Meanwhile, back in the real world...

Ivan's map mostly corresponds to reality. However, in *Going Forth*'s leg of the trousers of time, Chernobyl still had functioning nuclear reactors in 1990, Yugoslavia hadn't started to break up, and East Germany was still firmly in the grip of the Soviet Union.

All the towns and nuclear sites mentioned in the whole book are real, and you really could trace almost all of the expedition's journey on the ground, in considerable detail.

The derelict factory in the photograph on the cover of the book is not actually on the route. It's really in Armenia, at Tumanyan. It's been abandoned since the collapse of the Soviet Union. The places that are ruins covered in vegetation in the book mostly aren't yet ruins in the real world.

Laima and Persie's understanding of the hazards posed by abandoned nuclear reactors, uranium mines etc. is entirely accurate.

Their speculations about climate are reasonable, and could well be generally correct – see *How Did Humans First Alter Global Climate?* by William F. Ruddiman (Scientific American, March 2005). However, while a cessation of fossil fuel burning in 1990 and a worldwide regrowth of forests probably would eventually result in a resumption of a normal cycle of recurrent ice ages, it's unlikely (though we don't know enough to be sure) that cooling would really have been so noticeable within a span of only 34 years. (If these things happened today, global warming would most likely continue for a considerable period before starting to reverse. Levels of atmospheric carbon dioxide are significantly higher today that they were in 1990.)

About the author:

Clive K. Semmens was born in London in 1949, and grew up in Yorkshire and then Hertfordshire, in England.

In 1967, he gained a scholarship from the United Kingdom Atomic Energy Authority to study Nuclear Engineering, a course intended to lead to a career designing nuclear power stations and associated infrastructure. His studies and experiences in the nuclear industry led him to the conclusion that nuclear power generation is a very bad idea, and he changed course.

Since then, he has had a wide-ranging professional career in engineering, education, technical writing and academic publishing.

He describes his hobbies as travel, photography, reading, writing and innovative DIY (anything from microelectronics to major building projects).

He knows French, German and Hindi well enough for them to be useful, but in his own words "would certainly not describe himself as fluent or accurate in any of them." He's particularly interested in people and their lives, trying to see things from the point of view of people from very different backgrounds, to avoid as far as possible making errors of judgement arising out of the unconscious assumptions of his own background. He is also very interested in the world around people and is well versed in the issues surrounding energy production and consumption, resource consumption, and environmental pollution.

He first visited India in 1983. He rapidly got involved providing technical advice for a charity, and met his future wife, who hails from a remote village in central India. He spent six months in India on that occasion, and again a year later. Since then, he, his wife and their two children have visited her relatives in India about once every couple of years.

Today they are retired and live in a small English town. They still travel, and take part in political, technical and cultural discussions and he writes essays and novels.

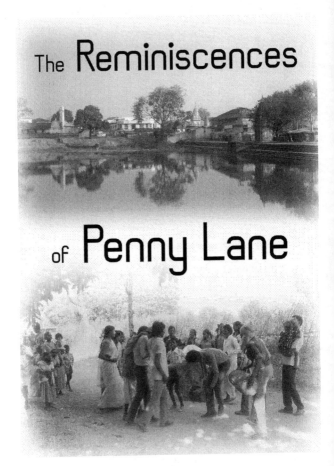

The Reminiscences of Penny Lane